MEPHISTO ARIA

Visit us at www.boldstrokesbooks.com

What Reviewers Say About the Author

Advance praise for *Mephisto Aria*

"Justine Saracen's latest thriller, *Mephisto Aria*, brims with delights for every sort of reader…delight at love's triumph, and at Saracen's queer reworkings of the Faust legend, are not this novel's only pleasures. Saracen's understanding of the world around opera is profound. She captures the sweat, fierce intelligence, terror and exultation that characterize singers' daily lives, in rehearsal and performance, she evokes well the camaraderie that a production's cast and crew share, and she brings to literary life the curious passions that bind people who make music together. Brilliantly fusing the insights of twenty years' worth of feminist and queer opera criticism to lesbian fantasy fiction, Saracen has written a passionate, action-packed thriller that sings— indeed, that sings the triumph of *Rosenkavalier*'s trio of lovers over *Dr. Faustus'* joyless composer. Brava! Brava! Brava!"—Suzanne G. Cusick, Professor of Music, New York University

Acclaim for *Sistine Heresy*

"Justine Saracen's *Sistine Heresy* is a well-written and surprisingly poignant romp through Renaissance Rome in the age of Michelangelo… The novel entertains and titillates while it challenges, warning of the mortal dangers of trespass in any theocracy (past or present) that polices same-sex desire."—Professor Frederick Roden, University of Connecticut; Author, *Same-Sex Desire in Victorian Religious Culture*

Praise for *The 100th Generation*

"[T]he lesbian equivalent of Indiana Jones…Saracen has sprinkled cliffhangers throughout this tale…If you enjoy the History Channel presentations about ancient Egypt, you will love this book. If you haven't ever indulged, it will be a wonderful introduction to the land of the Pharaohs. If you're a *Raiders of the Lost Ark*–type adventure fan, you'll love reading a woman in the hero's role."—*Just About Write*

By the Author

The 100th Generation

Vulture's Kiss

The Sistine Heresy

Mephisto Aria

MEPHISTO ARIA

by
Justine Saracen

2010

MEPHISTO ARIA

ISBN 10: 1-60282-139-9
ISBN 13: 978-1-60282-139-2

THIS TRADE PAPERBACK ORIGINAL IS PUBLISHED BY
BOLD STROKES BOOKS, INC.
P.O. BOX 249
VALLEY FALLS, NY 12185

FIRST EDITION: JANUARY 2010

CREDITS
EDITOR: SHELLEY THRASHER
PRODUCTION DESIGN: STACIA SEAMAN
COVER DESIGN BY SHERI (GRAPHICARTIST2020@HOTMAIL.COM)

Dedication

This novel is dedicated to opera singers Derek Ragin and Sylvia McNair, who allowed me into their backstage lives, and to Frederica von Stade, the quintessential "boy" mezzo-soprano.

I also wish to honor three other *Rosenkavalier* ladies I watched tromping around stage in knee pants and waistcoats singing love songs to other women: Tatiana Troyanos, Anne Howells, Brigitte Fassbaender. I do not know if real desire warmed their voices, but I claim the right to such a fantasy.

Acknowledgments

Over the years, numerous other singers have shared their wisdom and experience with me, and I would especially like to thank: Brigitte Fassbaender and Pan Conrad for detailed explanations of what it feels like to be Octavian; (the now deceased) Beverly Sills for allowing me to attend weeks of rehearsals at the New York City Opera; Ann Howells, who told amusing *Rosenkavalier* stories at Glyndebourne; and Laura Claycomb, who talked at length about stage craft and opera acting.

If one can honor a city, I wish to pay tribute to Salzburg, Austria, for giving me some of the most beautiful musical evenings of my life. And while I'm reminiscing, I'd like to thank Doris Kaufman, pianist, for entrapping me in classical music in the first place.

For technical details, thanks to wigmaker Sarah Opstad for trade secrets on the making and fitting of opera wigs.

Literary sources I drew on were first and foremost Wolfgang Goethe's *Faust* and *Urfaust*, Thomas Mann's *Doctor Faustus*, Alexander Werth's *Russia at War*, and the Hamburg performance of *Faust*. Gustav Gründgens, performing *Mephisto* at the age of sixty, has haunted my imagination for nearly half a century.

One also needs dedicated colleagues in "the biz" to make this string of themes and scenes into a printed story. Above all, I want to thank Jennifer Knight for encouragement and advice on how to sell my soul to the devil, and Shelley Thrasher, who has been a constant help as both editor and friend. Sheri has pulled another fantastic cover out of her magic lantern, and Stacia has deftly done the precision work of final editing.

Above all others, I owe this book to Radclyffe, the heart and soul of Bold Strokes Books.

I
OVERTURE

Berlin 1982

Katherina Marow staggered toward the parapet, at the end of her strength. She heard her own panting and the footfall of the men behind her, in close pursuit. Her knees were stiff, from kneeling by the body, and both of her palms were perspiring where she clutched handfuls of her bulky skirt. She focused on the steps, the speckled gray-green of weathered stone, and watched each foot landing, fearing above all that she might stumble. Finally, she reached the crenellated wall of the castle.

She stepped up on it, paused a fraction of a second to gather her courage, and turned her face to the light.

"Avanti à Dio!" she cried with her last breath, and threw herself off the wall.

❖

She landed smartly on the perfectly placed cushion and stayed on her knees until the final chords of the opera sounded. The two stagehands, who always stood by during her plunge, appeared without speaking and helped her to her feet. She thanked them with a nod, adjusted her costume, and stepped carefully around the set for her curtain call. The firing squad was just coming offstage.

Dazed, her heart still pounding from the exertion of the final scene, Katherina joined the cluster of singers waiting their turn to go before the curtain. The others glided out and returned, singly and in groups, from their applause.

Finally the tenor ventured out for his solo bow. His applause was long and enthusiastic, and she waited patiently while he savored his moment of glory. Then she strode out, passing him in the alley formed by the stagehands holding apart the overlapping curtains.

Katherina stepped out into the light and the Berlin audience erupted into ovation. Clearly, they adored their Tosca. Detached and enthralled, she gazed dreamily into the interior of the theater, absorbing the acclaim. She swept her eyes across the entire hall then glanced to her right, toward the space between the fluted columns that made up the patrons' box.

Of the several people there, one stood out by virtue of his height. Gray-haired and debonair, he had an air of authority. Even his clapping was reserved, as if his admiration were somehow different from that of the crowd. But at that moment, she belonged to the adoring world, and she shifted her gaze toward the highest balcony, where the students sat.

Exuberant applause washed over her from the dark mass above and below her and blended with the fierce glare of the footlight so that the sound itself seemed to radiate color and warmth. Intoxicated, she closed her eyes, letting the wave of adulation envelop her; she could almost lean her head against it.

Flowers landed at her feet and she gathered up the ones she could easily reach, holding them overhead in both hands. The volume and duration of applause was greater than it had been for the others and greater than she was used to. It suggested she had just advanced a stage in her career.

After a final inhalation of the sound, she curtsied deeply and exited the stage.

In the wings, the other singers had dispersed and the general manager stood alone, his expression somber. "Can we talk in your dressing room?" Without waiting for a reply, he took her arm.

The general manager closed the dressing room door behind him with excessive care, as if fearing to disturb anyone. Given the noise and activity everywhere else in the theater, his restraint was ominous. Katherina's joy drained away to dread.

"Is something wrong?"

"I am sorry, Katherina." He handed her a small note and waited silently, his eyes averted. She read the brief message, understanding the words but not the meaning. She forced her eyes over the senseless paragraph a second time, and as its sense gradually seeped in, her jaw trembled. "Is it true?" she whispered, hoping for denial.

The general manager nodded. "I'm afraid it is. I can assure you, the staff will keep the utmost discretion. I knew your father. Dr. Marow was a quiet man, but suicide was the last thing I would have expected."

II
DOLOROSO

Katherina taxied directly to the morgue, as if confronting her father's body would provide some explanation. The attendant led her along a corridor of white tile into a room of steel tables. The faint odor of decomposition and the stronger pungent smell of cleaning agents assaulted her. Only one table, to the left of the door, held an occupant, draped in a green cotton sheet. She hesitated for just a moment, knowing who it was and not wanting it to be so.

The attendant uncovered the cadaver to the chest and backed away. "His housekeeper has already identified him," he said. "But the police may want your statement too. You can stay with him as long as you'd like."

Katherina brought her hand automatically to her heart as she caught sight of the mortal remains of her father. But for the slightly blue lips, his sunken face was colorless. The jaw that fell back in the relaxation of death held beard stubble, giving him a look of shabbiness he did not deserve. She tried to convince herself it was a stranger. His head was wrapped in surgical gauze, which mercifully concealed the gunshot entry and exit wounds, though she could not help but imagine the mess they had made of his skull.

Suicide. She struggled to understand him. What could have brought him to that extreme? She yearned to talk to him, for just a moment, to ask why he had chosen that evening, the night of her great success, to abandon her.

She adored both parents but, even before her mother's death, had always felt she was her father's daughter: solitary, introspective, musical. She had inherited his cynicism and even looked like him.

Her earliest recollections were of their quiet conversations, mostly the undoing of the nonsense other children taught her. She had absorbed his little lessons on their trips to the zoo on winter days, when almost no one was there but the two of them. Holding her hand as they stood before the animal cages, he disabused her both of religion and of fairy tales. Cinderella and religion, he said, told the same lie, because they made you believe that someone good would always rescue you. But there was no rescue, not without payment.

He had lavished attention on her, but in a curious emotionless way, like a doting teacher rather than a father. No matter what she asked for, voice lessons, concerts, clothes, he gave them to her, though in postwar Germany everything was hard-wrought. Her mother had been an open book, a gentle, uncomplicated person. But even in their most tender hours, Sergei Marow was opaque.

She wept quietly, grasping his cold right hand—the hand that had held the pistol that sent him from the world.

❖

Katherina climbed out of the taxi in front of the house in the Schlossstrasse. A lovely old brick structure in the Wilmersdorf suburb of Berlin that had withstood World War II, it seemed a luxury when they moved into it during the 50s. East Berlin, a few kilometers away, became a foreign land, all the more so in 1961, when the Wall was built. After a year, they added an office space to one side, to house her father's modest but slowly growing dermatological practice.

She let herself into the house. "Tomasz? Casimira? Is anyone here?" No one answered. She set down her suitcase and wandered from room to room.

The house was immaculate with every object in its place, which she found somehow disquieting. No one lived here any longer who might create disorder. Deliberately, she tossed her coat over the staircase banister and climbed the stairs to her old room.

Pensive, she stood at the window, gazing down into the frost-covered garden looking for the gardener and housekeeper. Their cottage, which had also been added to the house, made the property seem like a miniature estate. Even now the grounds had a sort of elegance, derived from the gardener's constant maintenance.

Tomasz and Casimira Mazur had lived here since her mother died, and she was grateful that they were here now. She had no idea what to do with the house, so their presence—and the stipend from her father's financial estate that she would see to—allowed her to postpone any decisions.

"Katya!" A familiar voice called her by her childhood name and she turned around to the warm face of the housekeeper. The gray-haired woman embraced her unreservedly. As always, she smelled of cooked potatoes.

Tears welled up, but Katherina cleared her throat. "Thank you so much for taking care of things, Casimira. I'd be lost without you."

"*Liebchen*. You know, we's all family here. But come on now. Dry your face. There's an 'in-queerey,' of course, and the detective is already here. We was showin' him around the basement, but he's in the kitchen now lookin' to talk to you."

In fact, the detective already stood in the doorway behind Tomasz. "Walter Froelich, Berliner Polizei." A portly balding man in a dark green suit came forward and shook her hand, his grip loose and impersonal. "I am sorry to bother you in this difficult hour, Fräulein Marow, but there are questions I must ask."

"Of course." Katherina blew her nose in a tissue and composed herself.

The detective took out a tiny voice recorder and held it inconspicuously in one hand. "Since the deceased left no note, I must ask you, do you know of anyone who might have wished him harm or, at the very least, triggered the…act? Someone who stood to gain from it?"

"No, he never spoke of anything like that. But of course I was not usually here. Tomasz and Casimira would be in a much better position to answer that."

The detective turned his attention to Casimira. "Did you notice anything different on the day of his death, or shortly before? Any strange people in the neighborhood?"

"No, sir. Only a black dog, a big raggy poodle loose on the street. Sign of the devil, some folks say."

Katherina winced. "Casimira, where do you get those medieval ideas? It was probably just some stray."

"I'm sure you're right, Katherina dear. But you never know, do you? They's all kinds of things—"

The detective ignored the little side discussion and moved on. "What about letters or telephone calls?"

Casimira shook her head. "The telephone didn't ring that day at all. Herr Marow got his own mail every morning. 'Course I checked his desk. Nothing there but the electric bill."

"Did he say anything to you that might have suggested something was bothering him? Anything out of the ordinary that had happened to him recently?"

"No, sir." Tomasz rubbed his cheek, recalling. "But he was real quiet that day. Just sat in his study all afternoon, with the music going. Then, some time during the night, when we was sleeping, he went out and…and shot himself. The noise woke us up, and then we found him in the snow. We called an ambulance right away. The police was here too and they took the weapon."

"Yes, I have examined it," Froelich said. "An old Russian sidearm." To Katherina, "Did you know that he owned this pistol?"

"I had no idea. If it was Russian, I would assume it was a war souvenir, taken from the enemy. I don't know how else he would have a gun, least of all a Russian one."

"Suicide with the enemy's gun. That would be ironic, wouldn't it?" Froelich said softly. Then, resuming official procedure, "Have you examined all the likely places for a note? And the less likely places? Desk drawers, wardrobe, coat pockets, the floor under his bed or desk?"

Casimira's chin went up. "I keep a clean house, sir. They's nothing on the floor. We checked the drawers and Herr Marow had only one coat. Its pockets were empty."

The detective raised an open palm, as if to placate her. "All right. We'll leave it at that. It's possible that something may turn up later. In the mail, for example." He drew a business card from a side pocket and laid it on the table. "Please keep me apprised of anything unusual."

He clicked off the tiny tape recorder, signaling the end of the interview, and Tomasz led him to the door.

Katherina followed the housekeeper out of the kitchen. "Casimira, do you know if my father was seeing a doctor?"

"No, dear. Not for a long time. He was as healthy as any man his age. But the last day he did seem depressed. Moody, like after your blessed mother died. Come to think about it, he mentioned her."

"Really? What did he say?"

"That her death was his fault. Don't know why he said that. It wasn't nobody's fault. Tomasz and me, we didn't arrive here 'til she was gone half a year already, but we knew it was the diphtheria. That was the year of the epidemic. We was just glad *you* made it through."

Katherina dropped her eyes at the mention of the double disaster that had been visited upon them. It was a wound that had never closed.

Casimira went on. "Then he talked about the war, and about people who came home alive, but all broke inside. 'Soulless,' I think he said."

The housekeeper began dusting while she talked, moving around the room and wiping already clean surfaces with her dishtowel. Katherina watched the woman who had stepped into the role of caretaker for both her and her father. She had been a godsend, a calm, efficient presence around the house, cleaning up after them, sensing where she was needed.

Casimira had instinctively found the middle place between housekeeper and parent, and had seen to a child's physical needs without trying to meet the emotional ones, unless invited. And she was almost never invited. For all her kindness, she could not fill the void that opened up the day Katherina's childhood ended and guilt began. For Katherina remembered the last warm embrace of her mother, that feverish night. The embrace that killed her.

Katherina rubbed her face, dispelling the memory. "Thank you, Casimira. I won't be needing anything else. Just some quiet."

"All right, dear. Call us any time."

Casimira and Thomasz left the house again, and Katherina closed the door behind them.

For lack of other occupation, she wandered into her father's study, though she hesitated again in the doorway. It seemed an invasion of a place and a life that had always been private. She sighed inwardly. But death was the ultimate forfeiture of privacy, wasn't it?

His small oak desk was tidy, as always. She could not remember it any other way. The shelves behind it held his well-worn books: hardbound medical ones on the left side and light literature on the right.

Idly, not looking for anything in particular, she opened and closed the desk drawers. He kept a detailed account book and a folder of his bank statements and correspondences, of which there was little. His lawyer had the will, she knew, and her father did not seem to have left any urgent business undone. For that she was grateful.

She wandered around the room, touching books, familiar objects, then thumbed through his collection of record disks. She smiled wanly; he was the only person she knew who still listened to vinyl disks and did not mind having to clean them and the phonograph needle before every playing. The recordings were all familiar. Symphonies and operas and chamber music that she had heard over and over as a child. Some of the jackets were torn and taped together. She wondered which ones he had listened to on his last day. Which of them had inspired such melancholy that he had taken his own life?

Then it struck her, and she shook her head at her own obtuseness. A disk was still on the turntable and the empty record jacket still leaned against the cabinet wall beside it. She recognized it immediately. It was the new Munich recording, in the original French, with Joachim von Hausen conducting. Berlioz' *Damnation of Faust*.

She tapped the On switch and the turntable arm lifted, pivoted a few degrees, and dropped gently onto the outermost groove. Choral parts played first, and Katherina sat down to study the handsome record jacket in her hand. Faust and Marguerite stood shoulder to shoulder. But Faust's face was twisted in terror as he looked into Hell while next to him, gazing upward, Marguerite was radiant. More than radiant. It was Anastasia Ivanova, the stunning Russian singer who had defected from the Soviet Union five years before. Katherina remembered the rather sensational news and realized she had never seen Ivanova's face up close. She studied it while she listened to the dark mezzo-soprano voice that poured from the speakers.

"*Autre fois, un roi de Thule...*"

Under the penitent's shawl, the face was slightly Slavic except for the slender nose. Soft lines curved from the nostrils around the mouth that was wide and expressive. But most fascinating were the mist-gray eyes: full of expression and intelligence. At the corners, both eyes had faint lines, as if at the very moment of redemption, Marguerite squinted with a hint of skepticism. Worse perhaps, while she gazed upward toward divine grace, she emanated an unrepentant allure, a sensuality that belied the chaste remorse.

Yet her voice contained a powerful poignancy. Katherina could imagine her father, already despondent, being urged by the plangent melody into the abyss. It gripped her too, exacerbating her guilt and regret.

Brooding, she reached for the paper sleeve that had held the disk. As she grasped it, an envelope fell out.

The letter inside was on official government stationery, with letterhead: Liaison Committee for the Commemoration of Stalingrad. But most baffling of all, it was addressed to "Sergei Marovsky." The postmark was recent, she noted breathlessly; he could even have received it on the day of his death.

But "Marovsky"? How could that be?

Mephistopheles was singing now, in a robust bass voice. "*Esprits de flames inconstantes...*"

She frowned at "inconstant" and focused again on the letter. It was in detached official language, but it did refer to him as a hero, a survivor of the gargantuan battle on the eastern front. She dropped the letter onto the desk again. It was simply too much for her to absorb, too much to learn about a man she had thought she knew. The ground beneath her seemed to have opened up.

Sergei Marow had once been Sergei Marovsky and he had fought at Stalingrad.

He had survived the most brutal battle of World War II, the battle that had seen the fall of an entire German army and reversed the direction of the war. Why had he not told his family?

Several scenarios offered themselves. Had he been in captivity and released among the few lucky ones in the first year? Maybe he had been one of the tiny number of wounded soldiers who were taken out by air before the final defeat. Was it even possible he had been among the pathetic handful that survived years of captivity in Russia?

She read the letter to the end, but it gave no more information about the man, only the commemorative event to which he was invited in the coming February.

Her mind spinning, she laid her head in her hands. That he had never talked about his war experiences had not seemed odd. Few people spoke of them. As a child, she had grown used to hearing adults reminisce about the hunger of the years of occupation right after the war and, less often, about the air raids and the fires during the war itself. But now that she thought about it, she had never heard the men talk about the battlefront.

And why should they? No one wanted to boast about fighting for National Socialism. In a global campaign that had become genocidal and had annihilated whole cities on both sides, individual acts of bravery held little meaning.

But Stalingrad was different. The whole world spoke of Stalingrad in hushed tones. Stalingrad was Armageddon, a cataclysm where whole armies threw themselves at each other in the bitter winter of 1942–43, where men were reduced to savagery, to cannibalism, to daily hand-to-hand slaughter of the enemy. No matter that the German advance was one of pure aggression. To have survived Stalingrad was to have emerged from the mouth of hell and to have, in some sense, been purged of the national guilt.

She got up to pace again, needing to think, circling the room, trailing her fingertips along the furniture. His oaken armoire stood in front of her. She opened the door cautiously, as if not wanting to disturb his spirit that still dwelled in the row of worn suit jackets, all brown or gray. The slightly shabby attire of an old man who no longer went out very much.

To occupy idle, nervous hands, she removed the jackets and laid them on the rug in several piles. One pile for Tomasz—the two men were about the same size—one for charity, and the third to be discarded. A mournful job, and yet to do nothing but sit wondering would have been worse.

A leather satchel lay on the bottom of the wardrobe. Old leather, cracked with age, but a handsome bag. Maybe she could rescue it with leather oil. She took hold of it, surprised at its weight, and dragged it out onto the floor.

It was locked, but the lock was old and flimsy and she forced it easily with the point of a scissors. Dust flew up into her face as she pulled the two sides apart exposing a crumpled rucksack.

She tilted the satchel on its side to slide the rucksack out and only then did she see the faded lettering on the side. Russian letters.

War booty? Cellars and attics all over Germany held articles brought home from the front and then forgotten. She stared at it for a moment, as if it were a strange brown animal curled up at her feet, while on the record player Berlioz' chorus lamented of damnation.

Finally she knelt down and undid the rucksack's buckles. The leather strap was dry and pieces of it crumbled to reddish-gray dust between her fingers. Something bulky and soft was inside, and she slid it out.

A light brown tunic and dark trousers were neatly folded and tied around with a belt. The belt buckle held an unmistakable insignia, the hammer and sickle. She slipped the tunic out and unfolded it. A Russian soldier's uniform. She stared, dumbfounded. The name stenciled onto the inner yoke of the tunic was Marovsky.

Sergei Marovsky had been in the Red Army. Realization struck her and brought another wave of tears. If that was so, the pistol with which he had shot himself was probably his own.

She glanced around the study, a room that now belonged to a stranger, and everything that was once familiar seemed to mock her. Even his music, which poured from his antiquated record player, seemed filled with mystery.

She reached into the rucksack again. There was more.

Under the uniform was a notebook held together by a frayed cotton cord. She broke the cord easily and leafed through the lined book, the sort that school children used. Its pages were covered with text, each section precisely dated, in her father's neat script.

The first entry was headed February 20, 1943. My god, she thought. Sergei Marovsky, who never said a word about the war and the occupation, had kept a journal.

She set it aside carefully and peered at what had been tucked into the front. A few sheets of folded paper, with a string threaded in and out of the spine to create a sort of booklet. It was badly soiled, with water stains along the edges and grime in every fold. The entries were also dated, and most of the text, though smudged, was legible. Not comprehensible, though. The cursive script was in Russian Cyrillic. The smattering of the language that she had picked up as a child extended little beyond mastery of the alphabet. She could make out only the dates, all in February 1943, and the word "Stalingrad" in the heading.

With reverence, and a touch of dread, she laid the pages carefully on top of the notebook and resumed emptying the rucksack.

The last item at the bottom was a cloth bag sewn shut. Both thread and fabric were badly disintegrated, so she simply pulled the bag apart. She stared, perplexed, at what fell onto her lap. A black leather glove. It was filthy, and the cracks in the leather were filled with grayish grit.

Not a glove exactly, she realized on closer examination. A gauntlet, with a cuff reaching halfway up the forearm, of the sort that had not been worn for centuries. Ah, it was for a costume, she could see that now. Inside the cuff, in block letters, it read, *Stalingrad Opera*.

Katherina had been kneeling and now she rocked back and sat on the rug. The sheer weight of the revelations exhausted her, and there was no one to ask for an explanation. Tomasz, perhaps? Unlikely. Master and gardener had always been only cordial, even after many years. It was impossible to imagine her father would confide private things to Tomasz that he did not even tell his family.

The music had stopped. The first disk had come to an end and, half in a trance, she got up to turn it over. She dropped again into the desk chair as Anastasia Ivanova began to sing the most poignant of the Faust arias.

"D'amour l'ardente flame consume mes beaux jours" flowed along the back of Katherina's mind as she tried to make sense of the discoveries. How were they related? A hidden identity, a heroic and possibly horrifying past, and finally an invitation by the German government.

The letter; maybe it held more clues she had overlooked. But no, it was the simplest of invitations, in the dry formal language of the German government. In the spirit of *glasnost*, a commemorative concert in Volgograd, built on the ruins of Stalingrad. A concert by invitation only, for politicians and for survivors, both Russian and German.

Then she noticed the penciled words, barely legible at the bottom. It seemed to her now that while her father had listened to the Berlioz recording, he had read the letter and then scribbled at the bottom of the page.

Letters, apparently written by a trembling hand, formed the words, "Florian, forgive me."

III
MALINCONICO

Night fell finally, and the shock of discovery had muted to burning curiosity. Tomasz and Casimira, as she expected, knew nothing about another family name, and Katherina declined to inform them of the journal. Clearly, if there were answers to the mystery of her father, she would have to look for them in his writings.

Tentatively, as if before a hazardous venture, she settled onto the sofa and studied the slender volume. The few Cyrillic pages tucked in the front were a puzzle and would have to wait for a translation. She thumbed through the rest of the journal. Though written in a variety of pens and pencils, sometimes hurriedly, other times with precision, all the entries were in the same legible hand. She hesitated again, as she had before her father's study, reluctant to intrude even farther into an obviously private domain. But then she asked herself, Why does a man write things down unless he wants someone to read them?

She wiped her hand once again over the cover, brushing away dust, and folded it back to the opening page. She was not prepared for the shock of the first entry.

February 20, 1943
I cut off Georgi Adrianovitch's legs today. More precisely, I assisted at their amputation. But when he regained consciousness, it was me he saw, and he screamed. Finally we calmed him down and got him to understand that it was an exchange he had to make, his deal with the devil. He bought his life, and a trip home, but he paid with his legs. I could sympathize. I've made a deal too, but I paid with my soul.

I've started my journal again, this time in German. If it's

confiscated or captured, all that anyone will find are the broodings of a coward. No military information here, not a word about Stalingrad.

Commander Chuikov needs me for only half an hour every day; the rest of the time he's ordered me to the field hospital. I'm assigned to gangrene amputations. Cutting away dead flesh suits my state of mind. I'm dead myself.

Georgi Adrianovitch was a special case, a Stalingrad hero, wounded twice before and sent back to the front. Not this time. He has a new row of shiny medals for his chest, but no legs. And this is me now, with legs but no heart. No more writing pretty phrases in Russian. That was the Sergei of Stalingrad.

Katherina laid the journal aside for a moment and rubbed the bridge of her nose, as if that could dispel the confusion. Then she read the entry a second time, trying to absorb it.

Apparently, Sergei Marovsky had been a front-line surgeon with the Red Army. That explained the uniform. Well, no. It didn't so much explain it as add another layer of mystery. How had a German citizen become a Soviet doctor? Had he defected to the Russians? If so, why had he never mentioned it? What had happened at Stalingrad? Most unfathomable of all was how he could have served Vasily Chuikov. Even she knew he was the commander of the Russian troops that had invaded Berlin with the savagery of a Mongol horde. And how, after all that, did this Doctor Marovsky metamorphose into a soft spoken-German dermatologist with a tiny practice in the suburbs of Berlin? So utterly illogical. The journal seemed like a piece of fiction, and if she closed it, reality would return. Except that her father would still be dead, and the Russian uniform would still be lying unfolded on the floor.

"Katya, there's a telephone call for you." Casimira stood in the doorway wiping her hands on the dishtowel she seemed to always have. "She says she's your agent."

Katherina followed her back to the living room and lifted the handset. "Charlotte? Yes, the interment is tomorrow. After that I suppose I'll stay here for a few days to put things in order." She looked around a living room that was already immaculate.

"You want me to do what? *Carmina Burana*? I don't know." She shook her head, though there was no one in the room to see it. "I can't think about a concert right now."

Charlotte Lemke persisted. She pointed out that the engagement was three weeks away, in Hamburg—an easy train ride from West Berlin, had an undemanding part with only three rehearsals, and paid a good fee. More importantly, she went on, it was with Joachim von Hausen, who was conducting the next season in Salzburg. What's more—Charlotte tossed her last card on the table—in three weeks Katherina would prefer to work any place at all rather than stay at home staring at the walls in deep mourning.

Katherina glanced back toward the study where a performance that Joachim von Hausen conducted had hypnotized her for an hour. He seemed a witness to the family mystery now.

"All right. Tell them I'll do it."

IV

Affannoso

Clasping his hands in front of him, the minister droned, *"Vater unser, Der Du bist im Himmel..."*

Katherina glanced around at the circle of people gathered at the grave. She recognized all of them: her father's colleagues from the hospital where he had worked on Fridays, musician friends, various neighbors. None was called Florian. A man stood off in the distance, elderly and distinguished, but was not part of the funeral party and he wandered among the other tombstones.

Katherina had debated briefly whether to invite people at all to the interment. There was something so archaic about a public burial. But she also decided that ceremony and a symbolic joining of friends' hands negated some of death's terrifying arbitrariness. Besides, not to have a public service with parson and prayer would have suggested shame at her father's suicide. She was not ashamed. Suicide was a tragedy, not a sin. They were not in the middle ages.

Pious Catholics that they were, Tomasz and Casimira had lowered their heads and closed their eyes during the prayer, moving their lips along with the pastor's recitation. But Katherina did not pray for her father and knew she would not meet him in the hereafter. The only part of him that "lived after" was that part that lived in her. When she brooded, listening to music, a bit of him nestled in her mind. She felt her gentle mother too, whenever she was girlish or fussed over small soft things, but mostly it was her father whom she could sense looking out at the world through her eyes. Yet now she wrestled with the contradiction, that she could sense him that way and yet not know him.

"...denn Dein ist das Reich und die Kraft und die Herrlichkeit in Ewigkeit. Amen." The minister finished, and the men donned their

hats again against the increasing wind. The pallbearers stepped forward quickly and took hold of the ropes to lower the casket into the ground.

When it reached the bottom of the pit and the ropes were drawn out, Katherina limped on cold feet to the pile of sod. Snow had begun to fall during the ceremony and the pile was already covered with a dusting of powder. The handful she grasped was a mixture of dirt and ice. She leaned out over the grave and murmured to the coffin, "Who were you, then?" She crumbled the dirt through her fingers and shuddered as the heavier lumps thumped onto the casket lid.

The snow became heavier, and crystals soon covered the casket in the grave pit. Katherina shivered with the cold and with the thought of her father being consigned to so awful a place. She called up childhood memories of him, the bulwark of their little family.

He had been attentive, though given to bouts of melancholy, which he often cured by listening to music. Throughout her childhood, he had taken her and her mother to concerts, cultivating her taste in music. Curious, she recalled for the first time in years that the terrible sickness had struck her at the opera. Though it had happened twenty years before, she remembered now precisely that it was Gounod's *Faust*.

It was a strange evening. As the three of them took the *Strassenbahn* to the opera house, her father talked about the libretto, rambling on about guilt and retribution. Faust, he said, was the story of all ambition. Nothing good was ever gained without payment. And everything could be taken away again. "Like *that*," he said, and snapped his fingers for emphasis. The warning made no sense to her then, but it had stayed with her.

Someone coughed, signaling that the ceremony was over. The others all had thrown down their handfuls of sod, and the gravediggers had arrived with their shovels to finish the job. She thanked the minister, shook hands mutely with all the visitors, and began the walk back to the car with Tomasz and Casimira.

She touched the gardener's sleeve. "Tomasz, did my father know anyone named Florian? Someone he might have quarreled with, or who might have visited him recently?"

Tomasz thought for a moment. "Not that I recall. 'Course he might've had friends we didn't know. Not many people visited. He was kind of, you know, solitary."

Katherina shivered again, numb from standing in the cold and from the emotional strain. As she left the cemetery grasping Casimira's arm, she glanced around to see if the distinguished-looking stranger had found the tombstone he was looking for, but he had disappeared.

❖

Tomasz and Casimira followed her into the house, wiping damp shoes on the mat in the entryway. "Shall I make tea, dear?" Casimira asked.

Katherina understood that the offer was simply a way to delay leaving her alone, but, in fact, she did not feel like talking. There would be things to discuss in the coming days: whether and when she might move back permanently, how to finance the continued maintenance, when to meet with the lawyer. But not now. The shock of a family suicide had dissipated, and fatigue had dulled her mourning. Now she felt something else, the hint of anger. It had nibbled at the back of her mind while she made the funeral arrangements, but now she felt cheated, doubly bereft, for Sergei Marow had both died and robbed his daughter of himself. A stranger lay in the family plot, someone who'd had a different name, worn a different uniform, done battlefront surgery on Russian heroes.

And yet, she was intrigued. Who was Sergei Marovsky? Was he someone she might have liked? There was only one way to find out.

Casimira still stood with the kettle in her hand, waiting for an answer.

"Oh, no, thank you. I'd really like to be alone for a while. I'll be fine." Katherina kissed her on the cheek and nudged her gently toward the door.

❖

Strange how there are different kinds of quiet, she thought. Her father's house was not just soundless now, it also held no expectation of sound. He would not stride through the door with the mail or stand in front of her talking, jingling the change in his pocket, as he liked to do. She remembered that about him now, that he sometimes played with coins, rubbing his fingers over them absentmindedly, as if reassuring himself that he had them. He was otherwise neutral about money, neither a big spender nor particularly thrifty. He simply seemed to be glad that there was money in the house to take care of things. Did that attitude come from the postwar years, when trade was the main currency?

It was as good a reason as any to see what his journal would say about him. She made her own tea, then took up her post on the sofa with a blanket over her legs and resumed her reading.

March 1, 1943

So this is what I'll be doing for a while, at least until they decide they have no need for traitors and cowards. For now, I serve the commander and that protects me from suspicion. When his hands get bad, he summons me. I take him clean gloves and wash his sores. When they start to heal, he sends me back to surgery. The others were wary of me for a while, but now they let me do my job. They don't seem to think I will desert at the first opportunity. They're right. What would be the point?

But I have constant nightmares, all variations on the same thing. Last night it was Zharptitsa, flying over the frozen steppes, tossed by the wind. I tried to catch him, to save him from the cold, but he disappeared into the snowstorm. I knew he would soon freeze, far away from me, and his beautiful wings would lie open and rigid on the snow. I fell to my knees, crying. When I woke up, I ached from the sorrow.

March 15, 1943

I finally have a uniform, after a month of living in a padded jacket from a dead Russian infantryman. The supply lines have opened up again so not only do we have fresh bandages and antiseptic, but I have a new *gymnasterka* tunic, complete with epaulets, medical corps insignias, and the rank of corporal. Probably the only corporal in the Red Army performing surgery. Best of all, I replaced my old wool cap—held by a scarf tied under my chin—with a thick *ushanka*. What a relief to be able to pull the flaps down when I'm outside. First time in weeks my ears are warm.

As a doctor, I can usually stay indoors. But in the deadly cold outside, civilians or German POWs work in burial parties to gather the corpses that are lying all over the city. The work parties carry them on sleds or in handcarts and stack them by the roadside. Almost all of the horses have been slaughtered for food, but a few camels are left to harness for the job. The ground is still too hard to dig new graves, but the anti-tank ditches dug last summer are good for burying the dead. Already there are signs of typhus among the work teams.

The Allies have promised ambulances, but for now we have only old city busses, outfitted to carry wounded. For warmth, they have little metal stoves stoked with scraps of wood, and they all smoke terribly. The wounded men not only suffer from the lurching of the busses over the horrendous roads, they choke on the air inside. Better than freezing, but only a little.

April 5, 1943
The spring thaw has started and everything's turned to mud. Less fighting now since nobody can move artillery on either side. Russian troops are slogging toward Kursk and our medical team is packing up to follow them.

Still don't sleep well, no matter how tired I am. Nightmares, again and again. Of birds, of children, of beautiful things that I've let die.

May 22, 1943
The Stalin propaganda is in full force. Everyone has forgotten the purges of the '30s and the millions who died. Now everyone parrots "the Stalinist strategy" and "the military genius of Stalin" as the cause of every victory. The younger men seem proud to be one of "Stalin's soldiers" and hungry for the new medals and distinctions. It's the older ones who sense that their entire generation has been sacrificed. But all of them are brave, almost suicidal in their courage. The men

are talking about a battle where sixty tanks puttied up all their openings and forded a river underwater.

June 14, 1943
Red Army medicine is not as good as in the German field hospitals. Only the lightly wounded are saved. The Russians cry for their mothers just like the Germans did. The ones who can still fight are bitter, hungry for vengeance, and there is an almost universal hatred of the German invaders. Fortunately, my Russian conceals the fact that I was one of them. But the hour of vengeance is beginning and the Allies are already wreaking havoc on Germany's industrial areas. The radio reports heavy bombing raids on the Ruhr, on Cologne, Mainz, Frankfurt. Germany is lost. How many will die before Hitler's government understands this?

Fewer nightmares now. It must be the warm weather, the disappearance of snow.

July 28, 1943
Hamburg has been heavily bombed and there are reports that the Allies have begun raids on Berlin. My home, my family. All that I thought would stay safe while I was at the front. Has our house been hit? No way to know. And if it hasn't been hit yet, they'll be back again. The Allied bombers control the skies.

August 20, 1943
In Kursk now, treating the wounded from the great tank battle.

I thought Stalingrad had hardened me, but this was a different sort of horror. A soldier doesn't shrink from the thought of death from gun or explosion. But no one imagines being crushed under a churning tank tread. The battlefield is a butcher's block, with scraps of meat that a day ago were men. It was no better to die by fire inside the tanks either, the still-living ones pulled out without faces or hands. Fortunately we still have morphine for them.

The commissars have called the battle a great victory for Russia.

September 17, 1943
Most of the field medics are women, and they are unbelievably tough. In Stalingrad I saw them carry wounded men on their backs. Not much like the German *Mädels*, who are supposed to stay home and bear children for the Führer.

There is a shortage of cotton for bandages. We manage at the field hospital by tearing up bed linen and boiling it, but the medics at the front can't do that. They're re-using bandages and sometimes even moss or linden tree shavings as absorbent. Infection is rampant.

Italy has capitulated. Italian *faschisti* in the German-held territories will be put to work for the Germans. Doctors like me, working for new masters, treating soldiers of a different nationality.

What was the reason for this war? I can't remember.

Katherina set the journal aside and rubbed her face. She wanted to read on but her eyes burned, and though she read and reread the last page, her sleep-starved mind wandered off each time in the same place. Revelations overwhelmed her, and every new entry brought as many questions as answers. What was Zharptitsa? A bird, obviously, but why did losing it cause a soldier to break down and cry?

Why the large gaps between the entries? Presumably he was simply too busy at the surgeon's table to have the leisure to write. She knew that 1943 was a decisive year in which the German army was slowly pushed back toward the homeland. Embedded with the Russians as he was, did he think of that as defeat or victory? Did he care who would win the war?

Katherina was nodding off, but she did not want to go upstairs. Her childhood room, across from her father's empty bedroom, seemed even more desolate than the living room. She also could not bear to lie in the darkness and so she tilted the shade on the lamp away from her and left it burning, a sphere of comfort in the night.

Her sleep was troubled. The light shining on her face and the narrow sofa cushions kept her in shallow sleep, and she dreamed fitfully. Scenes came to her in patches, fraught with anxiety. Her father, in Russian uniform, seen in the distance through wind-blown snow. She struggled toward him with weighted feet, as he disappeared into a long black line of men winding toward the horizon. Then something fluttered in the snow just ahead of her and she clambered toward it. A bird, she thought with horror, with broken wings. But no, it was a glove, a black gauntlet, lifted slightly by the wind. She woke, shivering, in the unheated living room, her blanket on the floor.

V
CARMINA BURANA—VIVACE

Joachim von Hausen was rehearsing the chorus and the *pas de deux* of the dancers when Katherina arrived at the stage entrance. He was slight of build, but the energy of his person and his stature in the music world lent him height. She had taken to him immediately at the first rehearsal.

From the stage-left wings, she watched admiringly as the two lead dancers executed their most strenuous leaps. Carlo's tight musculature, vaguely Greek features, and long wavy hair made him the object of nearly everyone's desire. And the press adored him. Sabine, who partnered him, was just as striking, even in rehearsal, when she left her mane of red hair loose. As she leapt and spun, it flew around her like a flame in a breeze.

Part of the dance brought her sweeping far stage left. Scarcely a meter away, Katherina could see every taut muscle in the dancer's body. Unlike the other ballerinas, Sabine had visible breasts, and as she arched her back they swelled provocatively under her leotard. She curled forward, then straightened and danced in open-armed pirouettes back toward her partner.

"Nice, huh?" someone said at Katherina's elbow.

"What? Oh, Ulrich. I didn't hear you arrive. Which of them are you admiring, Carlo or Sabine?" she teased the baritone.

"Our lovely ballerina, of course. I wouldn't mind having a go at her. With muscles like that, it'd be like screwing a leopard. I've heard they call her the 'man-eater.'"

"It could also just be one of your lust fantasies."

"For sure, it's that too." He smirked as he moved away.

"You and every male in the chorus," she called after him. Suddenly she was not sure she had brought her score. She knelt down and fumbled through her shoulder bag until she found the stapled pages. Relieved, she stood up again and found herself face to face with Sabine, panting from her last pirouette. Droplets of moisture dotted her forehead and upper lip, and she tugged at the cloth of her sweat-damp leotard.

"Hello," the dancer said, between breaths. Then she stepped back for a moment and scrutinized Katherina, as if appraising her.

Katherina tried to think of something clever to say, but at that moment the conductor called her onto the stage for her solo.

❖

Ulrich glanced at his watch. "I think we were terrific today, and look, it's only five o'clock. Anyone interested in a beer and sausage across the street? I'll pay." His invitation was loud enough for all to hear, but it seemed to Katherina that he intended it primarily for Sabine.

In fact, she accepted, along with a handful of others. "You're joining us too, aren't you?" Sabine caught her eye.

Katherina thought of what awaited her at home. Nothing awaited her. "Sure, why not?"

"Let's go then." Ulrich threw a quick "See, I told you" glance toward Katherina, then helped Sabine on with her coat. In a moment, everyone was gathered and he herded the cluster of his new friends through the door.

The group migrated across the street to the Café zum Engel, and Katherina fell in step with Dieter. The tenor was a short amiable man with chipmunk cheeks, who, in spite of his youth, was already losing his hair. His equally amiable and colorless girlfriend was on his other arm.

They arranged themselves around the large common table. Ulrich was quick to help Sabine off with the coat he had just put on her. She smiled prettily at her unsubtle suitor and sat down between him and Katherina.

"I just adore *Carmina Burana*," one of the other dancers said as the beer and sausage orders went out.

Ulrich laughed. "Of course you do. It's work for dancers, right? Besides, nobody *doesn't* like *Carmina Burana*. It's the rock-and-roll of classical music. You'll see. The audience will go nuts for it."

"I wish the public would go nuts for opera. That would give *us* more work," Dieter added. "Sometimes I think it's just a matter of getting people into the opera house. Once they've heard it, they love it, but how do you lure them there in the first place?"

One of the dancers said, "You should give them prizes the first time they come."

"You mean souvenirs? Like a Desdemona handkerchief or a Tosca fruit knife?" Katherina laughed.

"Well, there could be a whole subcategory of knives." Ulrich warmed to the subject. "The Madame Butterfly dagger, and the Carmen pocket knife—sort of a Swiss Army knife thing, but Spanish—and then a Rigoletto knife."

"No, for Rigoletto they really ought to have a souvenir sack." Dieter's girlfriend joined in. "Like the one he carries his dead daughter around in for two days before she sings her aria."

Sabine leaned onto the table. "How about a line of clothing? A Lucia di Lammermoor nightgown, complete with bloodstains, a Pagliacci giubba."

"What's a giubba?" a dancer asked.

"It's that big clown shirt with pom poms that Pagliacci wears."

"Okay, a Pagliacci giubba." Dieter pretended to be writing a list with his finger on the tablecloth. "And a Don Giovanni address book. Organized by country. With extra pages for Spain." He paused. "What about Fidelio chains?"

The beer pitcher arrived and Ulrich poured a round of glasses. "Who's going to want chains, for god's sake?"

"Well, who's going to want a giubba?" Katherina laughed.

"Good point," Ulrich conceded. "Ah, I've got one. You want something practical? How about a Salome serving platter?"

"You mean like the one that holds the head of John the Baptist?" Dieter asked.

"That's disgusting." Katherina feigned horror. Suddenly she became aware of pressure against her left leg. She moved a millimeter away, but Sabine's leg followed.

Katherina was confused. What did it mean? She moved away a second time, but the touch was there again a moment later. Above the table too, Sabine's well-muscled upper arm brushed against her. Was she simply trying to get Katherina's attention?

Katherina leaned toward the arm and spoke quietly under the din of the group laughter. "Is there something you want to say to me?"

Sabine pressed closer in response, but was silent. Katherina could smell her perfume. Then Sabine whispered, "I saw the way you looked at me. The way you've *been* looking at me."

"I don't know what you mean." Katherina's throat was tight.

Ulrich made some bawdy remark about dancers' derrieres, and the group burst into laughter again. Sabine said under her breath, "Do you want to see more?"

Someone held the pitcher over Katherina's glass and she raised her hand to signal no. Her heart was pounding. "I have no idea what you're talking about," she whispered. Her left leg where Sabine's knee was pressed against it began to tremble. The sudden tightness in her sex was unwelcome, frightening.

"Of course you do. I know you. You're just like me."

Katherina slid her chair away from the table so suddenly that the table shook. The laughter stopped and a dozen eyes focused on her.

"I…uh, I'm sorry. I just remembered I have to be at home this evening. A visitor arriving. So stupid of me to forget. Thank you, Ulrich. I…uh…I'll see you all tomorrow at dress rehearsal."

Half a dozen heads nodded and murmured polite agreement. Swinging her coat over her shoulders, she left the Café zum Engel without looking back.

VI
Lamentando

Katherina sat at her father's desk. Though she had been home for half an hour, she still felt slightly breathless, as if she had fled something terrifying and only just found refuge. She felt foolish now, having left the café so abruptly and run back to her father's house. The people in the restaurant must have thought she was crazy. What was she running from anyhow?

She shook her head in a sort of internal dialogue. Two weeks before, she had been so sure of herself. She knew where she had come from and where all signs indicated she was going. But the floor seemed to have dropped away from under her. The man who had been the rock on which she had built her identity had been living a lie before he killed himself, and now a woman she had just met claimed to know her deepest desires. What *were* her deepest desires, anyhow? She wasn't ready to explore that darkness.

She glanced around the room, at Sergei Marow's books and records, and the journal of his life, and laughed bitterly. Her plight was so trivial, so banal compared to his. He—his whole generation, in fact—had looked into the abyss, had seen cruelty and evil in its pure, uncompromised form, while all she had to anguish over was flirtation. She felt suddenly ashamed, wallowing in her silly fears when in front of her lay his chronicle of cataclysm. She owed him her respect and her attention, so she opened the journal again to where she had left off.

❖

January 29, 1944
The Russians have broken through to Leningrad. Incredible, that the Germans besieged the city for nearly 900 days. I get

sick thinking of what it was like to be locked inside, trying to survive on the tiny trickle of food brought across Lake Ladoga. There are stories already now of people living on snow and sawdust, and Moscow reports that some million people died of starvation. What has happened to my cousins, I wonder. Kyril and Irena, I think they were called. Most likely they're soldiers now, but what about the others? Strange, you go to war thinking that the people back home somehow stay safe.

The retreating Germans wrecked the Catherine and Alexander Palaces and destroyed most of the other historical structures in the Tsar's park at Tsarskoe Selo. Even the Bolsheviks didn't do that.

February 2, 1944
It's been a year exactly since Stalingrad. Hollow nausea when I remember, and yet I can't get the images out of my mind. Karlovsky tormenting me with a cruel choice. Then the devil's gauntlet on the floor. Accusing me. Will this weight ever be lifted from my chest?

February 14, 1944
Headquarters has moved the medical staff again, following Commander Chuikov's troops westward. I'm slowly heading back to Germany. Back to what, I wonder.

There are round-the-clock bombings of Berlin now. The US Air Force bombs during daylight and the RAF at night. Dr. Tchelechev was gleeful at the news. I keep thinking of my parents. Are they still alive? Joining the Red Army, I have betrayed them too. Will Berlin surrender? Probably not, and so I will be part of a military storm that may destroy it.

March 24, 1944
Transferred to Poznan but was called on again by Commdr. Chuikov. His hands are infected again. When he lets them get dirty we go through the same round. He's a simple man and

thinks of munitions, not microorganisms. They both can kill, just as painfully.

I've treated him off and on for over a year now, in the beginning daily, now maybe once every two weeks. Although the men like him a lot and he is almost fatherly to them, he's never talked much to me, except about his disease. I can't blame him; he knows I came from the other side. But having your hands held for over a year does form a kind of bond. Out of nowhere he asked, "When the war's over, what will you tell your children?"

I was caught off guard. "Assuming I survive so long, I can't imagine having children. Not after all the horrors I've seen."

He shook his head. "The horrors are why we must have children. To have hope."

I had no hope, but had to answer something. "I'll tell them about the hero I was privileged to serve."

He was no fool. "What a liar you are," he said, and cuffed me on the shoulder. "You serve me because the alternative is captivity. Now get out of here and go save more of my soldiers' lives."

It made me think. What *would* I say to my children? "Don't be like me," I'd say to them. "Show more courage than I did."

April 8, 1944
We are meeting partisans now as we move west. Sometimes small bands of men who fled to avoid being rounded up for slave labor in the Reich or for forced service in the Wehrmacht. Half guerilla fighters and half bandits, they've spent the years derailing trains, disrupting German supply lines, and are a world unto themselves.

But in heavily forested terrain, like the Briansk, they are in their hundreds, well organized and supplied from Moscow. Sometimes, when they know we are approaching, they occupy a town, preparing for our arrival. Where possible, the army drafts them into its ranks, using them for reconnaissance missions. I've examined a lot of them before their induction and most are in poor condition. Some 20% have tuberculosis. The young ones are still fired up, ready to fight for the Motherland, but the older ones seem just relieved to have regular meals again, even if it's kasha and American Spam.

May 12, 1944
We've moved again, to yet another evacuation hospital. Chuikov's army is advancing so rapidly westward that we're short of plasma again due to distance from the nearest field depot. Some of the men presented with typhoid symptoms and we transferred them to another hospital to avoid contamination. The more wounded we treat, the more Moscow sends in medals to boost morale. Ribbons for dying, ribbons for killing, ribbons for managing to stay alive. All the new officers' uniforms have gold braid, and with their rows of dangling medals, they look like opera costumes.

June 6, 1944
The English and Americans have landed in Normandy. Troops and materials flow over France. The direction of the war seems irreversible now. It's all the same to me. I was part of Hitler's war machine, and now I'm part of Stalin's.

But the news of the invasion made the commander cheerful today. The minute I arrived, he asked if I liked music. I thought he meant something Russian—a patriotic song or something sentimental with the balalaika. I said yes, and he uncovered a little record player that he had acquired some place. He laid on a disk and it was, of all things, opera arias in Russian. I hadn't heard opera in over a year, and so it was almost blissful to tend to his hands while familiar arias played in the background. From *Boris Godunov, Rusalka,*

Onegin, Mazepa. Then, halfway through the disk, the music wrenched me away from that peace. Though it was sung in Russian, I recognized the words *ego gorjachie laski,* "burning caresses." It was the Berlioz "D'amour l'ardente flamme," and it pierced my heart like a blade. I remembered the hand that caressed me and then was mangled. A hand that now most certainly is withered and dead.

The commander had his eyes shut, caught up in the music while I rubbed cream on his hands. "Music is a blessing to the soul," he said with Russian pathos.

"A curse, too," I mumbled, though I don't think he heard me.

July 23, 1944

Chuikov's troops have liberated Majdanek in Lublin, though it looks like it was evacuated some time ago. The only prisoners left behind are Russians, defectors from the Red Army. They were half starved, but I doubt things will get better for them in the camps the Soviets will transfer them to. There are also a lot of Polish peasants and Byelorussians, partisan fighters and their families. Some of them, the ones who are still somewhat fit, have joined the Russian forces to drive the Germans out of Lublin.

They tell us that the fields all around are strewn with ashes from the crematorium. Fields covered now with cabbages. The men are reporting the piles of shoes, thousands of shoes. No one knows why.

Katherina knew why. With the advantage of nearly forty years of hindsight, she knew of the industry that supplied prison goods and prison labor. A whole economy built on forced labor and the recycling of prisoners' possessions. Majdanek, she had read in school, was in part a factory that took the shoes of the dead and repaired them for use in Germany.

She also knew what had to come in the following diary entries, since the Red Army was advancing through Poland. She held the yellowing paper of the journal in her fingertips for a moment, and then, bracing herself, she turned to the next entry.

She was right. The terrible word burned on the page.

Auschwitz.

January 29, 1945

I have met evil and it has my face.

Two days ago the Russian 60th Army liberated Auschwitz. I was here at the medic station in Cracow, and some of us were assigned to go back there to make a medical report.

Not much to see at first. It consists of three camps spread over wide areas. The usual wire fences and barracks. A few hundred survivors standing around. No exact count yet, but there are about 6000 or 7000 prisoners still there—Poles, Gypsies, Jews. Frail, some too weak to stand. We examined a few dozen of them, took pictures, brought in bread and kasha. They had already organized a kitchen. I talked to them in German.

The SS had evacuated all the other prisoners westward. In fact, we saw some corpses along the road about ten kilometers before the camp, shot, I suppose, when they couldn't keep going. Otherwise, it was a camp like all others.

Then one of the freed prisoners must have heard me speaking German because he approached me. "Come with me," he said, with no explanation, and I followed him. He led me across a wide field to a two-story warehouse. "We call it Canada. 'Cause it's the land of plenty."

I had to get used to the dim light inside the great hall but then I saw what he meant. Luggage. The room was filled with thousands of suitcases, satchels, bags, some of them spilling out contents, but most still unpacked. "The last arrivals," he said. "SS didn't have time to process the luggage. But upstairs is the stuff from the trains before." He led me up a flight of stairs to the second story of the warehouse. The rooms were filled with articles sorted by category. Porcelain, household items in one room, men's clothing in another. Farther down the corridor he led me to rooms containing women's dresses, shoes, children's outfits, infant clothing.

"The Germans brought infants to this camp?" I asked.

He didn't answer and just led me through a doorway to a second hall and more tables. On one row of them lay framed pictures, writing materials, books. On another, walking sticks, crutches. A corner table was heaped high with eyeglasses. Thousands of eyeglasses.

"You'll *love* this," he said, and guided me toward a room at the end of the corridor. Unlike the others, it was locked, but he carried a key. Just inside the door was a covered wooden box, which he opened dramatically. Inside were lumps of gold. I examined one and then dropped it, my stomach heaving. A gold tooth. The box was filled with gold teeth, caps, and fillings, which had been pried out of people's mouths. Kilos of them.

Next to the box, sacks of hair. Soft brown hair from young women, crisp gray hair from the old ones. Harvested hair.

"Is that it, then?" I asked him. I wanted more than anything to get out of there.

"No," he said calmly. "Just one more thing."

He led me outside and down a long path to a red brick building. It smelled of charcoal or soot or something I couldn't name.

"The SS dismantled and blew up a lot of things before they left, but you can still see some of it," he said, going in. The remains of two brick chambers stood on one side of the room behind a small hill of rubble. "The crematorium," he announced unemotionally, and added, "The inmates died in lots of ways—some of them fast, others slow—but here is where they mostly ended."

The smell and the thought of what had gone on there was unbearable, so I fled. He followed me, not letting me escape. "Oh, but it wasn't *all* bad." His tone was suddenly sarcastic. "During all that..." He tilted his head toward the crematorium door. "We had classical music. Inmate orchestras, a couple of them. They played concerts when the transports arrived, when the labor details marched out, when the unlucky ones went to the gas chambers. Cheered things right up! So very German, don't you think?"

He looked me in the eye for the first time, I suppose because we had been speaking German and he wondered about me.

"I have to go now." I offered my hand but he wouldn't take it. "I'm not one of them," I said, half lying.

"We're all 'one of them,'" he answered coldly. "I'm a *Kapo*. Do you think I could have stayed alive here for three years if I hadn't helped them?" Then he added, "But I'm a Pole, and you look too much like the SS man on the railway platform. The one who took my children." He walked away.

I've known since Stalingrad that there's no god, only the devil, and he's tainted me. Apparently, you can even see it in my face.

February 14, 1945
The British and Americans have firebombed Dresden. City of refugees and a treasure house of Baroque architecture. No military reason, no strategic advantage. Simple revenge—tenfold. Clever how they do it. They just keep bombing until the whole city catches fire and everything in it cooks.

A hundred thousand people? Two hundred thousand? All civilians, refugees. Roasted.
It seems the Allies cremate people as well, though it's while they're still alive.

Appalled, Katherina let the journal fall onto her lap and stared at the closed volume as if it held demons. She had learned about the concentration camps in school, but had always remained detached from the subject. It did not occur to her that they could touch her own family. But her father had been there—thank god, on the side of the liberators—and had stood on the blood- and guilt-soaked ground. She had a new respect for him now, though the entry told her nothing about the personal guilt he carried with him. Clearly there were more revelations to come.

She was equally horrified that the music of Bach and Mozart was used to lure the innocent into the camp or to render them docile for slavery or execution. She winced, imagining the sad concerts. Music was all she had, and it sickened her to think it had become a tool of monsters. She had the final rehearsal of *Carmina Burana* tomorrow, but how could she care about it in the face of what she now knew?

Unable to sit another moment, she got up from the sofa. She needed air. Her coat hung just inside the back door and she threw it on before stumbling into the garden. The ground was still snow-covered, but the path from the door was swept, so she walked a bit, to have movement and cold air on her face. Overhead the midnight sky was clear and stars were everywhere. Brilliant, guiltless stars. She envied them their innocence.

In a spontaneous movement, she scooped up snow from the top of a hedge and rubbed it over her face. The shock of it was cathartic, and she felt briefly cleansed by the chill. The journal was of the past, after all, and she was in the present. The music that she sang was innocent, like the stars. Now she could go back into the house and sleep.

VII
LUSINGANDO

Dulchiiissime! Katherina held the high note until the conductor's signal. Then she let her voice tumble through the delicious melisma to *totam tibi subdo me*, and the chorus followed with the warm swell of *"Ave Formosissima."* She thrilled at the ecstatic conclusion of *Carmina Burana*, the pumping heartbeat of the final chorus and the ever-repeating "bodoomp BOOM" of the timpani. It was a wild dance, the very essence of pagan erotic passion that mocked the monastic origin of its text.

The final fortissimo section crashed to an end and the orchestra fell silent. The conductor waved the chorus and dancers off the stage, dismissing them until the Friday performance. Only the soloists had to do another run-through. Katherina was slightly annoyed; she would miss the early train back to Berlin.

Ulrich seemed disappointed too and his eyes followed Sabine as she strode in long graceful steps into the wings. He acquitted himself well in his song, though he was obviously bored. Dieter forced his voice one more time into the falsetto lines of his swan aria. Finally it was her turn and she focused her full attention on *"Stedit puella in rosa tunica."* She loved the delicate sensuality of the words. "The girl stood in a red dress, and when she moved, the tunic rustled." She sang the passage without looking at the score, directly at the conductor, and ended the long "Eiiiah" on pianissimo.

Von Hausen was obviously satisfied. "Good work. All of you. Bring it with you on Friday and we'll have a hit."

Relieved, Katherina followed the other soloists back to the dressing rooms.

Her room was small and sparse, but afforded privacy since, as the only female soloist, she had it all to herself. She would use it on performance night to change into her concert gown. The wide cushioned bench at one end was an amenity she had not expected to need. Today, however, when she had an hour to kill before catching the late train, it was welcome and she dropped onto it gratefully.

The chorus had left and so had the dancers, and Ulrich's dismay was apparent when he stuck his head through the dressing room doorway and said good-bye. He had obviously not gotten very far with Sabine the night before and could not fathom why. Katherina did not intend to inform him.

Staring blankly at her score, she let the images of the flirtation drift again through her imagination. She had been brooding the entire day on it, for it had exposed a part of her that she had always carefully guarded. Without a current boyfriend, even the shallow kind like the ones she'd had at university, she felt unprotected.

Well, that was over now and she could let it pass from her mind. She tried to study her notes, but fatigue and the warmth of the room made her drowsy. She slouched against the wall and allowed herself to doze.

Katherina dreamt she was at the table in the Café zum Engel again, but not only the *Carmina Burana* singers and dancers sat there with her. Directly across the table was her father. Sitting shoulder to shoulder with him was Anastasia Ivanova, as on the record jacket. And similar to the photograph of Faust and Marguerite, her father seemed penitent, terrified, while next to him, Anastasia smiled. The rest of the group at the table seemed oblivious to them and to the woman next to Katherina, who began to caress her breast. Katherina dared not move, for fear of drawing attention to herself, so she allowed the caress, growing both more aroused and more frightened. Her father glanced first at her, then past her to someone who stood behind her. She wanted to turn around, but something held her in place. She could only ask, "Is that Florian?"

She awoke, abruptly, to some sound.

Sabine stood just inside the dressing room. "I see you waited after all. I'm glad."

Katherina tried to clear her sleep-addled brain. "What? No, I wasn't waiting for anything. I mean, my train leaves in an hour and I don't want to sit in the station."

"If you say so." Sabine swept gracefully toward the soft bench and sat down next to Katherina. She rested leisurely against the wall and surveyed the room.

"Nice. The privacy, I mean. Not like washing up with six other half-naked dancers." She shifted her position to face Katherina. "Funny how one naked woman is erotically appealing but six of them are not. I wonder why that is."

Katherina could think of nothing to reply.

"Do you like naked women?" Sabine's voice was suddenly soft, suggestive.

"What?" Katherina drew back as if pricked. "What kind of a question is that?"

"You don't have to be so afraid of the subject. I look quite good naked. I bet you do too."

"I suppose so, but it's not something people talk about."

"Why not? It's something we all think about. What other people look like naked. I know you wonder about me. I've seen you looking at me."

"You flatter yourself. I look at everyone."

"But not the way you look at me. What do you think about? Do you wonder what it would be like to touch me?"

"Of course not." Katherina's blood was pounding in her ears as it had done in the café. She licked dry lips.

Sabine bent toward her and murmured, "You do. I know you do. You think about what it's like to be intimate with a woman. Well, I can tell you. It's…exquisite."

"How can you say those things to me? Look, I don't even want to have this conversation." Katherina threw her weight forward to stand up, was halfway off the seat when Sabine caught her wrist and pulled her back down.

"Oh, please. Don't be so dramatic. I'm not trying to embarrass you." Her voice became softer, cajoling. "Look, I just want to get to know you, honestly and without pretense. Here we are, in a nice quiet room all by ourselves. No one here to see or know anything. Really. Nothing to be afraid of."

She was close to Katherina's face now. Katherina could feel the warm breath on her cheek, smell the soap she had just washed with. "I…I don't know," was all that Katherina could manage.

Sabine's hand rose and touched her softly on the cheek, brushed away a strand of hair, then came to rest on her chin. Katherina turned her head with the pressure of the hand and found Sabine's lips centimeters away from her own. Sabine gazed into her eyes dreamily. Then her bright expression clouded with desire and her mouth came down on Katherina's lips.

For the briefest moment Katherina resisted, her back stiffening. She froze, as if waiting for some third party to arbitrate, then relented. Her defenses fell—to the heat of Sabine's mouth and the flickering invasion of her tongue, to the strong arm that slipped around her back, to the hand that dropped from her cheek to her breast.

Her own hands did not know where to go. They landed, helpless, on Sabine's upper arms and her fingers curled feebly to clutch Sabine's sleeves. She inhaled Sabine's breath, tasted Sabine's saliva mixing with her own. The hand on her breast squeezed and caressed, then ventured farther, down the side of her leg and under her skirt. When the intruder's fingertips touched the skin on the inside of her thigh, something in Katherina broke away. Will and flesh seemed to separate, and the flesh surrendered.

This is not me. I am not doing this. Katherina told herself, *This is another part of me that is just for now, that will go away again afterward.* The thought seemed to free her to throw herself into the maelstrom that drew her ever downward.

She melted, her sex pouring out hot syrup over Sabine's invading fingers. Tiny demons gathered in her groin, flickering like fireflies, growing in number and intensity.

Was she still kissing Sabine? Yes, their tongues still slipped past each other, their panting breaths—the only sound—blew across each other's cheeks.

The flashing demons congealed, deep inside of her, merged into a burning ring that set her trembling. Tighter and hotter the ring closed, until she could no longer endure it and she moaned into Sabine's mouth. Then it broke. She shuddered as the convulsions erupted through her, then collapsed against Sabine's shoulder.

Spent, Katherina rested for several moments with her forehead against Sabine's neck. As the euphoria evaporated, she became aware that nothing more was happening, no further tenderness, no gentle promises. "What do we do now?" she murmured.

"Now?" Sabine answered. "Now you have a train to catch."

VIII
Alla Marcia

Katherina huddled in her bathtub, brooding, trying to make some sense of what had happened two hours before. She was not a child, she told herself. She knew what sexual pleasure was; she had experienced brief moments of it with the boys at university. This was simply more intense—probably because it was more forbidden. If she was ashamed, it was only because she had let it be imposed on her. She had consented, of course, but only just. Sabine's actions were somewhere between assault and seduction, and deeply unsettling. More than that, it was indecent to do such a thing scarcely two weeks after her father's suicide. She was supposed to be in mourning.

At the same time, her body remembered Sabine's prurient touch, the way the lascivious fingertips had brushed along her thigh, then slipped so easily inside her. Lewd though the whole experience had been, Katherina's body craved the invasion again. She hated only that the conquest had been so simple and that she was the one conquered.

Was that the entire range of sexual intimacy? The fumblings of well-meaning young men that ended up in pregnancy and then marriage, or lascivious encounters that set her on fire but left her humiliated? If that's all there was, she would rather give herself to singing. That at least gave her a sense of elevation.

She stepped out of the tub and dried herself. It was still early in the evening and she was restless, with no one to talk to. The afternoon's event had added more questions to the ones already buzzing in her head. Her confusion about herself seemed of a piece with the enigma of her parents. So many mysteries, and they all weighed on her like a phantom on her shoulders.

She settled into bed. When it was certain that sleep would not come, she picked up the journal again. She could hardly bear to read more reports of battlefront wounded, concentration camps, or firebombings, so she jumped ahead to the spring of 1945, to the final Allied victories.

April 22, 1945—On the Brocken

You can feel it everywhere, exhilaration on one side and terror on the other. These are the final days. The Red Army is well inside Germany now and a race is on with the western Allies to see who will get to Berlin first. In the Harz Mountains, there are scattered American units as well as Russian. Both wanted to claim the Brocken Peak and its radio transmitter. The Soviets got here first.

I spent three days patching up wounded Russians for transport by truck to the evacuation station in the valley. The dead were buried, to prevent disease, the German wounded rounded up for the POW camps. My work is done now. Since the trucks are gone, the orderlies are bringing horses around for us to ride down into Wernigerode, where they'll ship us back to Chuikov's main force.

I asked myself if I should try to escape the Red Army now that I'm in Germany. Woods are all around and I could easily run. But then I realized that's insane. The Russians are the victors; why would I want to join the defeated? Besides, I made a deal, after all, and this is where it got me. I'm at the Brocken Stone now, the highest rock on the highest mountain in Germany, writing this by first light. The air is crystal clear. Looking out over the hills in all directions, I have the sense I'm seeing the whole world. Unbeliever that I am, I can't help but think of the Temptation of Christ. Except Christ refused the devil's offer. Foolish man; it got him crucified. But this is a more pagan place, possibly even a place of sacrifice. They call the rock I'm sitting on the Witches' Altar. Something about a mountaintop stirs the imagination—toward gods in the morning and demons at night.

I hear the horses they've got waiting. A bell is ringing, calling us to the canteen, and the sun is up.

April 25, 1945

The Red Army has linked up with the Americans on the Elbe River. Big celebration, back-slapping, photos, exchange of cigarettes. Berlin is encircled. It's only a matter of days. Both armies are rushing from their respective positions; each one wants to be the first to take the city. I fervently hope it is the Americans. Doctors bring up the rear in the line of battle, but I still can't bear the thought of following troops that storm through streets where I've lived, or shopped, or shared a beer. I dread to find my friends and family among the dead.

The army paper, *The Red Star*, is full of Ilya Ehrenburg's articles fomenting rage in the troops, as if it needed fomenting. His propaganda is extreme these days, even for him. "Germany is a witch," he writes, and, "The Germans have no souls. Not only divisions and armies are advancing on Berlin. All the trenches, graves, and ravines filled with the corpses of the innocent are advancing on Berlin. All the cabbages of Majdanek and all the trees of Vitebsk on which the Germans hanged so many people. The boots and shoes and the babies' slippers of those murdered and gassed are marching on Berlin. The dead are knocking on the doors in all the cursed streets of that cursed city."

May 2, 1945

Berlin has fallen to the Russians. Yesterday the city still thundered with desperate battle but now there's an eerie stillness. I sit here on the front of a Russian tank and watch the Soviet flag flutter on the roof of the Reichstag and I feel nothing. I'm without allegiance, cold as the wind blowing through these streets. This is day zero, month zero.

This city was my home and now it's a cadaver. Covered with soot that the slightest breeze stirs up. Streets full of craters. Broken pipes spew water or gas, which burns with a blue flame. The dead are everywhere: Wehrmacht, SS, the old men of the Home Guard who stood on their pathetic hills of dirt and shot at us. They lie in the streets and on the barricades.

And the suicides. In the parks, on the benches or the ground, like picknickers who fell asleep. In the houses, whole families of the dead sit poisoned around the table or they hang in their cellars. They hang by the neck on the lampposts too, but these are executions. One of them, only a boy, had a sign pinned to his shirt: Coward.

This is Germany's payment for its devil's pact.

Some of our troops are out of control. Stealing anything that shines. And raping any woman they find. Brutally. I've heard horrendous stories. They remember what the Germans did when they blasted their way east and are giving it back double.

I finally got a few hours' leave and went to Babelsberg to see if my house was still standing. Everything was gone, the neighbors' houses too. Elsewhere, walls and pillars are covered with chalk scribblings, desperate messages: "Looking for Karl Hartmann. Notify Red Cross—his brother Rudi," or "We are alive, Hr & Fr Stolz." But in the ruins of my street there are no walls left to write on.

I'll search until I find out for certain, but I think my parents are gone. If they were killed, it was by Allied bombs, but in a war that Germans started. Yet if they had gone back to Russia, Stalin would have killed them too. There's no side I want to take. I wash my hands of all of them.

It's day zero for me too.

June 10, 1945
They are everywhere, the *Trümmerfrauen*. Women in filthy dresses with woolen scarves or rags around their heads. Clearing the blockage from the streets, they labor for food coupons—only workers get a livable ration—or to collect the bricks for themselves. They knock off loose mortar with their rusty hammers, pile up the bricks in carts, and strain starving

muscles to drag them away. Other diggers ferret in the hills of gravel looking for firewood, flooring or broken furniture. They crawl over the mountains of rubble, digesting them like microbes, carrying away the useful particles to live.

The city is quiet. All you hear is the clopping of wooden shoes, the 'tok, tok' of hammers, the rattle of handcarts. And everywhere ragged coughing.

I see practically no men. Only the old and a few pathetic, broken soldiers in the ragged remains of Wehrmacht uniforms. Everyone is hungry and everyone smells bad. Only the allies have soap. The Germans have *Ersatzseife*, crumbly stuff that smells carbolic and even that's scarce.

How many years will pass before Germany recovers normalcy? Its dignity? Will children born tomorrow still suffer the guilt? Will mine? *The sins of the fathers shall be visited upon the sons...*

Black market is everywhere and cigarettes have more exchange value than Reichsmarks. A pack of British or American cigarettes will get you sex for the night. The victors have everything, can get anything, and what they trade out—cigarettes, cans of Spam, marmalade—filters out into the population.

Commander Chuikov, who is in charge of Soviet occupation forces now, has not called on me for months, which makes it easier for me to lie low. I answer only to Dr. Tchelechev, who ignores me as long as I do my work. There are still sick and wounded to treat even while the division is reorganizing. It's a good time to break away, but I can't go back to being the felon that I was before the war, so I'll stay on awhile with Chuikov's army, for the regular meals, if for nothing else.

June 15, 1945
I tried again at the Red Cross to get information on Michael

and Alma Marovsky, but found no record of them. Had an hour left on my leave so I walked around the Brandenburg Gate. In the Friedrichstrasse, only the façades of the national library and the opera are still standing. I watched two old men digging out a corpse. A woman, in an evening gown, of all things.

A man leaning against a lamppost called out to me. I thought he wanted to strike some kind of deal, but I had nothing to trade. He had pale eyes, a thin blond beard along the edge of his chin. Well fed, he wore clean, tailored clothing. He pointed toward the opera house. "*Staatsoper.*" He spoke beautiful German, like an actor. "Strauss conducted here, and von Karajan." He smoked leisurely, not like a hungry man. "And the singers: Melchior, Lehmann, and Chaliapin. Unforgettable." He seemed to assume that I would know all the names and of course I did. "People poured in to listen, right up until '45, when it was bombed." He smoothed his fine leather gloves. "But it will be back," he said, puffing on his cigarette. I could smell that it was good tobacco. Not like the trash the Red Army was issued. We watched the diggers heave the black corpse into the rubble cart. "It has a certain poetry, doesn't it? Dying at the opera, I mean," he added.

"Not for me." I thought of Stalingrad.

"You seem like an intelligent man, an ambitious man," he said. "I collect things and have things people usually want. Try me." He offered his hand. "Peter Schalk. Businessman."

"I'm just a Russian soldier," I said. "With no money."

"A Russian soldier who speaks perfect German. As for payment, there are many ways to pay. Pledges, goods in kind, counter-favors. I prefer long-term clients. Loyalty has its own value, don't you think?"

"How could I find you? If I did want something?"

"Around here," he said, sweeping his hand across the ruins. "If you don't see me right away, just come back later. This is my terrain."

I walked away from the opera house and it struck me. There *was* something I wanted. I needed to kill Sergei Marovsky.

IX
Minaccioso

A dog blocked Katherina's path to the stage entrance to the concert hall. Plump and sleek, his coat long and black, he hardly seemed like a stray. But he had no collar and there was no one in sight who could claim him. He was neither hostile nor friendly, did not bark or wag. She took a tentative step forward, and still the beast did not move. He simply glared at her through orange-brown eyes, panting softly. Then, finally, he turned and trotted away.

A bad omen for a performer, she thought, then scoffed at the superstition.

❖

Joachim von Hausen was nothing if not a man of the theater. To dramatize the opening sound of the great choral work, he had all house lights turned off, even the emergency-exit signs. For one long moment, the audience sat in chilling darkness. Then, as if some transcendent being had opened its eye, a single needle of white light shot down from the rafter onto his upraised baton. Another thirty seconds passed and the tension in the hall was palpable. The baton sliced suddenly downward like a whip and BOOM! The timpani thundered its opening crash.

"Ooooooo Fortuna, veeeelut luna" the chorus sang, full-throated, ominous and ecstatic at once.

The emotional level set, the work took off at full throttle. Pastoral maidens, randy suitors, roasted swans, drunken monks, all sang of lust and power and inebriation and doom, their chants sending wave after rhythmic wave of sound over the audience. Finally, Orff's thundering great wheel came full circle. The opening chorus became the last, culminating in the shattering, orgiastic, nine-measure-long fortissimo chord of lament, *"Plangiteeeee."* Hardly had the cry ended when the audience rose to its feet in ovation.

Now Katherina stood in the post-concert reception line in the green room. In a few moments the well-wishers would flutter in like a flock of doves into a dovecote. Friends, fans, and regular—mostly elderly—concertgoers who viewed the reception as part of the evening's performance. Usually they settled for a handshake, a few moments of small talk, an autographed program.

Someone said, "What a lovely concert," and another, "Such a beautiful voice." She smiled and nodded toward the line of faces, familiar with every compliment. Sometimes they admired her concert dress or the way she interpreted the music. Katherina had struggled to craft a different response each time until she realized it was unnecessary. The hand-shakers did not really want to exchange ideas; they simply wanted to connect in some way with the musician, to prolong the evening.

She replied to each remark and tried not to glance over at Sabine, who was in animated conversation with her own admirers. Katherina had not spoken to her since the evening before and Sabine showed no interest in her.

Seduced and abandoned, Katherina thought to herself with bitter humor.

The crowd of admirers had shifted again, and she focused on the next person. White-haired, probably in his seventies, he was elegantly dressed. Sleek, she might have said, except that sleek implied softness and he had nothing soft about him. He was trim, his haircut professional, as perfect as his charcoal suit. He offered his hand and she took it, found it cool and soft.

"I trust you received my letter," he said.

She was confused for a moment.

"Forgive me. I suppose it would be helpful if I told you my name." He chuckled softly. "Raspin. Gregory Raspin. I sent the letter right after your splendid Tosca last month."

"Oh, yes. I did get it. Thank you. So much has happened recently, I haven't had time to reply."

"That's quite all right. It pleases me just to be sure it arrived so that you know how much you are appreciated. I am familiar with every nuance of the great women's voices, and you should know I count yours among them."

"You are very kind," she replied, as she always did to excessive flattery. In most cases, she knew, the fan said it to every singer they got the chance to meet.

"I am also fortunate to be able to support great vocal music—in my way," he added cryptically.

The public had begun to filter out of the green room. "I believe your conductor wishes to speak with you." Gregory Raspin touched her elbow delicately with a fingertip, causing her to turn. Then he stepped away and joined the mass of departing well-wishers.

"I'm sorry I didn't have time to talk to you earlier today." Joachim von Hausen was already at her side. He guided her back to the rear door of the green room. "Too many last-minute preparations for the concert." His eyes sparkled and he paused, like a person about to bestow a gift. "As you might know, I've been rehearsing *Rosenkavalier* in Salzburg. Agnes Schongauer, who is singing the role of Sophie, has had a car accident."

"An accident? I'm so sorry to hear it. Not serious, I hope." Katherina wondered why he was telling her that. She did not know Agnes Schongauer.

"She'll be all right—just a few broken ribs—but she has had to cancel, obviously. Salzburg does the casting, you know, but I have recommended they offer the part to you. Assuming your agent likes the contract, Salzburg's approval will largely be a formality. They've never said no to me before. So the question is, can you learn the part of Sophie in two weeks?"

Katherina felt her jaw drop and she closed it again. She was being offered the opportunity of a lifetime.

"Yes, of course I can. I am already familiar with it," she lied. No matter. She could learn it. She felt something tugging her arm and realized von Hausen was shaking her hand.

"Excellent. It's settled then. I'll have Salzburg contact your agent tomorrow. It would be lovely if you could manage to fly to Salzburg on Tuesday."

Katherina nodded energetically, prepared to agree to anything. Tuesday, Monday, in fifteen minutes, if necessary.

Something moved in the distance and she glanced past von Hausen's face back into the green room. Sabine was gone, but on the far side of the room, Gregory Raspin was smiling in her direction.

X
AFFRETTANDO

Y ou were right after all, Charlotte," Katherina said into the phone. "Things are really beginning to fall into place. Just imagine. Three engagements in three months: *Tosca, Carmina Burana*, and now *Rosenkavalier*. Does this mean I'm 'arriving'?"

Charlotte's voice seemed even chirpier than usual. "I told you this would happen. You're a great soprano and I'm a great agent. It was only a matter of time. Salzburg is a major step. If the right people hear you, and they probably will, a recording could be next. I'll put out feelers with Deutsche Grammophon. Then, if we could just get you a broadcast, your career would take off like a rocket."

"It's all happening so suddenly. I keep looking over my shoulder to see if I'm going to be hit by a bus or something."

Charlotte's high voice made her chuckle sound almost like a giggle. "Oh, Katherina. You're always making deals with the universe, as if every bit of good fortune had to be offset by a disaster. Just relax and enjoy it. You're doing everything right. Just learn your role, be nice to everyone in Salzburg, and let me take care of all the rest, okay?"

"I'll do all those things. It's good to have you on my side. If I need anything in Salzburg, I'll give you a call." Katherina hung up, then sat for a few minutes savoring the sense of accomplishment. She *had* worked hard, done everything she was supposed to, and success was the result. Charlotte was right, it was silly superstition to think that good fortune and bad fortune had to balance out. That attitude had come from her father, she knew. His cynicism was natural, she supposed, seeing that he had lived through so much horror and difficulty, but she wished now that he were still alive so she could both prove him wrong and make him proud.

Well, if she could not talk to him, she could at least "listen" to him for an hour—and pay him a symbolic visit. She had finished reading all the war entries, things could only get better, and now she was curious again. The journal was where she had left it, on the table next to the sofa, so she settled in again and opened it. She had left off where he had decided to change his identity. Did he describe meeting his wife— her mother? The birth of their daughter? It occurred to Katherina there might be descriptions of her. It was time for another descent into the past.

Berlin, October 7, 1945
Schalk was as good as his word. I met him at the opera house and we made the deal. Ten days later he had new papers for me. *Zeugnis*, medical certification, *Soldbuch* identifying me as a field doctor with the Wehrmacht. An exact duplicate of my original German papers, but under the new name.

I've nothing material to go back to anyhow. Family and house destroyed. Nothing left to claim, and under German law, Sergei Marovsky was a criminal. He's one of the war dead now, and Sergei Marow, who suddenly exists, is a civilian registered in the British sector.

I gave Schalk all the money I had, but he said he was more interested in my future services. Loyalty during the hard times, he explained. It's a deal I'm willing to make.

Berlin, October 17, 1945
I've found a room with Herr and Frau Wengler, in exchange for work. Frau Wengler, who is old and weak, stands in the food lines while Herr Wengler and I forage. We scavenge for coal near the railroad lines, but it often isn't enough. We have better luck with a handsaw in the bombed-out houses. We dig down under the brick and usually find wood left from the interior walls.

I've begun to forage in the countryside on the Wenglers' bicycle. I pedaled to the Autobahn and found I could grab hold of one of the wood-burning trucks. They don't go very fast, so I can hang on to the rear and be dragged along for kilometers. The farms and villages outside Berlin are reachable now and have food to sell or exchange. I brought back potatoes and carrots.

November 1, 1945
It was inevitable, I suppose. The victors have set up a military tribunal in the Palace of Justice in Nuremberg. They're trying the leadership of the Nazi party, the SS, the SD, the Gestapo, the SA, and the High Command of the German Armed Forces. The charges are crimes against peace (I wonder what that means), wars of aggression, war crimes, and crimes against humanity.

Victor's justice. Plenty of loathsome Germans in the dock, to be sure. Mass murderers and accomplices of mass murderers. They are drenched, up to their filthy necks, in blood. Not only for the industrial-scale slaughters of Jews and Gypsies, Slavs, and dissidents and homosexuals, but for ripping away civilization altogether, making us all savages for five years.

But who will try the victors for *their* savagery? The British and Americans who roasted 200,000 civilians in Dresden? The Americans who bombed Hiroshima and Nagasaki? Who will—some day—try Stalin and Churchill and Truman for *their* blood thirst? Probably no one. Their history books will change the whole story to a tale of good and evil, removing the nuances. No army or nation ever says, "We were monsters, but we won."

January 1, 1946
Everyone lives from day to day. Last night Wengler exchanged a load of firewood with the neighbor for some schnapps. A foul homemade brew bartered from some farmer. It didn't take much to make us all drunk. I went outside to clear my head and it was snowing again, a bad sign for the New Year. I can't see a snow-covered field without remembering snow drifting down on the frozen Volga, blowing over lines of men

as far as the eye could see, marching into captivity. Soldiers, wounded boys falling by the roadside, covered by snow while they're still alive.

The flakes dissolved on my arm, all around me countless snowflakes falling. Like the millions lost. All of them loved by someone. Snow is my shame and accusation. I spent the first hour of the New Year in mourning.

March 30 1946
I've found work at the Johannes hospital. Doctors of any sort are scarce and they're glad to have me. Very different from war hospitals; no battle wounds or trauma to treat. Patients arrive with pneumonia, typhoid, diphtheria, but we have no medicine. And they are so undernourished they can't recover. Children and the old die quickly of dysentery, tuberculosis, jaundice, and even the young women look old and haggard.

Wards crowded and dirty. Hygiene impossible with dust and dirt everywhere, on everyone's clothing. So little plumbing in the city; people bring their filth with them into the hospital. No soap to launder the bedding, no bleach to wash the floors.

Schalk has begun calling in his payments. Private appointments for his "clients," men with political ambitions in the new regime, and their women. I do the occasional abortion for their girlfriends, or treat their syphilis, and they supply the penicillin themselves. God knows where Schalk gets it for them; we have none in the hospital. He's a master of exchange and he uses some war-proof currency.

I wonder if I dare ask him… No, not yet.

April 2, 1946
Berlin has no food but concerts everywhere. In schools, garages, sport halls, living rooms, any place with a roof. During daylight hours when the streets can still be traveled.

People arrive by the odd streetcar—a few are still in
service—or by bicycle, by foot, sometimes from far away.
Germans, Russians, refugees. It distracts from the hunger,
and the misery.

I even ventured into the Russian sector to the Admiralspalast.
Streets festooned now with red banners and portraits of Stalin.
The Russians trying to incorporate Eastern Germany, and
Berlin, into the Soviet block. The audience had a scattering
of Russian officers, whom I carefully avoided, a few British,
many Berliners. We paid in cigarettes, eggs, bread, potatoes.
The hall was freezing and we sat in coats and hats. The singer,
Lucia Berning, wore a heavy woolen shawl over her concert
gown, and when she sang, we could see the steam rise from
her mouth. She sang a few Schubert lieder and then popular
songs: "Mack the Knife," "Pirate Jenny," "Falling in Love
Again," "Lili Marlene."

Went to talk to her afterward. She's very small. Dark hair.
Fine nose, eyelashes black and long over bright blue eyes,
lips like a Renaissance cherub. An echo of the one who
haunts me.

April 8, 1946
I've been to all of Lucia's concerts, and she seems happy to
see me. The last time I gave her a package of ersatz coffee and
sugar, and I've promised to bring her some coal. No one else
is looking after her. She's frail and of course malnourished,
and I can't understand how none of the sicknesses that have
swept through Berlin have gotten her. She is just as hungry
as the rest of us, but when we were sitting a few days ago
outside the clinic eating our precious bread, she fed a small
portion of hers to some sparrows. I said it seemed wasteful,
and she answered, "Don't you want the birds to return? It's
their land too." I agreed, and asked how, in the middle of
squalor and defeat, she managed to be almost cheerful. "Not
cheerful," she said. "Just grateful for surviving. You could
show some gratitude yourself and spend a few crumbs on

the poor sparrows." Just then one of the birds landed on her palm, but by then a little bit of my heart was there too.

April 25, 1946
I visited Schalk again. I'd been treating his friends for weeks so I thought by now I had credit with him. I asked him to get me some fresh meat so I could give it to Lucia. He got it, of course, but in return I had to do an abortion on a young woman for him. He said she was eighteen, but she looked fifteen. Or forty. There's no way to tell in these hard times when no one is a child anymore. This one wouldn't talk, just came and went silently. I have no compunctions about terminating a pregnancy, but in this case, I couldn't escape the feeling of being complicit in something awful, though I didn't know in what.

Lucia showed up at the clinic again. We see each other a lot now and she has offered to mend my torn jacket for me. Although battlefield surgery taught me to use a needle and thread better than any seamstress, I was touched that she offered. I've decided "Lucia" is too opera-heavy for her, tiny thing that she is. I call her Lucy.

May 14, 1946
Finally, Lucy let me come home with her. On a street where every house has been blasted, her building had lost its top floors, but two stories were left. Miraculously, there was still plumbing, and they ran a cable down the street to a line for electricity during the hours when the grid was on.

We talked about her background and mine. Her father a socialist, killed by the Nazis, her mother a *Volksdeutsche* killed by Russian troops invading Berlin—the soldiers I arrived with. My parents killed by Allied bombs. Plenty of guilt to go around. She shares a kitchen and bathroom with two old gentlemen, brothers, I think. I saw them when I passed their room in the morning. They just nodded.

Lucy's room was small and cold, and we lit a candle. We shivered for a while until we got used to being in each other's arms. There was no talk of love, or passion. The world has just fought a war with passion and we've had enough of it. We settle for solace, a little warmth at night.

Katherina held the journal open on her lap to the May 14 page and brooded on the entry. It was strange to read about the courtship of her parents. It seemed emotionless. Was it the difficult times that rendered romance a luxury? Was her father simply incapable of expressing his feelings? Or did they both have some emotional deficiency that she had inherited?

It would explain the lack of excitement in her relations with men, the disconnect between her heart and her sex. All through school, she had no shortage of good comrades, men whose strength and laughter she found endearing. But none had ever swept her off her feet. And the very few she had been intimate with had stirred only the minimum of physical response.

What did it mean, then, that Sabine Maurach had reached a part of her that none of her lovers at university had? Sabine, whom she didn't even much like.

Was her emotional coldness an effect of childhood guilt? From the knowledge that her feverish embrace had transferred a deadly infection to someone who loved her? Was she crippled by the knowledge that she had killed her own mother?

Plagued by self-doubts, she fell into troubled sleep.

❖

Katherina had the dream again, the recurring nightmare she had suffered while recovering from the sickness. It was of a performance she *had* to give, but only after she had paid some terrible price. Again and again she dreamt of having to exchange something precious for stage success. This time the negotiation was with Sabine. And when Katherina tried to step out on stage, she opened her eyes in her own childhood bedroom.

She breathed slowly, letting herself waken fully, then turned on the light beside the bed to clear her head of the terrible images. The dream had appeared so often in her youth that she knew its pattern, but now she seemed to understand its source. It was the "every good is paid for" fixation of her father that had become her own. The dramas of his life had been radically different from hers, but his part in them seemed frighteningly familiar. It was as if the same mentality lived in them both, that they had, in effect, been in two different operas but sung the same role, and it was one that involved guilt.

The clock read 3:00 a.m. No matter. She switched on the light and reached again for the journal, realizing that she was hooked. Looking for references to herself now, she opened the precisely dated volume and leafed through it until the year of her birth.

XI

Piangevole

June 25, 1948

Just when Germany was beginning to recover, disaster has struck. I was on a train to Magdeburg when Russian soldiers boarded, demanding exit visas. No one had them, of course, because they didn't exist until that moment. The soldiers pushed us back into our seats and barked, *"Pass geben!"* and *"Nicht reden!"* and I didn't dare ask what was going on in Russian, for fear of drawing attention. I just sat in helpless fury like the others.

After an hour of confusion, the train finally reversed direction, taking us back to the *Hauptbahnhof.* We found out that the whole city was blockaded. No traffic at all toward the west. I'm sure the same thought occurred to everyone. The west is where most of our food comes from. What will the British and Americans do? Their front-line soldiers have been sent home, while Berlin is still crawling with Russian troops.

Hoarding has begun again, and ration cards—and hunger.

August 14, 1948

Will it work? The British and Americans are trying to supply the city by airlift, but their planes are too small and too few to carry everything a city needs. They arrive haphazardly and are subject to weather. Yesterday in heavy fog, a C54 carrying coal crashed and burned at the end of the runway. The one landing right behind it blew out its tires trying to avoid the burning wreck. A third had to touch down on a small side runway and skidded in loops. The whole airfield was in chaos. It feels like war again.

September 20, 1948

Lucy is pregnant. It couldn't happen at a worse time. Food is rationed again and the black market is back overnight. Lucy has stopped giving concerts, though I can see it breaks her heart. Her health is poor and it's a strain for her to go by foot to all the halls and stages. When we go on the train to the east zone to get produce from the farmers, she can't carry any weight. Routes toward the east aren't blocked, but you have to travel farther and farther out from the city to find anything, and in the winter, it's grueling for her.

November 8, 1948

Most of the available coal goes for industry and there's little left for heating. People go out at night and cut down the trees in the parks for firewood. People are pulling up the grass and mixing it with their potato ration, just to have a little more in their stomachs. Schalk delivers whatever I ask for, but I hate the counter-favors. He sends me his other "clients" for special medical treatment, usually for syphilis. Some of them are very young, which sickens me. How do twelve-year-old children get syphilis?

December 19, 1948

The planes roar into Tempelhof in an endless stream, one every three minutes. They arrive so close together now you can't separate the engine sounds. It's all just one long drone, soft, then loud, then soft again. At first we couldn't sleep, but we've gotten used to the great dark wasps that bring in food and coal. I've volunteered to help unload the flights. There's no payment, but they feed us a hot meal afterward along with the airmen. The G.I.s are huge, sleek and well fed, the way victors always are. Some of them very handsome. A few have been arrogant, but most are cheerful, open, and friendly in a superficial way. They all chew gum, their jaws constantly moving up and down, like they never finish eating.

Except for "Kommen Sie hier, Fräulein," none of them speak German, so conversation is impossible.

May 11, 1949
The blockade is lifted. A great embarrassment for the Soviets, who had to back down. The supply planes are still arriving, though. I suppose because no one can be sure the whole thing won't be reversed. As soon as fresh food was available, I used all our food coupons to buy milk, meat, and vegetables for Lucy, though it may be too late to help her or the baby.

May 15, 1949
Three years as a battlefield medic did not prepare me for this. I stood by, helpless, while Dr. Weidt attended. I argued for a caesarian section but Weidt said ether was "too scarce to waste on childbirth." So my poor Lucy suffered twenty hours of labor before the first baby was delivered. A girl. But the long labor caused hemorrhaging in the second infant.

Lucy was in agony, I could see, but she was so weak she just moaned. It was an hour of horror as the foetal shoulder presented instead of the cranium. Lucy screamed while Weidt forced it back and tried to turn it.

The baby presented, not the cranium, but its face, already gray. Blood trickled from the tiny nostrils. Bright blue eyes opened wide, seemed to look at me, begging for life, then closed again. Lucy was moaning, deep, desperate moans. Weidt pushed the forceps around the face, lacerating it, and slowly extracted the baby. A boy, fully developed, perfect.

Suffocated.

Weidt applied oxygen, trying to revive the infant, but nothing helped. "Natal asphyxia," he said. "I'm sorry."

I held Lucy's hand, both of us sobbing, until the afterbirth came.

❖

Katherina closed the journal and let it fall to the floor. Another revelation. She'd had a twin. A brother who lived for just a moment. Why had they never told her? She tried to imagine him, the child who had been the focus of all their hope. She could not conjure a face, only wide imploring eyes before death snatched him away at the very entrance to life.

But it was the last line of the entry that struck her like a blow. In clear script, as if her father had written it with loving care, were the words, "We named him Florian."

XII
SALZBURGER FESTSPIEL

Katherina stared out of the train window at the winter landscape just before the Austrian border. The air was frigid, but no snow had fallen and the hills, meadows, and woodlands of Bavaria were various shades of gray.

It was good to get away from Berlin. Too much was unresolved, confused, churning in her head. Too much hinted of wrongdoing, shame, absurdity. What did a stillborn infant have to do with a suicide thirty years later? Why ask forgiveness from a child who never lived? She no longer knew her own family, what she came from or who she was.

Well, Sabine had known her all right. Had known something very important, for about fifteen minutes, and then never called again. The journal and Sabine's conquest had been like blows from two directions. Katherina felt suspended, thrown from the safe space she had inhabited her whole life, and not yet landed in any new place she understood.

The journal had become an obsession, like a mystery she could not put down. She had read the early entries with morbid fascination but the stream of revelations had overpowered her; she needed time to absorb them lest they drown her.

She had resolved to stop reading at least for a few days, to clear her head and focus on the Salzburg engagement. Meanwhile, she carried the journal with her in her music bag like a talisman charged with the presence of her father, even while she no longer knew who he was.

More urgent matters demanded attention now. For the last week she had studied the *Rosenkavalier* score day and night until she knew every note and syllable of her part. Now she needed to integrate the stream of music in her head into a stage performance with other singers.

More importantly, she needed to hear the other voices, to rehearse the ensembles: the several duets and the spectacular final trio. She hoped the sheer force of will was enough to accomplish in seven days what the rest of the cast had been doing for a month. Yet, the pressure was in its own way a blessing; it took her mind off her personal problems.

She pulled her charcoal gray cape up higher on her shoulders. An expensive cloak, an extravagance, really, that she had allowed herself as a form of solace. With its hood and sweeping width, it was a bit theatrical, but blissfully warm, and there was no harm in an opera singer dressing like...an opera singer.

The train crossed the Salzach River and she pressed her head against the windowpane watching the morning sun illuminate the medieval *Festung Hohensalzburg*, the prince archbishop's fortress on the hill that was the icon for Salzburg on every guidebook in the world. Including the one in her hand. In the remaining minutes before arrival, she glanced through the first page.

"The Old City of Salzburg on the banks of the Salzach River can be traversed by foot in its entirety in a single afternoon. It has 16 churches (11 on the left bank and 5 on the right) and a plethora of concert halls, ecclesiastical residences, princely palaces, cloisters, and fountains and gates and monuments as would dazzle the most jaded eye. It is a Catholic city, which flaunts an extravagantly gilded Baroque Christianity. Its rooftops are patina'd domes, its gardens thoroughfares of relief and statuary, and its angels and Madonnas and Infants, its halos and coronas and explosions of flora are so laden with gold that even in the murkiest sanctuary and crypt, it shimmers. It is a supremely religious city, but its religion is art."

Katherina smiled at the description, wondering why there was no mention of opera. Ah, there it was, on the next page.

"And even more than the eye, Salzburg beguiles the ear, for no city in Europe is more closely identified with classical vocal music than this one. Mozart was born here in 1756 and Herbert von Karajan in 1908. For over two hundred years, gorgeous music has been performed in its glittering palaces and churches, music that purported to glorify prince or deity, but was always in fact its own glory. Mozart festivals began in 1877 and the first summer festival was given in 1922, the year that the Kleines Festspielhaus was built. In 1960 the Grosses Festspielhaus was added, its anterooms fashioned out of the massive stables of the prince-archbishop, and its stage and backstage area blasted out of the stone of the Monchsberg behind it."

A theater cut into the rocky slope. Music versus the mountain, and music won. She liked the idea.

❖

Confirming that she had her shoulder bag, scarf, hat, and both gloves, Katherina struggled out of the taxi on the Linzergasse and blinked in the bright winter sunlight. Yes, this was clearly the historical part of the city, Mozart's Salzburg. Hefting her suitcase, she trudged up the tiny winding Steingasse to the Pension Stein. She'd originally planned to stay at the Hilton Hotel, but when the Festspiel administration told her about the quiet pension on the Kapuzinerberg overlooking the town, she moved her reservation to the Stein. The fact that Anastasia Ivanova was also staying there might have played a role. Still, she had not considered how difficult it would be to drag her luggage up the endless stone steps to the entryway.

"Gnädige Frau." A plump, ruddy-cheeked woman opened the oaken door all the way and stepped back. *"Ich bin Frau Semmel,"* she said, and offered her hand. She had the slightly flat face and the singsong lilt of the Austrian peasant. Katherina took the hand and was drawn into an entryway. The adjacent breakfast room was Alpine-cute, with whitewashed plaster walls above pine wainscoting. To their immediate left was a steep wooden stairway that led to the upper floor. As they climbed the stairs, Katherina detected the unmistakable smell of soap and wood polish.

Having reserved late, Katherina had gotten the last room available, and it was small. The few furnishings and the double bed appeared to be antique, as did the enormous wooden crucifix that hung over the carved headboard. Almost a meter in height, it held a figure whose agony was carved and painted with morbid precision. Tiny trickles of blood ran down the face and neck of the Savior, and larger streams bulged like knotted velvet cords from the side and hand wounds. The bone of one knee was exposed through an ulcerous black-rimmed wound.

She had scarcely unpacked when the phone rang, the rehearsal secretary calling, slightly out of breath and obviously relieved to have reached her. A sudden change in rehearsal plans. Could Katherina begin this afternoon instead of tomorrow?

Yes, of course she could. Katherina snatched up her cape and scarf, and reversed the path she had made scarcely half an hour before. At the end of the Steingasse, she crossed the large stone bridge and continued past shops with wrought-iron signs hanging over their doors: *Amadeus Schokolade, Figaro Café*. In a few minutes she was at a square where a stone balustrade marked off a large pool of water. The watering pool for the Prince Archbishop's horses. At the rear of the pool, a wall held seven equestrian panels. Ramps led into the pool from two sides, and in its center a bronze stallion reared up over a squire who still held him by the reins. An apt image of her current state of mind, Katherina thought, one part of herself trying to gain control of the other.

Just across the street toward her left was the concert-hall complex of the Festspielhaus. A long and unimpressive concrete box of a building, it could have been a municipal structure in a middle-sized German town. Yet its three theaters were hallowed halls for aspiring opera singers, and to sing in any of them meant you had made it. She hurried through the wide foyer into the main hall.

❖

The first act was halfway through when Katherina crept into the auditorium. Baron Ochs was handing over the rose casket with just the right balance of lasciviousness and charm. Singing the bass role, Hans Stintzing executed a marvelous rococo bow, as elaborate as a dance step. He drew a lace handkerchief from his cuff, waved it in a half circle, then blew his nose into it as he lumbered from the Marschallin's boudoir.

Then the Marschallin began her long monologue and Katherina had time to study the stately soprano who performed her. Sybil Ruiz, a black Puerto Rican–American, had a creamy soft-grained voice that was perfect for the role. Katherina became caught up in the musings of a woman fearing age and the passing of time. Katherina was always amused by the way the soliloquy ended, with the campy observation, "Ah, but style makes all the difference."

Suddenly the door behind the Marschallin flew open and a slender, gorgeous boy in riding clothes strode across the stage. High suede boots went up to his knees and covered the bottom of his gray-green breeches. Over a soft white shirt he wore a brocade vest that ended at mid-thigh, and over that a green riding coat. Wide cuffs were trimmed in black velvet slashes, each vertical slash ending with a brass button. Down his chest, on both front panels of the coat, rows of gold braid and stamped brass buttons ran from collar to hem. The pommel of a dress saber jutted from an opening at the hip of the coat, and whenever he turned, it swung after him.

Anastasia Ivanova was stunning in the trouser role, and Katherina was hypnotized. It was the same sensuous face she had seen on the record jacket of Berlioz' *Faust*. How fascinating now, to see her move and gesture, confirming the authoritative presence Katherina had discerned on the *Faust* photo. But now she had a male swagger. The Slavic features were still striking, though the nose in profile was longer than expected. Although she had a rehearsal costume, she wore neither of the two wigs that would be required in the performance, and her blond hair hung loosely clipped behind her neck.

Androgynous though the role was, Anastasia did not blur the sexual identities so much as project both sexes at once. A strikingly attractive female face sang in a high, bright timbre, and it remained obvious that a woman's body was under the breeches and coat. At the same time, every word and gesture bore masculine authority.

The idea of being on stage with this woman, singing amorous duets, suddenly excited her.

❖

"I'm sure you're beat from travel and then four hours of rehearsal." Anastasia opened the door to her room at the Pension Stein. "But stop in just for a moment and see the view from my balcony."

Katherina followed her inside. "It's a fantastic room. Not only do you have a crucifix that's much less gory than mine, but a balcony opening to the whole city!"

"Yes, come outside and have a look, but be careful of the step down." Anastasia reached in front of her and opened the glass door. "It's almost too pretty to be real, isn't it?"

They stood side by side and looked out over the cold evening landscape. The Salzach River crawled below them, slightly silver under the blue-gray sky. Lights had gone on in places among the low houses of the old city across the Salzach, concentrations of warmth and solace against the frigid oncoming night. Among the low houses, the churches stood like shepherds watching over a flock of sheep, their domes ornamented and patina'd. Behind these, stark and grim in the falling light, the ancient fortress crouched atop its hill.

"If it would only snow," Anastasia said. "Then Salzburg is sublime. It crouches in the mist like a phantom city. But that's just my fantasy, I suppose. I adore snow."

Katherina hugged her cape around her. "I don't care much for it myself. It makes my legs stiff."

"Let's sit by the fire then and warm up. I'll pour us a little port." Anastasia retreated into the room to ignite the gas jet in the tiny fireplace in the corner. As Katherina came in behind her, she was drawing up two stools.

"Snow for me is childhood innocence," she continued. "The quintessential image of Russia."

"I suppose that's why it's on all the postcards. What city did you live in?"

Anastasia reached into a corner cabinet and withdrew a bottle of something deep red, along with two tiny glasses. "The Communists call it Leningrad, but my mother never stopped calling it St. Petersburg. For her the Revolution was just a passing phase. Insane, of course, because she married a communist. They must have really been in love." She handed over one of the glasses and filled both of them with the crimson liquid.

"And the snow part?" Katherina sipped from her glass. The port was silky sweet and she held it deliciously on her tongue before swallowing.

"That's from my mother, who lived in a fantasy of Old Russia. When it snowed, she lit our samovar and reminisced about her childhood under the Tsar. Her name was Olga Adrianovna Romanova Kalish, and she had some distant connection to the imperial family."

"You have Romanov blood? I'm impressed. I guess that explains your name."

Anastasia snorted, and the unexpected sound bursting from her elegant face was hugely comical. "You don't know the half of it. My full name is Anastasia Olga Vasillievna Ivanova, but you have to appreciate what a joke it is. My mother gave herself those "ova" endings when in fact she was something like a second cousin to a second cousin on the female side. Anyone with real Romanov connections went into exile, and the fact that she stayed safely put in Russia tells you how thin her imperial blood actually was. In fact, her own brother, my uncle Georgi, was a hero in the Red Army during the war."

"I suppose it would be pretty foolish to claim royal privilege, wouldn't it?"

"Not only that, the whole idea of Romanov blood is meaningless. They were a rather dull family, whose only distinguishing trait was hemophilia, certainly not intelligence. The Romanov monarchy, for all its history, was a kind of splendid opera. All theater, with no inkling of the rumblings among their own people. Of course the most operatic of all was the end of the dynasty, with the Tsarevitch and Rasputin and the slaughter of everyone at Ekaterinburg."

"Fabulous costumes, though," Katherina quipped. "A shame the communists are so drab."

Anastasia laughed softly. "My thoughts exactly. Why can't they have their collective farms and tractor factories and still leave us a few nice outfits? I suppose that's why I love our little operas. We get to dress up and play miniature versions of the big operas of empire and no harm is done."

"Oh, I agree." Katherina took another sip of the sweet wine. Was it the port or the closeness to Anastasia that was making her giddy? "But we were talking about snow, weren't we?"

"Yes, well, the fantasy my mother built around herself and around me, little Anastasia, was right out of Russian folklore. As she got older, she suffered from dementia, so all the while we were in communist Leningrad, she was living in that postcard illusion. Toward the end, she claimed to have been at a ball at the Winter Palace. She could even describe mirrored halls, the servants, the women in long gowns and the men in smart military uniforms. There was always snow in her story, and people arriving at the palace in horse-drawn sledges. For years I had a doll called Snow Maiden, a character in Russian folklore. I suppose if anything, Snow Maiden was the symbol for our perfect world, the world of our dreams."

For a moment, Katherina felt a stab of envy. Having a delusional mother was vastly better than having none at all. Then she remembered the hardships of Soviet life. "I have trouble imagining what it would be like to become an opera singer in Communist Russia. It must have been difficult."

"It wasn't, really. The education is free. If you have musical talent, the state will support you and there's always work. After I finished Rimsky-Korsakov Conservatory, the Leningrad Symphony engaged me right away. I sang the mezzo solo in Prokofieff's *Alexander Nevsky*. A couple of years later I was invited to sing with the Leningrad Opera.*"*

"Then the Bolshoi discovered you?"

Anastasia laughed again, her voice as creamy as the port wine. "The Bolshoi doesn't 'discover' anyone. I had to audition with a dozen other singers hungry to leave the provinces. But they signed me on. In the second season I sang Joan of Arc in the *Maid of Orleans*. The Russians adore their Tchaikovsky."

"When did you start singing *Rosenkavalier*?"

"Not until Paris. I love Octavian, but it's a very demanding role. Not only are you on stage all the time, but the running around and the costume changes are a strain. I'm always afraid I'll forget a sword or a glove." She bent toward the fire to warm her hands. "And once I sang with a Sophie who dropped the rose."

"In performance? How awful. Well, I think I can promise not to do that, but I'm still not certain quite how to play her. I find her a bit silly."

"You don't have to play her silly. I'd definitely welcome a Sophie with dignity. My Octavian is also a notch more introspective than usual. I think you'll like him."

"I'm sure I will." Katherina toyed with the empty port glass. Like Octavian? She was already smitten with him. "Do you think we might bring something new to their relationship?"

"A little more passion, you mean? That will depend on the kind of Sophie you are." Anastasia squinted with sudden seriousness. "I will be leaving a great woman for you, so you have to be very exciting."

Katherina stared back at intelligent gray eyes and wondered how much they teased. "Well, then, I guess I have to work on being a Sophie you can't resist."

❖

"No, no, no. You keep missing the cue." Exasperated, Radu Gavril signaled the pianist to stop. Sixty years old but with the energy of a man possessed, he marched toward Katherina in the center of the rehearsal room. Hans Stintzing sat next to her, as perplexed as she was by Radu's action.

"I'm having trouble getting off Hans' lap fast enough to start my line," Katherina said. "It'll be even harder in costume."

Radu gave a little puff of impatience. "Try it a beat earlier, then. And sing the line with more staccato. I'll show you." He called to the pianist. "Heinrich, take it from the first measure."

The stage director sat down on the knee of the bass, who sang his line unfazed by the man on his lap. At the specified moment, Radu leapt up and sang Sophie's line in a lively falsetto, mimicking girlish annoyance. An instant later he was himself again, somber, authoritative. "Do you see what I mean?"

Katherina nodded. "Yes, I think so. Sharper, with a notch more outrage."

"Yes, exactly." He signaled the pianist. "Start again from one."

Katherina was acutely aware that the piano rehearsal was for her benefit, as latecomer, since the rest of the cast had already begun rehearsals with her predecessor. Intensely focused therefore, she worked her way through the second act, getting to know the rhythms of each of the other singers, interacting physically, dramatically, and vocally. It was a joy to work with singers at the level of skill and professionality of the other cast members.

Hans Stintzing exuded a carefully calibrated lasciviousness for his Baron Ochs without losing the air of a nobleman. Anastasia maintained a subtle presence at the edge of the scene without drawing attention away from the Baron and Sophie.

Back and forth she went with Hans' Baron Ochs—he singing lewdness in short waltz motifs and she responding with dissonant rejection. Then it was Katherina's time to linger at the periphery while the two "men" had their duel.

To the general amusement, Anastasia proved far more skilled with the foil than the burly bass. Finally, exasperated, Radu took the Baron's foil.

"The orchestra gives you plenty of time for this, Hans, so you don't have to get too excited. There are only a few steps before Octavian pokes you." He assumed position, toe to toe with Anastasia. "Start on your cue," he said to Anastasia, and the brief duel began.

After assuming the *en garde* position for a fraction of a second, Anastasia feinted and then advanced in a series of lunges. Radu parried each one, talking all the while. "You see, Hans. You just have to match her steps backward, and...parry...parry, then, *riposte*."

"Now, you try it." He handed the foil to Hans.

The two singers practiced the choreography until the stage director was satisfied. At the right moment, Octavian flicked the foible of her blade across his upper sword arm and Hans' comic genius took over. Clapping his meaty hand over his wounded arm, he stood gawking in astonishment. His lips quivered hilariously for a moment; then he sang out "Mur-der! Mur-der!" and swooned into the arms of his servant. "A doctor. Bandages! Police!" he sang. "I'm hot-blooded. I'll bleed to death in a minute. Stop him! Poliiiice!"

It took another hour to block the remainder of the second act: servants conspiring, Sophie protesting, father ranting. But finally, the outraged Baron was placated by a "fine old Tokay" and was carried off, murmuring naughty innuendo in the melody of a waltz.

❖

The air outside the festival hall was biting cold and Katherina spoke through the layers of scarf that covered her mouth and throat.

"Radu Gavril is amazing, isn't he? He's got so much energy. He seems to be running on better fuel than the rest of us."

Equally muffled, Anastasia pressed close to Katherina to be heard, taking hold of her arm. "A good thing, too. Hans needed work on his fencing. I've been worried all week that he might put a hole in me." She laughed.

Katherina felt like a schoolgirl, walking arm in arm with Anastasia, and though thick layers of wool separated them, the pressure of Anastasia's shoulder seemed to add warmth. "You want to stop for some coffee?" she said suddenly. "The Café Tomaselli is just around the corner in the Alter Markt."

Anastasia shook her head. "It's apt to be full of tourists. Let's make it supper and go to the Triangel. The headwaiter is a sweetheart. He'll give us a quiet table if the place is not too full."

The Triangel *was* full, but the headwaiter lived up to his reputation. A round ruddy face with wide nose and gray handlebar mustache radiated grandfatherly charm. Katherina thought of a somewhat aristocratic St. Nicolaus. He kept a pristine dishtowel folded over his arm as if part of a waiter's costume. His step was buoyant, and his eyes shone with pleasure when he recognized Anastasia.

"Ah, Madame Ivanova, what a pleasure to see you. And you brought another lovely lady."

"Looks busy tonight, Willi. I don't suppose you have a quiet table anyplace."

"*Tja.* It will be difficult I'm afraid. Friday evening, you know. But let me see what I can do."

Katherina scanned the café. The unpretentious room had only basic wooden tables and a few sets of goat antlers on the walls. The clientele was obviously from the Festspielhaus. Katherina recognized several of the administrative staff. Detlev from the wig department caught her eye and waved, and in the far corner, with her back turned, Sybil was having dinner with Hans.

Willi the waiter had returned. "*Glück g'habt,*" he said. "Gerda was folding napkins at the table in the back and I convinced her to move. If you don't mind being next to the kitchen."

They both shook their heads and he led them down the narrow space that branched off from the main restaurant. As the level of noise dropped off, the kitchen smells increased. A pleasant mixture of warm potatoes, sausage, and coffee.

Unwrapping meters of woolen neck scarves, Anastasia hung her coat on a wall hook and sat down. "I recommend the schnitzel. Best in Salzburg."

Katherina exhaled luxuriously in the warm air. "Sounds wonderful. Order for us both." She was still exuberant from the rehearsal. "Seeing you only as Marguerite, I wouldn't have guessed you were so good in a trouser role. And you fence like an expert!"

Anastasia laughed. "I only know those three steps, but that's all you need for Octavian. It's not much of a duel, after all. If I ever have to sing a pirate or musketeer, I'm cooked."

"*Are* there operas with pirates or musketeers? Outside of Gilbert and Sullivan, I mean."

"I can't think of one, but in any case, I'll stick with Octavian and

Cherubino. In fact, strike that. I'd prefer Mozart's Cherubino any time. So much easier to sing."

"He's fun to watch too. I saw my first *Nozze di Figaro* when I was ten, in German, of course. A birthday present from my parents. I was already studying voice."

"Really? I've always wondered what children think of him. Cherubino, I mean."

"I was bored at first. You know, the opera starts with Figaro measuring a room for a bed, and I couldn't get interested in *that*. But then Cherubino, this fantastic boy-girl creature in blue satin knee pants, burst into the room. It was like I myself was suddenly on stage."

The schnitzel arrived and Katherina bit into something exquisitely spiced. She chewed for a moment, reminiscing. "I didn't know what a trouser role was, and it was confusing to see a woman singing as a boy. It also was exciting, a kind of lawlessness."

Anastasia nodded, raising her fork for emphasis. "That scene is real comic theater. Then it gets even funnier, when he starts switching back and forth between the sexes. He's a boy, then a soldier, then a woman singing a boy disguised as a peasant girl."

"Yes, in every scene, Cherubino was all I looked at. He always came and went through the window, as if he lived in the air outside, not on earth. Frankly, I was smitten. You can imagine how thrilled I was when my mother took me backstage to meet the singer."

"That didn't destroy the illusion?"

"Not at all. Backstage was a magical place. Men carrying flowers knocked on doors with nameplates. When the doors opened, divine light seemed to shine out from the rooms."

"Oh my, you *were* smitten."

"I was so excited, wondering how this otherworldly being would look up close. Then the door opened. It was a woman, of course, but she wore slacks and a blue shirt, almost the same color as her costume. Her hair was shorter than the wig she had worn, but some of Cherubino was still there in her face. She seemed to look through me."

"Who sang that Cherubino?" Anastasia asked.

"Claudia Martin." I never saw her again after that performance."

"Oh yes, she was a good mezzo. Almost a contralto. She stopped singing early on and went to live in the country with her girlfriend.

The Cherubino that stepped into her shoes was of course the American Frederica von Stade."

Katherina ignored the "girlfriend" remark. "Yes, I love von Stade, too. But the meeting with Claudia Martin changed my life. She asked me if I wanted to be an opera singer and at that moment, I knew with certainty I did. Strange, isn't it? I was ten years old and I was ready to sell my soul. In fact, she warned me that I had to make sacrifices and asked me what I was willing to give up. I told her *everything*. And it was true. Something had happened to me that night and I was willing to abandon everything I knew and run away to 'join the opera.'"

"Not the circus?" Anastasia mocked gently.

"Not even close. Anyhow, that was it. Just then my mother showed up to fetch me and we went home. I'm sure I babbled on and on about Cherubino, but my mother seemed to understand."

"The opera bug was from her side?"

"From both sides, actually. My father loved opera and my mother was a singer. Of popular songs, like Hildegard Knef or Edith Piaf. She died when I was young and after that, there was just my father. But opera was always in the air, as long as I can remember."

"You lost your mother. In my case, it was my father. He was killed at Kursk."

"So many died in the war and in the hard years right after. There must have been millions of children on both sides raised by one parent, or none."

"That's true, though I did have a second father for a while. My uncle Georgi, my mother's brother. We heard that he had been lost at Stalingrad, but he showed up five years later at our house. He had two artificial legs, but he was alive."

Katherina shook her head. "The war, the purges. It all seems such an appalling waste. We had Hitler and you had Stalin. A hundred million dead. How many people did the Soviets lose? Twenty million? So much sacrifice and the Kremlin still is imprisoning its own people. It's hard not be cynical."

"That's so true. No sign of a god, but it's very easy to believe in the devil, isn't it?" Anastasia poured more coffee into both their cups. As if they were a couple, Katherina thought.

"Well, there's plenty of evil to go around, that's for certain, but I think we make a mistake to see it only as something alien and absolute. We are sometimes its victims, but I think we carry it around inside ourselves too, and it stays docile only as long as the going is good and we're not threatened."

"Let's not talk about good and evil. You are far too somber today, and there's no reason for it. Here, this is what you need."

She held up a cube of sugar for a moment and then dropped it into Katherina's coffee. Was it flirtation or just silliness, Katherina wondered as she lifted the cup to her lips. Whichever it was, the oversweetened coffee was, in fact, delicious.

XIII
Duetto

*E**r kommt! Er Kommt!"* On the upper floor of the stage set, the maidservant sang as she ran from window to window, describing the street, the gathering crowd, the ornate carriage, and every movement of the arriving cavalier.

Below, on the main stage, Katherina gathered the crinoline of her Sophie costume and turned in circles of girlish joy.

Then the double doors flew open. Two lines of Hussars entered, with high fur hats and pale green, fur-trimmed jackets hung on one shoulder. Scimitars swung from their sides and elaborately ornamented white boots rose to their knees. They stood at attention, forming a phalanx on each side of the open doorway.

A fanfare sounded, and the rose cavalier appeared. Abruptly, the orchestra dropped away, leaving only the violins on a high, sustained tone, full of suspense.

Octavian glittered like an ice sculpture at the center-rear of the stage. His left hand rested at his waist on the bejeweled hilt of a ceremonial dagger, and his right hand, raised slightly above his head, held the silver rose. His immaculate white satin knee pants and rhinestone-studded jacket caught the various spotlights and he sparkled.

He began hesitantly, "I have the honor…most noble lady…" and stepped slowly with lowered eyes toward the waiting Sophie. Little by little he neared her. At the words "this rose" he bowed from the waist and, keeping his eyes averted, held out the silver flower.

With measured hesitation, Katherina took the rose, touched it to her nose, and sang her reply to the silver-white top of Octavian's head. "It has a strong fragrance, like living roses."

"Yes, a drop of Persian rose oil is on it," he sang, and the lovely head rose slowly, mist-gray eyes capturing her.

For an instant, Katherina felt as if the ground had dropped away and she was suspended, held in place by Anastasia's eyes. Sensing the rose slip through her fingers, she tightened her grip and sang, "It pulls me, as if chords were around my heart."

They sang together to the thrilling climax of the duet, then moved downstage for the sweet dialog in which she sang his baptismal names to him: "Octavian, Maria Ehrenreich, Bonaventura, Ferdinand, Hyacinth."

How delicious it was to play at falling in love with Octavian, letting her Sophie character ramble on while the glittering rose cavalier sang back, "My God, how lovely she is." That they were on a brightly lit stage in front of press and dress rehearsal invitees did not dilute the thrill of playing at romance.

Anastasia sang with the full conviction of a young man falling in love, looking directly at her and then away, as if caught in too great an intimacy. Then she faded back, stage left, to allow the husband-to-be to ply his troth. Hans von Stintzing played the boorish Baron Ochs with gusto, and his hands were all over her.

Then Octavian was at Katherina's side again, and the satin-clad arms held her for their next duet as they looked into each other's eyes. Their vocal lines interwove, tone for tone, the brief dissonances resolving into thirds, their two agile voices in tense and thrilling interplay. "Your eyes, your noble air...I know nothing more of myself, only you. Oh, stay with me, stay by my side." Katherina had never sung a love duet with a woman before and was unprepared for the effect it had on her.

Then the Baron returned for the duel, which Hans had finally learned. Baron Ochs was made for him and he milked every drop of humor from the scene. At exactly the right moment, Octavian administered the wounding prick and Ochs collapsed. "Mur-der! Mur-der!" he called out, and was carried away, singing of martyrdom and the need for a nice aged Tokay.

❖

Finally the dress rehearsal was over. Bone weary, Katherina slipped out of her costume and emerged from her dressing room looking for Anastasia. How nice it would be to walk back to the hotel together again, arm in arm, talking about intimate things.

Radu Gavril was suddenly in front of her, still full of energy, as if the day had just begun. "We need to re-block a little bit for the lighting," he said, urging her back onto the stage to show her the exact spot. "It will just take a moment."

Ten minutes later she was free again and hurried backstage.

"Oh, Miss Marow, do you have a moment?" A slender man minced toward her.

Katherina exhaled in resignation. "Yes, Detlev?"

"I am *so* sorry. I know everyone's leaving, but the director has decided that Sophie's wig doesn't go with your face and he wants me to fit another one. Can you spare me just a teensy bit of time?" His voice grew playful. "Or are you late for evening mass?" The tips of his long fingers formed a little tent and his eyes rolled heavenward.

Her annoyance evaporated and she poked him gently on the shoulder. "Does *anyone* around here go to mass?"

"Not in *my* circle of acquaintances." He turned away with a slight flourish and she fell into step behind him, following him down to his subterranean workshop.

The wigmaker's shop was small and cluttered. On two sides, glass-covered cabinets held *Perüken* of every size, from mass-produced spear-carrier wigs to flamboyant Baroque monstrosities. On a table to the right, wooden dummy heads wore the various *Rosenkavalier* wigs, natural-colored ones for the first and third acts, formal white for the second act.

Katherina sat down on the chair at the center of the shop and drummed her fingers on the armrest.

"Just sit still and it will be over before you know it," he said, tugging her hair back into a tight ponytail and tacking the tail flatly on her head with hairpins. With a single adept movement, he slid a tight nylon cap over the entire mass.

"Here is your new Sophie look," Detlev announced. He set the wig on her head and adjusted it back and forth until he could match it to her hairline. Though it was pure white and made her look doll-like, it was less extravagant than the previous one, and for that she was grateful. She sat patiently as he traced her hairline with a brown marker, moving only her eyes to study the wigs in her field of vision. One of them caught her attention.

"Is that the Queen of the Night?" She gave a faint tilt of the head toward the wig that took up a whole cabinet shelf.

"Oh, yes. Don't you just love it?" He finished his work and fetched the wig dummy from the cabinet, setting it on the table in front of her. The wig was enormous, as if inflated, and was surrounded at its edges by glistening white curls. In among the filaments that made up the hair was a sort of metallic confetti, which caught the light and sparkled. A dozen thin wires jutted from the crown like spokes in a wheel, each with a tiny diamond at the center and on its tip. The effect was a sparkling double halo around the wig. On a dark stage, with dramatic spotlights, it must have been scintillating.

"My finest work," he announced, resting his open hand on one hip, then sighed. "I've always wished I could sing Queen of the Night," he confided "Can you *imagine*?"

Katherina knew he was serious and didn't laugh. "Think you could do the high notes?"

"F above high C? Guess not. But, when you're young, you have your little fantasies, and she was mine."

"Mine too, actually," Katherina confessed. "I saw *Magic Flute* about fifteen years ago. Ruth Welting sang her. This black mountain rolled in from the rear of the stage. There she was on the top, all sparkling with an enormous diadem of diamonds radiating out against the blackness. When she started singing I dissolved into a pool of longing."

He removed the Sophie wig and held it up like a puppet on the fingertips of one hand.

"Don't you hate that they made her the villain? I mean, it's…I don't know…like a big lie. Something beautiful and natural portrayed as evil, while Sarastro, the *kidnapper*, for God's sake, is Mr. Benevolent. I wanted to sing the Queen just to be able to tell him where he could stick his magic flute."

Katherina laughed. "Actually, I wanted to be her daughter Pamina. I couldn't imagine anything more exciting than having her as my mother." She stroked one of the sparkling curls.

"I had just lost my own mother, you see. To illness. So I was…" She shook her head. "Sorry, I didn't mean to tell you my life story."

"Oh no, dear. It's a beautiful story." He nodded sympathetically. "And believe me, I know all about longing." He pressed a fingertip on his lips, as if formulating something.

"Opera is a wonderful place to escape a cruel world, isn't it? That's why there are so many people like me in it. In opera everything happens—great love, horrible deaths, tragic sacrifices, terrible crimes—and the music purifies it all."

She smiled up at his melancholic expression. "A little like being intoxicated, isn't it?"

"Oh more than a little! It's a big emotional orgy. And *we* do it. The singers, musicians, wigmakers, we get a thousand people drunk for the night."

She giggled. "You make us sound immoral."

Detlev pursed his lips. "Well, we *are*. Maybe that's why Mozart made the Queen of the Night into the villain. On the other hand, she has the best costume and the best aria. And let's face it, she's the one everyone wants to hear. Who would you rather go home with after the party, a smug-face, rule-enforcing patriarch, or the Empress of the sparkly Night?" He pirouetted, holding the wig over his own head.

"I'm guessing not the patriarch."

"No, the Queen!" Detlev retrieved his wig dummy and danced gracefully toward the display shelves. "Long live the Queen. Long live the Night!"

"Long live the night?" a voice in the doorway said. "That sounds ominous."

XIV
Capriccioso

"Maestro." Katherina felt like a truant, caught out of school. "I thought everyone had left the theater."

"Everyone has. We're the last." Joachim von Hausen took her cape from her hand and draped it over her shoulders. "Come on. I'll walk you to your hotel, if you don't mind making a slight detour to pick up my wife. I'll give you a little tour on the way."

Emerging from the subterranean halls, they went through the glass doors of the Grosses Festspielhaus into the frigid evening air. Katherina wrapped her scarf once more around her throat and chin.

Von Hausen began his tour, sweeping his arm in an arc across the square. "This, as you know, is the Max Reinhardtplatz. Did you know that he was one of the founders of the Salzburg Festival? The Austrians thanked him for it by forcing him into exile in 1938. He made a big career in the U.S., though, and after the war, they forgave him for being Jewish and named this square after him."

"Do I detect a hint of cynicism?" Katherina decided she liked this man.

"Cynical? Me? Just because Salzburg is a blend of museum and toy shop that makes an industry out of Mozart, whom they practically expelled, and whose main products are concerts, kitsch, and chocolate?"

"Aren't you being a bit harsh? Salzburg is the biggest musical scene in Europe. The public gets to hear some of the best opera, and thousands of musicians and theater people have work."

"Yes, they do, I admit it. I am one of them. I'm just not enchanted by the city the same way the tourists are. It's one great big anachronism, and too cute by half."

They had reached the archway to the St. Peter's Church courtyard.

"My wife, however, is far less critical. She adores Baroque art, and for her Salzburg is heaven. Particularly the Peterskirche. Are you familiar with it? So Baroque, it will give you a headache." He swung open the heavy wooden door to the sanctuary and they walked side by side down the center aisle.

Piers on both sides of the aisle held murals of saints flanked by faux Baroque columns and fronted by a line of fir trees glittering with tiny yellow lights. Von Hausen was right. The combination of excessive ornament and extreme piety was overwhelming. Presumably, that was the point.

At the last pier to the right side of the altar, a woman stood with a sketchpad.

"Ah, there she is. My lovely wife."

The woman turned as they approached and smiled recognition. She closed her sketchbook and tucked it under her arm.

"Katherina, this is my wife Magda. Schatz, this is Katherina Marow, our Sophie."

Magda wiped her charcoal-smudged fingertips on a handkerchief, then offered her hand. "Pleased to meet you." Katherina set her shoulder bag on the arm of the pew and accepted the handshake.

Magda von Hausen was an attractive, well-kept woman a few centimeters taller than her husband. Her perfectly coiffed hair was artfully blonded to conceal her fifty-something age, and her makeup was flawless. The look of a woman married to a famous man. For all that, her manner seemed sincere, her handshake firm.

Von Hausen turned to a white-haired gentleman who had stood up in the meantime. Katherina had not noticed him. "And I believe you know Mr. Raspin, one of the festival patrons."

"Yes, of course I remember you. From the *Carmina Burana* reception." She recalled his flattery and his mysterious remark, "I support such music—in my way."

One of the festival patrons. Now it made sense. Her face warmed at her misjudgment and condescension. He was a financier of the festival. He paid her salary.

"How nice to see you again," she managed, offering her hand. His handshake was the same as before, a tight grasp with cold fingers. She resolved to show more interest in him this time.

"I ran into Madame von Hausen in the square and kept her company while she sketched," Raspin explained to the conductor, although it did not seem necessary. Von Hausen had opened his wife's sketchbook and was looking at the most recent drawing. It was a rather good replica of the oil painting over the church shrine. "Who is that?" Katherina asked.

Magda laughed, as she collected her charcoal pencils into a box and dropped it into a shoulder bag. "You'd better not let anyone hear you ask that. It's Saint Rupert, the patron saint of this city."

Katherina sat down on the pew and pressed a fingertip on the edge of the sketchbook. "May I take a look?"

"If you like." Magda drew on a fur coat over the already thick sweater she wore. "I make them just for myself, not to show."

Katherina turned the pages respectfully. A mixture of very skillful charcoal sketches, sepia drawings, and the occasional watercolor. Fountains and gates, a dozing Salzburg coachman, the glass tomb in one of the churches with its prelate's cadaver displayed in ecclesiastical regalia and, on the last page, a man with a fur-covered body and a red-painted, horn-topped head.

"Is this also something from Salzburg?"

It was Raspin who answered. "That's from Hofmannsthal's *Jedermann*. Have you ever seen Salzburg's annual morality play, Fräulein Marow? It's performed in summer in front of the cathedral in the medieval tradition."

Katherina shook her head, still studying the curious facial expression on the figure. It was rather soft, almost beguiling.

"Probably not what Hofsmannsthal had in mind, but I don't care." Magda took the sketchbook gently from Katherina's hand. "It's his play, but *my* picture, right?" She slipped the volume into her bag next to the pencil box. "In any case, I'm glad you're here. My fingers are like ice."

Her attention still on Magda, Katherina reached for her shoulder bag that lay on the armrest of the pew and knocked it over. It dropped with a soft thud and its contents spilled out onto the church floor: rehearsal notes, sheet music for the *Rosenkavalier* duets, a handful of pencils, and the journal, which fell open as it hit the marble.

Before Katherina could kneel down and gather her scattered belongings, Gregory Raspin was on one knee and already had everything in hand. He shuffled the notes and sheet music back into the canvas bag, then with particular care picked up the battered journal. Closing it gently, he held it out to Katherina. "You keep a journal, Madame Marow?"

"It's my father's," she replied, taking it from him. Embarrassed, she dropped it quickly into the bag, which she hooked over her shoulder. Von Hausen, meanwhile, had collected the loose pencils.

The two men were standing now and brushing dust from their knees. The crash had momentarily ended the banter and so, without speaking, the four of them made their way along the center aisle of the sanctuary.

Stopping just before the narthex of the church, von Hausen took a final look backward, drawing everyone's attention to the twinkling of the Christmas trees that added to the visual density of the Rococo church. "See what I mean?" he said. "Like marzipan. Too much gives you a headache."

Outside the night air was bitter cold again as the four of them strolled along the Getreidegasse. The sense of group gave the illusion of a sphere of warmth against the icy air. Most of the shops were closed, and only the soft yellow streetlights presented a brave front to the evening desolation.

They wound their way through narrow passages and ornate archways, and reached the Domplatz. Magda brought them to a halt at the center of the plaza before the Salzburg cathedral. Wide stone steps led to the arches of the façade and to the four colossal statues of saints. In the near darkness of the plaza, they rose up, blue-gray, and seemed ominous. "Here is where they perform *Jedermann*," she said. She pointed toward one of the towers, now black against the cobalt sky. "The angels 'fly' down from there on wires, and heavenly voices call out from as far away as the Peterskirche. The devil, on the other hand, simply strolls in from the street. Very medieval."

Von Hausen shook his head. "Yes, in a city full of anachronisms, a medieval morality play is the biggest one of all. Though, in fact, it's not medieval at all. It was written in 1911."

He looked up at one of the massive saints, as if disputing him. "You should read *Jedermann*, for laughs, Katherina. The devil's the only one who speaks the truth."

Magda linked her arm in that of her husband. "Joachim has always had a place in his heart for the devil. That's why I married him. Besides, everyone knows that evil is nothing but sex. *Nicht wahr*, Joachim?"

Gregory Raspin came alongside the couple "A common practice, to equate sex with the devil, encouraged by religions that seem to care an awful lot about the subject. But sex is just *one* of the avenues toward perdition."

"And what might the others be, Mr. Raspin?" Magda asked.

Raspin gestured toward the Festspielhaus. "Music, for one. Even Plato thought so. Mob activity, for another. And for a third, simple intoxication. All those things can unleash the demon. Or liberate the true vitality of the human being. We are, after all, a bundle of wants and urges, held in check by guilt and good manners."

"What a pessimist you are," Magda chided.

Katherina was not sure she liked the direction the conversation was taking, but by then they had reached the Salzach River. Streetlights glowing along both riverbanks gave slight comfort, while in the middle, the rapidly flowing Salzach was dark and menacing.

Gregory Raspin halted at the corner. "Alas, this is the street to my hotel. Much as I have enjoyed our little theological chat, I must leave you now." He took the women's hands one by one and pressed a cavalier kiss to the backs of their gloves. "Good evening, ladies." He hinted at a bow and turned away from them, quickening his step.

Katherina glanced back toward the bridge and the Pension Stein, and remembered now what had made her want to hurry. Magda was talking about painting the cityscape from the perspective of the Salzach bank, but Katherina was scarcely listening. She looked for a light in Anastasia's window and wondered if it was too late to suggest dinner.

Then she saw them. Anastasia and a man—a great bear of a man—emerged from the narrow Steingasse and walked toward a waiting taxi. The bear opened the car door, waited as Anastasia entered, then doubled over and got in after her.

Von Hausen saw where Katherina looked. "Ah, it appears Madame Ivanova is going out for the evening."

"Who do you suppose the man is?' Katherina asked lightly.

"Her husband, it looks like. Boris is his name, I believe. A big executive in Deutsche Grammophon. Yes, that was definitely Boris Reichmann."

XV
Mesto

Inexplicably depressed, Katherina climbed the stone steps to the pension in the dark. She was in Salzburg, she reminded herself, the opera capital of Europe, in a starring role. Everything she ever craved. Why wasn't she euphoric?

She was tired, of course, after a day of rehearsing, and the steps seemed steeper than usual. She panted, and inside her thick scarf her exhalations came back moist, warmed with her own heat.

Mercifully, the heavy oak door of the pension was unlocked so she did not have to fumble for the key. At the sound of the front door closing, Frau Semmel appeared in the entrance to her office holding a long white box. She was beaming.

"Isn't it wonderful? These arrived just a little while ago. You have an admirer, dear."

"An admirer?" Katherina repeated, dumbfounded. Her heart pounded. For the minutest fraction of a second, she hoped it might be from… No. She had just met the woman. But no one else seemed likely. Her manager never made such gestures, she had no family, and no one in the general public knew where she was staying.

Baffled, she unfastened the ribbon and opened the carton.

"White roses!" Frau Semmel exclaimed, hovering next to her. "And even before opening night. Romantic, *nicht wahr?*"

Tied to one of the stems was a little white envelope. The card inside was succinct. Frau Semmel read it out loud over Katherina's shoulder, as if to assist her.

"Sorry they are not silver. Yours truly, Gregory Raspin."

❖

Her room seemed smaller than before, the crucifix over the headboard larger. She sat down on the edge of the bed, confused.

She'd gotten flowers many times before—but never *before* a performance. It was a good sign, probably, that her career was advancing toward stardom. Performance offers, quality roles, fervent fans. Everything was falling into place. So what was causing her vague malaise?

Katherina stared at the white roses, still in their box at the foot of her bed. That was the answer. Gregory Raspin was paying court to her in the guise of the rose cavalier, if only for the length of a metaphor. He had stepped into the role that belonged to Anastasia. Dignified and debonair as he was, the thought of him wooing her in place of Anastasia was—distasteful.

She plucked one of the roses from its box, holding it by its head, velvety and fragrant and fraught with suggestion. She recalled the rose duet she had rehearsed that morning. The weaving of her voice with Anastasia's, not in banal and comfortable harmonies, but in a complicated back and forth through subtle dissonances. How skillfully Strauss suggested resolution, tantalizingly brief, before he pulled them apart again, leaving them to strain to be reunited until the whole duet climaxed in unbearable sweetness. Like courtship itself was supposed to be.

But Strauss, for whatever reason, had intended his rose cavalier to be sung by a woman. For a man to presume the role was, ironically, a travesty. Or at least the travesty of a travesty.

Detlev was right. Opera was its own world. Everything was allowed, as long as it was beautiful. She got up from the bed and stared out the window at the dark Salzach below.

Thoughts turned in her head like sea birds. Morality plays, the devil as sex, flirtation, identity, Raspin's reduction of the human being to a bundle of urges. She wasn't sure what it was, the discussion, the unwanted sight of Anastasia's husband, the unwelcome flowers, but she was morose. Her vision clouded and the spark of a dreadful memory glowed brighter—of the last night of her childhood.

She turned from the window and swept her eyes across the room to her canvas shoulder bag where the journal lay. Had her father recalled that night as well? Had he recorded it?

She fished the journal from the bag and leafed through it, skipping the entire 1950s. An important decade for Germany, she knew, but she would read those pages later. Finally she found the entries for the terrible week that had destroyed her childhood. They were all brief, scarcely a paragraph each, but their very brevity seared her.

May 14, 1960
Two new private patients this week. A sign of the times, that people now can afford the luxury of dermatology.

Katya's birthday is tomorrow. We offered to have a party for her but she said she'd rather we took her to the opera. Strange taste for an eleven-year-old, but she's been obsessed with singing since we took her to see *Figaro* last winter at the Staatsoper. The only tickets available on short notice were for Gounod's *Faust*, the one opera I would have preferred not to see. I explained the story of Faust to her, but she's too young to know what that means in real life. So I simply told her that all good fortune is paid for in the end. I don't think she understood.

May 16, 1960
An expensive mistake; I should have known. We didn't even get through the performance. Katya was restless through the whole first act and complained of a sore throat. Her forehead was hot, so I put my arm around her and told her we could leave at the end of the act. She half fell asleep resting against Lucy, and at intermission we took her home. She was coughing by then, and crying. We gave her aspirin and let her sleep with Lucy, and that seemed to calm her. Dawn is breaking now. When she wakes up, I'll take her to the clinic. The specialists there will probably confirm that it is just a bad cold and we'll put her to bed for a week.

May 17, 1960
Diphtheria. I should have suspected it, but she had no lymph-node swelling. There's been an outbreak in the city. The next morning Katya's throat was swollen nearly closed and she couldn't stand up. By the time we got a diagnosis and

medication, she was in respiratory distress. They've given her antibiotics, but she's unconscious. I sat by her bed all afternoon and it seems like she's breathing a little easier now, but I'm ashamed that I waited a whole night before getting her to the hospital. How much harm did I do my daughter in those twelve hours?

May 19, 1960
Katya is breathing better and is no longer in critical condition, but she's still delirious. She rambles on, semiconscious, about ghosts. And as if that's not enough disaster, Lucy has fallen sick too. The symptoms are the same, just as violent, but Lucy's heart has never been strong. The doctors are doing all they can, but meanwhile we are all in hell.

I pray to the God I don't believe in—let them recover. Don't make them be my payment.

Katherina's throat tightened and her eyes teared up. She knew what was coming as she turned the page.

May 25, 1960
Dear God. Lucy has died. Heart failure. She was the warmth and light of this family, and now she's gone. I force myself to keep going but I can barely walk from room to room.

I plod on, for Katya's sake. The antibiotics seem to be working and she's pulling through. The illness has deranged her, though. She's conscious, but when I told her—as gently as I could—that her mother had died, she barely reacted. She just turned her face away and said, "I'm sorry. I didn't mean it. I didn't think he'd do it."

Katherina closed the journal on her lap and dropped back against the bed pillow, letting the tears flow. She had not wept for her mother in years, but the brief entry in the journal made her recall the whole force of her childhood bereavement. Strange that her father had not understood that guilt and grief had weighed on her even more than it did on him. She was, after all, the cause of the death, infecting her mother the night she lay coughing in her arms.

She did not remember saying the words that he recorded, but she knew they had to be true; they were the logical outcome of the dream. And in over twenty years, she hadn't forgotten the dream.

In her fever, she had dreamt she was on a stage behind a curtain that was about to go up. On the other side she could hear the buzzing of a huge audience waiting for her to perform. Everything in her told her she had to sing, but she couldn't even take a deep breath to begin.

A man approached her, handsome in white tie and swallowtails. The conductor, she thought. He was supposed be with his orchestra, but had come to find out why the curtain had not risen. Claudia Martin, dressed as Cherubino, in blue satin knee pants, stood right behind him.

"Help me," Katherina begged. "I can't breathe."

"Of course I'll help you, but you have to pay for that. What are you willing to give up?"

Her chest heaved as she tried to suck in air. "Anything you want."

"I want the one you love the most."

"Yes, I agree," she'd said, gasping. "Just help me."

"Very good." He nodded and walked away.

At first she was disappointed because nothing happened, but then she discovered she could take a deep inhalation. She waited for the curtain to part, and when it did, she opened her eyes to the white walls of a hospital room and the somber figure of her father. That must have been when he broke the news to her.

Bitter memories. She was sorry now she had made herself relive them.

Soft tapping on the door wrenched her from her reverie. Katherina glanced at her watch. Nearly midnight. Who would bother her so late at night? She set the journal aside and got up from the bed.

Anastasia Ivanova stood in the corridor in her winter coat and fur hat. Her cheeks were still red from the frigid night air. "I'm sorry if I disturb you," she said, cold lips slowing her speech and thickening her Russian accent. "I saw your light…"

XVI
GRAZIOSO

No, not at all. Please come in." Katherina's mood changed instantly, as if the room had suddenly grown lighter.

Anastasia swept in bringing some of the night cold with her, and she waited for a moment just inside the doorway. She seemed nonplussed, as if she had not expected anyone to answer the door.

Katherina slipped the heavy woolen coat off Anastasia's shoulders and laid it across the foot of her bed, brushing away the box of roses. She gestured toward the one chair next to the gas fireplace. "Sit down. I'll turn up the flames. Is everything all right?"

Anastasia sat down delicately and bent toward the blue and yellow flames, rubbing the warmth into her upper arms. "Yes. Well, no," she said, then started again. "My husband's here." She hesitated again. "He's staying at the Hilton Hotel. We were separated, you see. I knew he was flying to Vienna this week, but he surprised me by stopping here first."

"I see." Katherina could think of no other response. She wished she had something to offer, wine or chocolate, but she had nothing, so she simply sat down next to the other woman.

"We've been married for five years," Anastasia went on, "but most of that time I've been performing. You know, touring, recording in London and New York, staying every place but home."

"I guess it's hard to be married and maintain an opera career. So much traveling. You have to really be in love to keep it going."

"In love? I have the feeling that love is a myth kept alive by novelists and librettists. At least it's never struck me. But Boris has always been a good companion. He was a godsend after I defected. That was the most difficult year of my life and he pretty much saved me."

"Yes, I remember the newspaper headlines. It was at the Paris airport, wasn't it? Very dramatic. Did you plan it that way?"

"I didn't plan it at all. I had been chafing at the restrictions at the Bolshoi for years, at the shabby housing, the political denunciations, the constant sense of being watched by KGB, all that. But I had no relatives or friends in the West. I had no idea *how* to defect."

"So what made you do it?"

"Snow."

"Snow? But there's almost never snow in Paris."

"There *was* that winter. I had just performed in *Boris Godunov*, and the morning I was supposed to fly back to Moscow I woke around 3:00. I looked out of my hotel window and it was snowing over Paris. It was like a revelation. I watched for an hour, a million thoughts in my head. Then it finally dawned on me that snow did not belong to Russia. All of those wonderful feelings and associations I had with snow I could have in Paris too. Or Munich or Oslo or New York. My mother had already passed away by then, or I would have telephoned and told her. But this realization was in the eleventh hour. Literally. A short time later, I was picked up and escorted by the Bolshoi 'colleagues,' who were obviously there to make sure I got on the plane. But as fate would have it, the flight was delayed—because of the snow. That's when I decided."

"What did you do?" Katherina was awestruck.

"I was terrified. My heart was pounding so hard I thought I would pass out. But then I saw two security guards strolling by, and I ran over and begged them to protect me. I told them I was being forced to get on a plane against my will. I don't know what made them act. I suppose a combination of French pride, chivalry, and the chance to rescue a pretty woman. In any case, they took me to security headquarters and called their captain. He called his superior, and the superior called *his*, and so forth. All this time, the two 'minders' were shouting about kidnapping and international agreements. There was a lot of confusion, but after an hour or so, I was taken in a police car to the *Ministre de l'immigration*, where I asked for asylum."

"And they said yes?"

"They said they would relocate me while my case was considered. But of course the press picked the story up and it was a coup for the West to have gotten a Bolshoi singer, so I was safe from deportation.

It took a lot longer to figure out just how I was going to live. Moscow, of course, froze my bank account. That's when Boris showed up. I had met him at a reception after one of the performances. When he heard the news he stepped in and took care of my financial needs, found me an apartment, and hired protection from the KGB. I owe him a lot. In any case, a year later, we were married."

"And that marriage worked?"

"We were happy enough. I provided him with glamour, an increase in record sales, while he provided me with safety and comfort. He was, and is, a decent man. You know, the kind who watches soccer matches on the weekend."

"That sounds boring, but also endearing," Katherina lied. In fact, it sounded stupefying.

"Boring, for sure. I can't tell you how many matches I had to listen to. Berlin versus Munich, Warsaw versus Cracow, Leningrad versus Moscow. Unfortunately, he also has an appetite for champagne and young women, and that got worse over the years. So just before I left for Salzburg, I told him he had to choose between them and me. It was all up in the air until he showed up here and now it seems like we might try to get things working again."

Katherina felt a string of reactions, one devolving into the other: sympathy for Anastasia's flight from the Soviet Union, revulsion for a husband who had obviously exploited her, and finally disappointment at realizing that Anastasia wanted nothing more than reassurance that she should reconcile with him.

"That sounds reasonable enough, if that's what you want." Katherina wondered if the dreariness was evident in her voice.

"The problem is that I want *everything*. I've spent my adult life developing my voice, but I want a home and children. Don't you?"

"Yes, I suppose so, one day. But for the moment, singing is more important to me."

"You mean the fame? That only lasts so long."

"No, not the fame." Katherina searched for words. "There is something that can happen on stage and nowhere else." Her glance drifted back to the fire. "I mean the moments when you are in perfect voice and your partner is too, when the orchestra is flowing all around you, and everything is working. You feel suspended and you can sense the audience suspended with you because they *know* it's perfect and you all share something…magical." She shrugged faintly. "I don't mean to suggest that as a substitute for family. But it's all I have, and for now, that's enough."

"Oh, I'm sorry. That's right, you just lost your father. I read about it in the paper." Anastasia laid her hand on Katherina's forearm. "You must have him on your mind a lot."

"I do. I'm reading his journal now, and I'm learning how very little I knew him. But please, let's not talk about him. Your problems are here and now. With your husband, I mean. What will you do?"

"Dither, probably. And talk. There are so many uncertainties, I just don't know yet." Anastasia glanced at her watch. "Oh, Lord, one in the morning. It's time we both got some sleep." She stood up and gathered her coat where it was lying next to the flower box.

"Oh, white roses," she observed. "An admirer, even before the performance. Should I be jealous? That he didn't send them to me, I mean?"

"I wish he had. I'm not sure how I feel about this kind of admiration. They're from someone named Raspin, who apparently is a Salzburg patron. He showed up at a concert performance I had too."

"Gregory Raspin sent them to you? That's no small thing. His company is a major sponsor of festivals all over Germany."

"You know him?"

"I know *of* him. He sort of collects people. Von Hausen is one of his protégés; rumor has it that Raspin got him the post as conductor of the Berliner Staatsorchester. He is very influential and if he likes you he can advance your career."

"That's good to know, I suppose. But I never heard of him before."

"Well, you have a chance to get to know him here. He's invited the principals to supper at the Goldener Hirsch tomorrow night. I'm sure everyone will accept."

"Will you go?"

"I don't know. If Boris is still here, I'll have to be with him." Anastasia stood in the doorway now. "Thank you for putting up with me so late at night. It's nice to have someone close by to talk to."

She leaned in, smelling of carnations, and gave Katherina a light kiss, though only her cheek, not her lips, touched Katherina's face.

"Read your father's journal," she said, "and be glad you had a father." Then she turned away.

Katherina closed the door softly and sat down again in the room that now seemed empty. The flowers were still on the bed, and as she lifted the bouquet a thorn pricked her thumb. "Damn!" she whispered, staring at the tiny dome of red that swelled up on her thumb. Gregory Raspin was beginning to get on her nerves.

XVII
Allegro Vivace

A freezing rain fell as Katherina reached the horse pond, where a delicate lace of ice edged the shallow water. Hans Stintzing and Sybil Ruiz were already waiting together under a large black umbrella, almost unrecognizable in heavy coats and with scarves wrapped around their lower faces. Katherina laughed through her own woolen layers. "You can sure tell the difference between singers and normal people, can't you?"

"Normal people don't have to worry about canceling engagements because of thousand-dollar colds," Sybil said.

"Exactly. So let's get out of this rain." Hans directed them across the Sigmundsplatz to the Goldener Hirsch.

Gregory Raspin was waiting at the door, in a green loden jacket and a felt hat, Austrian upper-class formal clothing that gave a nod to the traditional *Tracht*. "I've reserved a special table, ladies, over there." He pointed toward the corner where Joachim and Magda von Hausen already sat. Katherina noted bleakly that Anastasia was absent. Boris Reichmann was obviously still in Salzburg.

Katherina surveyed the room. In a décor that breathed class, the cream-colored walls held simple lamps alternating with oil paintings of bucolic and pastoral scenes, all so heavily blackened with age that she could scarcely make them out.

The new arrivals seated themselves, and Katherina found herself next to the host. She looked toward the door in a final frail hope as two women entered, but neither one was Anastasia.

"Will you have some champagne?" Gregory Raspin was holding a bottle of Veuve Clicquot suspended over her glass.

"Yes, of course," she answered, and waited as he filled all the rest of the glasses as well.

"Tonight is a celebration of all of you. I toast your talent and, with your permission, have ordered the house special of venison in wine. The chef has promised me absolute perfection."

With a general murmur of approval, everyone tapped glasses and Raspin continued. "Each one of you has, at one time or another, given me a wonderful operatic experience."

He turned toward Hans Stintzig. "For example, I saw your Wotan in *Die Walkuere* at the Metropolitan Opera. I'm sure you remember. It was the night the set caught fire."

"My Lord!" Sybil Ruiz pressed her fingertips to her cheek. "At the Met? How was that possible?"

Hans chuckled. "Wotan's staff held an exploding cap, so that when I struck the rock, it shot out real sparks. Then the special effects were supposed to make the mountain look like it was burning. At that performance, the sparks actually set fire to the plastic rock. Of course, the scenery at the Met is fire-proofed, so there was no big blaze, but this tiny flame kept melting the mountainside."

"But you never missed a note, did you?" Raspin said.

"I *had* to keep going. The conductor was in the pit and couldn't see the problem, so he kept conducting. Of course, the audience began to notice the flame, and I could feel the nervousness spreading throughout the house."

"And...what happened?" Katherina asked.

"Well, finally a stagehand crawled along behind the set with a fire extinguisher. You could hear the *Huussssshh*, and of course the audience could hear it too, right through the orchestra." He shrugged. "Sort of took the magic out of the moment."

Von Hausen gripped the bass fraternally on the shoulder. "Hans, the *Ring* is sixteen hours long. Five little minutes lost out of the middle is *nothing*."

Raspin turned toward Sybil. "You, on the other hand, Madame Ruiz, gave me a most memorable and inventive Tosca. I refer to the Hamburg performance, of course."

"Oh, dear." Sybil lowered her eyes. "I thought I had lived that one down."

"I definitely want to hear about *that*," Magda said as the waiter appeared with steaming plates of venison.

Sybil took another sip of champagne. "It was with Cornell Wilde, bless his heart. I had just finished *'Vissi d'arte.'* Cornell did all this stage business at the window and then he lumbered toward me for the would-be rape. I reached back to grab the fruit knife and…it wasn't there. A dozen panicky thoughts went through my head on how I could kill him. Whack him with the candelabra? Choke him with my bare hands? Then time ran out and I had to do *something.*"

She paused for effect. "So, I stabbed him with the banana."

Hans exploded with laughter, hitting the table with his fist.

"A banana?"

"Yes, it was that or the peach." She continued with a straight face. "It was wood so it held up when I poked him. But Cornell was so shocked, he missed his cue. Fortunately, he only had to fall down, while I, on the other hand," she laid her open hand on her chest, "had to continue singing while he writhed on the floor clutching his banana and giggling."

"A stunning performance." Gregory Raspin took Sybil's hand and kissed her lightly on the knuckles. "You must sing an opera especially for me one day."

Raspin looked toward Katherina. "And I have already informed Madame Marow that she swept me off my feet in Brahms' *Requiem.* Her solo transported me, beyond the concert hall, beyond polite society, I would even venture to say, beyond good and evil, like all great music."

"Beyond good and evil? Oh, dear. And in a sacred mass?" Katherina replied.

Raspin seemed amused. "Yes, the opera house is a veritable temple to the passions, a sordid place, after all. Quite the opposite of sacred."

"Beyond good and evil." Von Hausen chuckled, chewing on the last of his venison. "We Germans love our Nietzsche, don't we?"

Katherina raised her glass, changing the subject. "I propose we drink to our innocent little *Rosenkavalier* and leave it at that."

They toasted the opera, then the composer, then the Salzburg Winterfestival. Feeling the wine rise to her head, Katherina thought again of Anastasia. What was she doing while the others dined at Gregory Raspin's expense? Was she quarreling with her husband, or embracing him?

Then Hans Stintzing was standing up and helping Sybil on with her coat. The von Hausens too got up to leave, and Katherina wondered if she could also politely escape. Their host seemed to read her thoughts.

"Madame Marow, would you be so kind as to stay for another glass of wine. I have a business proposal for you."

"If you'd like." Katherina was nonplussed, but remembered who Gregory Raspin was and so waited through the awkwardness of multiple good-byes. In a few minutes, she was sitting alone next to him.

While waiters cleared the table and set out fresh wineglasses Gregory Raspin fumbled under the table—in his briefcase presumably— and a moment later he pulled out a thick manila envelope.

"You may have surmised by now that I have been monitoring, not to say guiding, your career," he began, and laid the envelope on the table.

Katherina frowned slightly, puzzled. "What do you mean?"

He spoke softly, like a father gently explaining the harsh realities of business. "I mean that it was I who got you the *Rosenkavalier*. The *Carmina Burana* too. Your success in the one led to the other."

"I don't know what to say."

"Say you are pleased." He slid the envelope closer. "So you can see, I have the highest regard for your talent and am devoted to advancing it. You will agree, I think, that you have done well by my assistance, not only financially, but also with regard to public exposure. In that light, I would like you to give serious thought to this proposal for your next engagement."

Katherina stared at the envelope without opening it. No law said that engagements could not be initially discussed directly with a singer rather than through an agent. Joachim von Hausen had in fact proposed the *Rosenkavalier* in this way. But something about Gregory Raspin himself bothered her. Maybe it was simply that he was not a musician, but a businessman. Maybe it was the roses.

"I am grateful for your efforts, Mr. Raspin. But generally engagements are negotiated through my agent who knows my schedule, repertoire, and fees."

He tapped the envelope. "I *know* your schedule, and I have already contacted your agent. This will be a world premiere of an innovative and at the same time ancient work, and in a format unlike you've ever worked in before. As such, it requires your understanding at the outset.

Do not worry about compensation. I assure you it will exceed your usual fee by a wide margin."

"A world premiere? Who is the composer? I haven't had any experience with experimental music, twelve-tone, and that sort of thing."

"Oh, you will find it is quite melodic. When you read the score you'll see how thrilling it is. Its initial staging will be on a mountaintop. Most striking, however, is the erasing of the separation between performers and audience."

Katherina's resistance weakened. "A 'sing-in,' you mean?"

"Something like that. The idea is to allow the audience to participate in the passion and the ritual of the music. A bit Dionysian, if you will."

"I don't know what 'Dionysian' means, but the idea does sound intriguing. You haven't told me the name of the composer."

"Friedrich Diener. I doubt that you will know him. The work is called *Walpurgisnacht.*"

"The Witches' Sabbath?"

"Yes. This is the libretto, soprano part, and contract." He tapped the envelope again. "I have already faxed a copy of the contract to your agent. You will note that it is to be performed on the Brocken Peak in the Harz mountains, the legendary site of the Witches' Sabbath. Although it is a high-security location, and generally closed to the public, I am in discussions with the East German government to televise a performance with an invited audience."

She took the envelope without opening it. "It sounds audacious."

"I know the offer seems precipitous, with the performance only five weeks away, but in fact we have been in preparation for weeks already and in negotiations for months. We simply needed to find the right soprano, and I am convinced you are it."

"I'll look at the opera, of course, as soon as I have opening night behind me. I'm sure you won't mind if I also discuss it with my agent. She has been looking after me for a long time now and I trust her judgment. Now, if you don't mind, it is quite late."

He leapt up and drew back her chair in cavalier fashion. "Of course. Take all the time you need." He helped her on with her cape and she thought he was planning to offer to accompany her back to the Pension Stein. Instead, as he buttoned his alpaca coat in the doorway of the restaurant, he looked at his watch. "I do apologize, Madame Marow, but I see we have chatted a bit long. I have a business call scheduled in just a few minutes. Please forgive me if I have to leave you here."

"That's quite all right, I don't mind at all," she replied, shaking his hand one last time. Watching him disappear down the cobblestone street that glistened slightly with frost, she felt inexplicably relieved.

❖

The Pension Stein was quiet as Katherina entered and crept up the stairs past Anastasia's door. For the briefest second she considered knocking, then thought better of it. Anastasia was probably at the Hilton with her husband or, worse, in her room sleeping with him. As long as Boris was in Salzburg, there would clearly be no more of their late-night talks.

Disgruntled, she unlocked her own door and kicked off her shoes. She stood in stocking feet, too tired to go out again, and to what? But she was also too restless to go to sleep under the pain-filled eyes of the wooden Jesus.

Vaguely disappointed that a pleasant evening had lost its cheer, she tossed her bag onto the bed. The bag landed on its side and its flap opened, spilling first her comb and wallet and then the envelope Raspin had given her. Recalling the same disgorging in the Peter's Church, the day before, she resolved to add a fastener to the flap. Idly, she sat down on the bed and gathered the items, and a wave of dread washed through her as she realized the whole bundle was too light. Something was missing.

With rising panic, she rummaged through the bag, then emptied all its contents onto the bed. The journal was not there. She glanced around the room. No, it was not there either. She had definitely taken it with her that evening to the restaurant. It had to have fallen out again.

Her mind raced to all the places where she had set down the bag that evening: the horse pond, the floor of the restaurant, the wall of the main bridge where she had stopped to watch the Salzach flow beneath her. She threw on her shoes and cloak and rushed out to retrace her steps.

❖

An hour later she came in again, sick with anger at herself. She had found nothing, and neither had the restaurant staff. How could she have been so careless as to carry around the precious family document with her every day? It was insane. She rubbed her knuckles across her lips. The book had to be some place in the city. She just had to make sure it was identified and not thrown away. She would go out early in the morning and notify the police to say a valuable document had been lost. Probably more importantly, she would contact the Salzburg sanitation facilities to make sure it was not swept up with the city's trash. Her costume fitting the next day was at nine o'clock, but before that, she would retrace her route meter by meter and stop at every shop nearby.

Fretting with alternating anger, determination, and guilt, she finally fell asleep only an hour before dawn.

XVIII
IMPETUOSO

I'm sorry to be so late, but I had an emergency," Katherina said, as she stepped up onto the dressmaker's stand.

"It's no problem, hun," the costume designer said cheerfully as she set to work, snipping through the thread that held the hem in place. "Is it solved, your emergency?"

"No, it's not. Something very valuable fell out of my bag yesterday. This morning I went back to every place I had been—for the second time—and then, when the shops opened, I stopped at each one just in case anyone had found something."

"I'm so sorry. Are you sure it wasn't stolen?"

"That would make no sense. My wallet wasn't touched. What I lost was my father's journal, and no one would be interested in a battered old book. No, I'm sure it fell out of my bag during the evening. I called the sanitation department to try to keep them from throwing it away with the city trash if they found it on the street. I'm still a wreck about it."

"It sounds like you did all the right things. Maybe someone found it and turned it in at their hotel. You should check with all the hotels in the area too."

"Yes, that's a good idea." Katherina felt a faint surge of hope and forced herself to concentrate on the work at hand. "Thanks also for making time to alter the costume. It was obviously made for a shorter, plumper soprano than I am."

"Don't worry about it, hun. It's easier making a wide, short costume smaller and longer than the other way around. And just between you and me, the dress looks loads better on you. But you didn't hear me say that." Anne's lighthearted analysis of every aspect of the Salzburg opera world was cheering, like her American-accented German.

"Thank you for the compliment. But the dress is beautiful. Did you design it?" Katherina held up a pinch of skirt, trying to feel interest.

"Yes, but dresses are not really my thing. I'm better at designing boys' clothing."

"Really? You did Octavian's costume, then? I mean the white one for the rose scene."

"I did them all. Octavian, the Baron, the palace guard, the whole shebang. 'Course I have people sewing for me, but I do the design. I did over thirty costumes in two weeks." Anne snipped the thread holding the hem in place and undid the fold at the bottom of the skirt. Then, getting to her feet, she inserted a row of pins down the two seams of the bodice, first on the left and then on the right.

"You must be glad that's over."

"It's never over, hun. I'm doing the Spanish soldiers in Hanover next month where Anastasia Ivanova is singing *Carmen*. One of my specialties is women's 'trouser' roles. I had a lot of fun doing her Octavian."

Katherina visualized the white satin breeches and waistcoat the young Count wore in the second act. On Anastasia, they were absolutely gorgeous. Even her full bosom was only hinted at under the glittering waistcoat. "Are men's costumes for women different from men's costumes for men?"

"Oh, absolutely. For starters, you have to compensate for all the round female parts. I once made a Cherubino outfit for a singer who was five months pregnant. Boobies out to here." She held a cupped hand a distance from her own chest. "But if I had my druthers, I'd do military. Soldiers, police, Cossacks. The Pentagon should hire me. I'd get those boys out of olive drab and into some really snappy outfits."

"Hello, ladies." A man stood in the doorway, mustached and avuncular. "This gonna take a while?"

"Hey, there's my favorite soldier." Anne twisted her head to glance back at him while she checked the lacing at the back of the costume. "Hi, hun. No, not much longer." She knelt down again and tugged on Katherina's skirt, pulling it to its new length. "What j'a think?"

"Dunno. It's not lit yet."

"Oh, sorry. Katherina, this is my husband, Chuck. He does the stage lighting."

"Yep. I'm the one who makes you look real purdy up on stage. No matter if you got a face to scare the horses. Once I got my lights on you, I can make you look like a million bucks."

"He's speaking in the abstract," Anne said reassuringly. "Chuck, hun. You make Katherina sound like an ogre."

"No, I understood him. He just means it's all in the presentation, and he's good at it. You both are. Reality doesn't stand a chance."

"Reality? What's that?" Waving her husband away from the room, Anne helped Katherina out of the costume. "We don't do reality here. We're in the business of illusion."

"That's what Detlev says. Though for him it's all in the coif." Katherina pulled on slacks and a shirt again and sat down to watch while Anne turned the costume right side out and hung it on a hanger.

"Detlev is a sweetheart, isn't he? And he's right. Good hair, spiffy clothes, great lighting, and you've got the world in your hand. Isn't it nice that he and Hans have hooked up? They make such a delightful, funny couple."

Katherina was taken aback by the American's lighthearted candor. "Detlev and Hans? I had no idea. But I'm not sure Detlev would like people talking so openly about his affairs. I mean, technically, it's still illegal in Austria, isn't it?"

"Hun, just don't you worry about Detlev. He's got past that fear thing a long time ago. It's no issue in the theater world anyhow, and Lord knows, if it was, you'd have to just about shut this place down. Fact is, we owe it to him *not* to whisper about him, thinking we protect him. We should celebrate out loud with him, just like we celebrate with other folks when they get engaged or have kids. Don't you think?"

Katherina hesitated. "It just seems like something intimate that people don't talk about. Shouldn't we respect his privacy?"

"Privacy? How's that? Is it private when I introduce my husband to you? Or when a woman announces she's going to have a baby? Why should it be private if someone like Detlev has a boyfriend? The subject isn't sex. The subject is husband, partner, baby. Oh, I'm sorry, hun. There I go lecturing again." She took a few stitches to repair the lace on the front of the dress and bit through the thread.

"You're right, of course. He shouldn't have anything to be secretive about. I just never thought about it that way."

"Well, I'm not going to tell you how to think. But if everyone gay was open about it, we might find we have gay brothers, plumbers, preachers, firemen, fathers, and opera singers. Then there'd be one less stupid thing for people to be afraid of." Anne hung up the costume and brushed it smooth.

Katherina collected her shoulder bag, recalling again what she was upset about. "I guess I'd better—"

"'Scuse me." Chuck stood in the doorway again. "Don't mean to be bothering you again."

"No bother, hun. What's up?"

"The boys and me, we was throwing out some old light bulbs and cables and stuff, and we come across this." He held up the battered journal.

Katherina gasped. "That's the journal I've been looking for. I dropped it someplace yesterday and I was afraid I'd lost it forever." She took it and brushed grit and sawdust from the cover. "Where did you find it?"

"In the trash bin out behind the theater. It didn't have no name in it, but there was a bookmark." He pointed to the folded schedule tucked between two pages. "Seein' as how it was your personal rehearsal schedule, I figured it might belong to you. On the other hand, it's all tore up, so maybe it was yours and you threw it away. I thought I'd ask."

"Oh, Chuck. Thank you. You've saved me so much anguish. But you're right. Someone has torn a whole section out of it." Bewildered, Katherina examined the dates before and after the gap. "They've ripped out everything from the 1950s."

Anne peered over her shoulder. "Well, it *was* a pretty boring decade, but ripping apart a journal for it seems a little extreme."

"Looks to me like whoever found it decided the only part they *liked* was the '50s and they tossed the rest."

"What happened in the '50s? In the journal, I mean." Anne asked.

"I don't know. I hadn't read that part."

"Well, I guess something's better than nothing," Chuck concluded. "Anyhow, I got to finish cleaning up. I'll swing by again in half an hour when you close up for the day," he said to his wife.

"Thanks, again, Chuck," Katherina called after the departing man. Bemused, she stared again at the eviscerated journal, wondering if she now faced the biggest mystery of all. What had happened in the 1950s?

❖

Back in her hotel room, Katherina set aside the music she planned to study in order to examine the remains of the journal. The entries at the beginning of the 1960s might give a hint of what had happened earlier. She lit the gas fire in the corner and sat down, letting the book open to the first remaining entry after the torn pages, at the end of 1962.

She did not recall much of the year herself. Motherless and struggling to recover from diphtheria, she had focused only on herself and had emerged a changed person. It occurred to her only now that her father might have also changed. In fact, the new entries seemed to come from a different man.

October 7, 1962

How is it possible to know a man for over fifteen years, to have accepted favors from him, done business with him, sat with him over beer, and not know that he was a monster.

Worse, I was part of his filthy network. But no more. I'm free of him and all the rest of it in Auerbach's Cellar. I'd go to the police but I know they'd send me to jail along with the others. Schalk knows it too; he knows he's safe from me. A stalemate then, that neither of us will report the other. But over the course of ten years, I've noted the names of his clients and their locations. Some day, maybe…

I wish I'd broken ties with him earlier. But I thought I needed him. Until I met Nikki, all on my own.

It was in a shabby little bar called the Insel that I'd heard about in Schöneberg. I wandered in, not expecting anything. Just a place to sit and listen to the sort of slow jazz they played on records A few men and women were dancing slowly, though I was sure the women were all prostitutes.

Then, from nowhere, an angelic creature glided in and sat down. Long wavy black hair, beautiful soft eyes with bottomless black pupils. Graceful gestures and full sensuous lips that sent heat to my groin. A Moroccan probably, I didn't ask. A single earring caught the light and sparkled at me. I bought the obligatory drink and we spoke a little—"What's your name?" and "You from around here?" A meaningless exchange to give the illusion we were getting to know each other. I did not give my own name, and I am sure that doe-eyed "Nikki" was lying too, but it didn't matter.

"They have back rooms," Nikki said. "If you want to go where it's quiet. You just have to order a drink, then pay for it with a fifty-mark bill and say, 'No change, thank you.' They'll give you a key."

The "quiet back room" was a filthy little closet with a bed that I'm sure we were not the first to use. But Nikki's skin was so fragrant and so soft, the body so graceful and supple and acquiescent that I was ready in one minute. I tried not to go too fast. I tried to be tender. But I had waited so long, I was like a teenage boy, bursting. In just a few moments it was done and I lay exhausted. Nikki made some excuse and left. I knew that I had paid for the semblance of love, but it didn't matter. I knew where to go for it now, I knew how to set it up, I knew how much it cost.

Sweet, soft, pliant Nikki. I wonder if I'll meet him again next week.

That was it then. The single word "him" was the piece of the puzzle she had missed. Her father was homosexual.

One more shock to add while she still reeled from all the others: that he had invaded Berlin with the Red Army and had fought with them at Stalingrad. He was, as Anne said, one of the brothers, plumbers, preachers, firemen, fathers who were forced to love in secret. He was, by the law of the time, a criminal. She didn't condemn him, but it sickened her to know about the other life, the underworld he lived in.

Even in the current day, he would be relegated to a special category of socially marginal people.

What perverse vein ran through the mind of a public that condemned *him*, but was delighted to see a transvestite soprano sing love songs to a woman? People paid large sums of money for the pretty titillation of a stage embrace. Was it morbid curiosity? A small safe step toward Gomorrah they could shrug off?

She wondered where she stood on the spectrum of hypocrisy. When she sang with Octavian in her arms, did she too simply thrill at the small taste of Gomorrah while remaining blameless? Or was there something more?

XIX
Trio—Amoroso

Katherina sat nervously at her dressing room table waiting for the cue for her final entry on stage. Opening night was going splendidly. The Great Festspielhaus was full. Every aspect, musical and dramatic, flowed along perfectly; and Anastasia's Octavian swept through each scene like a randy angel.

A loudspeaker broadcast the opera into her dressing room and she could hear that Act III had just begun. Octavian and the Baron were just sitting down at the table in the long tavern scene, and poor Anastasia was playing in double disguise, a woman dressed as a man dressed as a woman. How she managed the complex comedy of a twice-faked voice was astonishing. Hans too proved masterfully comic as his Baron was gradually made a fool of. There had been no snags or soft spots, and all boded well for the great final trio, the tour de force that was the musical heart and climax of the opera. Half the people in the audience, she knew, attended only to hear that trio, and every opera critic in Austria would certainly scrutinize it.

She checked her costume in the mirror, the one that Anne had adapted. It fit comfortably around the chest but still allowed for the deep inhalations. Detlev's wig was also perfect, the loose curl at her ear giving her a faint disheveled look that suited Sophie's distress.

The clock on the makeup table told her she had ten minutes to go. Next to the clock were the contract and the open libretto to *Walpurgisnacht*. To pass the time, she glanced through them both.

The libretto, if one could call it that, was clever: a parade of seductions by the seven deadly sins, not onstage, but of the public itself. The medieval setting reminded her of *Carmina Burana*. The music itself was built more on rhythm than on melody and seemed derivative, a sort of combination of Stravinsky and Orff. But the melodies were flashy and held no excessively high notes.

It was, like *Salome*, a single-act opera. The soprano was on stage almost throughout and, aside from the recitatives of the drama, had several duets and a final aria. It was musically undemanding and all well within her range. There was no indication of staging, though, which worried her. For new works especially, so much depended on the visual presentation.

A brief but firm knock at the door was followed by, "Miss Marow, five minutes until call."

"Thank you," she called back, and opened the contract again. It was boilerplate standard, listing dates, location, rehearsal obligations, and fee. A very generous fee. The only disquieting thing was that the producer, the entity to which she would be contracted, was Gregory Raspin himself.

Katherina's agent had assured her that morning that Raspin was a real presence on the musical scene. The engagement—a world premiere, Charlotte reminded her—would be good for her. It would generate a lot of publicity, even if the composer was anonymous, perhaps *because* he was anonymous. The very oddities of the engagement made it attractive, Charlotte said. Still, something about it made her uncomfortable.

Another brief knock. "Miss Marow. Two minutes until call."

She brushed aside the contract and stood up. Humming a scale, she felt her wig to make sure it sat firmly. Pacing herself to stay calm, she wound her way quietly along the corridors to the stage rear. Then she took her place in the wings, waiting for her cue to enter the scene.

"Mein Gott, Es war nur eine Farce." She sang her entry lines from the far right side of the darkened tavern, then slowly crept in, beginning the deliciously provocative back and forth of the three lovesick women. The opulent staging, together with the long tradition of travesty comedy, obscured the raw fact that emotionally and erotically excited women were negotiating sexual ownership, and not a man in sight. But the audience sensed the titillation, not the least because Strauss had charged every musical moment. Who had claim to the beautiful, sexually ambiguous, and permanently tumescent Octavian? The Marschallin, in full imperial splendor, a regal dominatrix in crinolines and pearls, who had held the cavalier between her legs two hours earlier? Or the appetizing Sophie in the bloom of youth, who offered her first passion and maidenhead? The whole stage was electric with sex.

Yet the competing lovers did not fight, but were generous in their love, each one recognizing the worth of the other. The Marschallin told Octavian, "Go, make love to her." Sophie sent him back, sighing, "Her Highness calls. Go to her." Octavian, befuddled, pledged obedience to the one, passion to the other. Then the two rivals faced one another. Sophie curtsied, pliant to the powerful Marschallin, who bore no rancor, only tenderness. "Your cheek so pale…you're pretty enough." And Sophie, sweetly responsive, "Your highness is graciousness itself…"

As the tender scene unfolded, the three of them moved gradually into place for the climactic trio, Sophie at stage right, Octavian in the center, the Marschallin stage left, a step above the others.

The transition chord, the diminished B, floated up from the strings, drawing away from the E major and coming to rest in E-flat major. For three full seconds, the house was completely still; every person in the theater had waited for this moment and the audience seemed to hold its collective breath.

Then the Marschallin began, seraphic, in E flat, with her warm golden thread: *"Hab mir's gelobt…"* Ten measures later Octavian entered, *"Es ist was 'kommen,"* and a moment after, Sophie added the brightest thread, *"Mir ist wie in der Kirche…"* Unrelated soliloquies that streamed around each other so that the melodies hooked and snagged as they passed. The lines wove in and out in a spiral of musical phrases, polyphony as ingenious as a Gregorian chant, and yet profane, perverse. Three women sang of love, fidelity, reverence, mixing silver and gold, meandering in and out of keys. Pieces of melody tantalized like kisses and forbidden touches as the vocal lines merged and separated and then joined again until the tension was unbearable.

Then the orchestra modulated upward from D flat to E major, bright, thrilling. The Marschallin held herself vocally aloof, sustaining her long high C while the two young lovers carried the exchange, shimmering vocally against each other.

Octavian had crossed the stage now to stand next to Sophie, and their three voices flowed upward like a column of water catching sunlight. Katherina swam together with conductor, orchestra, Octavian, Marschallin, all moving perfectly in the ecstatic culmination of the ensemble.

The three women faced outward toward the audience throughout the trio, keeping tempo with the orchestra, but on the final three measures, as the dazzling fountain of sound fell and the voices united in a harmonic chord, Octavian moved. The Marschallin sang her final word of renunciation, "understanding," gazing upward, while the two young lovers joined together on the word "love."

Then, unrehearsed, Anastasia turned and gazed at Katherina. Held captive by mist-gray eyes, Katherina held her note, ending with the others, but electricity went through her and warmth spread outward like a fluid from the center of her body.

After the final stage business, when all but the two young lovers had exited the scene, she sang the final duet as if in a dream.

A simple melody in thirds told of the simplicity of their love. Katherina's final pianissimo note was close to the top of her range, but she sustained it effortlessly for eight beats, drawing out the last glimmering filament of sound. Then, silence, and Anastasia kissed her delicately on the side of the mouth. The kiss had been carefully rehearsed, but it seemed personal this time. For two beats, Katherina heard or felt Anastasia's breath on her cheek, and then it was over. The rose cavalier offered her arm and they exited together through the door at stage center.

The applause began the moment the orchestra stopped and increased in volume as the large spotlight illuminated the curtain. Two stagehands took position and, at a nod from the stage director, drew the curtain back to form a corridor for the singers to take their curtain calls.

The secondary singers went out, first as a group and then each alone, from the smallest role to the largest. Then the three women, Marschallin, Octavian, Sophie, swept out onto the stage together. The audience roared. The two in dresses curtsied deeply, and Anastasia, in breeches and riding boots, bowed from the waist.

Breathless, moving in front of the curtain and into the waves of ovation and then back again, Katherina was close to tears. It was not the joy and relief she usually felt after a performance. Something extraordinary had happened, something attached to the music but outside of it as well. Though drenched in perspiration, she swam in a golden euphoria. It was an afterglow she recognized, but not from the stage.

XX
CADENZA

The house lights came up. While the audience streamed out of the Festspielhaus into the plaza, the orchestra members packed up their instruments and sheet music, stagehands broke down the set, and singers removed costumes, wigs, makeup. Faithful admirers, dignitaries, colleagues, and patrons hurried backstage for the congratulatory visits, kisses, compliments.

Gregory Raspin was at the end of Katherina's line. "You have surpassed yourself, Madame Marow. What I saw tonight was amazing and I am sure the reviews will reflect that. I will only say 'brava' and leave you to your evening." Then he stepped away to join the stage manager in some banter or other. He had not even brought up the contract.

Finally free of obligation, Katherina knocked on Anastasia's dressing-room door. No one answered. Then she felt a hand on her shoulder. "Good work tonight. Best Sophie I've heard in years." Joachim von Hausen placed a paternal kiss somewhere near her right ear and moved on to Hans Stintzing's dressing room.

She called after him. "Have you seen Anastasia?"

"Yes, she left right after the curtain. Exhausted, I'm sure. She's in every scene, after all," he said over his shoulder.

Detlev passed him, looking like a ventriloquist, with wigs on both hands. A Marschallin puppet on his left, an Octavian puppet on his right.

"Bravissima, bella!" he sang, and pecked at her cheek, birdlike. "You remember our Queen of the Night discussion? When we agreed that you should go home with the one with the sparkliest costume?"

"Yes, of course."

He shot a conspiratorial glance toward Anastasia's door. "Well, if you ask me, I think *that* one sparkled like a demon." Then, with swaying hips, he elbowed past her into the empty dressing room to collect the last wig.

❖

Still excited, Katherina mounted the slippery Steingasse steps, stopping midway to gaze back down at the cobblestone street. The wind had dropped and clouds obscured the night sky. There was no traffic at the late hour and the silent air seemed expectant. She let herself into the warm hotel, greeted the night porter at the front desk, and climbed up the last staircase to her room. *Sparkliest costume.* Detlev's words buzzed through her mind and, quickly, before she lost her nerve, she knocked on Anastasia's door.

The door opened to Anastasia in blue jeans and plaid flannel shirt. She seemed surprised but not displeased as she stepped back to let Katherina enter. She held a glass of port wine in one hand.

"I hope I'm not intruding. Were you getting ready for bed?" Katherina pointed to the plaid flannel shirt. "Or to cut lumber?"

Anastasia smiled softly. "Come have a glass of wine. I was just unwinding. It was a good performance, don't you think?"

Katherina stood awkwardly in the center of the room, noting that the blanket on the bed had been drawn back. It was clear she couldn't stay long, yet Anastasia was already pulling out a chair for her. Katherina loosened her cape, but did not remove it, and sat down.

"I'm sorry. It looks like you were about to go to bed. I won't stay long."

"Oh, no. Please stay. I've been wanting to talk to you, too. But I've been busy with…well, things." Anastasia held up the port wine bottle and an empty glass, a questioning expression on her face.

"Oh, no thank you. Not tonight. I'd fall asleep on your floor, and that would be embarrassing."

"I'm sorry we couldn't spend more time together. There were so many things we just got started on. Are you still working your way through your father's journal?" They sat down, knees to knees on the hotel chairs.

"Yes, and every page is a new shock. I don't think people should know their parents' secrets. I don't *want* to know them."

"Yes, but it's not just secrets. You're reading a historical document. You can stay detached about the errors of a young man, can't you? It was a different time."

"Detached? I don't know. The journal tells of more than just a few indiscretions. It reveals a whole other life. My father's family emigrated to Germany from Russia when he was a child, and he became a German citizen, yet somehow he ended up being a medic in the Red Army. He constantly writes about being guilty of something. I have no idea of what. I'm afraid I'll find out he was a war criminal of some sort."

"Even if you do, you shouldn't be quick to judge him. He lived through horrors you'll never experience, so whatever he was, whatever demons he had, none of it affects who *you* are."

"That's just it. His demons *do* affect me. We shared a vague guilt after my mother died, and it was a darkness in the air through all my adolescence. But now I find out something was haunting him even earlier, something apparently worse. I feel connected with him in this dreadful way and won't be free until I find out what it was."

"And you think the journal will have the answer to that."

"Yes, I'm sure it does, but part of it, unfortunately, is in Russian. I think it's about something that happened at Stalingrad. I speak a little Russian and can make out the printed letters, but not Cyrillic handwriting."

"I can take a look, if you like."

"Would you? It's only half a dozen pages. I'd be grateful if you could read them. I'll have a copy made for you."

"It will have to be after *Rosenkavalier*, I'm afraid. I can work on it while I'm in Hanover and mail you the translation. Will that be all right? And don't worry. I promise you complete discretion. You can trust me, I hope you believe that."

"I do. I feel like I've known you a long time, that we understand each other. It's too bad, you know. We both come and go this way from one engagement to the next. Opera gypsies. Keeping a friendship warm is a little like keeping a marriage warm, isn't it?"

Anastasia's eyes twinkled. "Without the sex."

Katherina thought of Hans and Detlev. "Or, sometimes with."

Anastasia looked puzzled and Katherina realized she hadn't spoken the Detlev-Hans part out loud. "I mean that some of the team have paired up. Haven't you noticed? Hans, for example."

"With Detlev? Yes. Who would have thought? And they're obviously having a lot of fun. I envy them, don't you? Their courage to live and love as they want to. The rest of us just put up with the loneliness."

"Were you lonely? You should have... Stasya, look!" Katherina interrupted herself abruptly and took Anastasia by the hand, pulling her up from her chair. "It's what you've waited for." Katherina slid open the balcony door. Dazed, Anastasia allowed herself to be pulled gently out onto the balcony.

The bridge, the shop rooftops, the churches, the Festspielhaus were sprinkled with white powder, and the air all around them roiled with snow.

"It's beautiful, but I'm sorry, it's cold out here." Anastasia hugged herself.

"Stay, please. I'll keep you warm." Katherina moved around behind her onto the higher step. She opened the heavy gray cape she wore and enfolded the other woman in front of her so that both of them stood within it. "Is that better?"

"Uh-huh," Anastasia answered uncertainly. Then a breeze caught the tiny flakes, causing them to swirl in a wide funnel out over the river. "Ohh, you're right. It's like a fairy tale."

"And you don't have to be in Russia for it."

The snow began to fall more thickly, spinning as it caught currents of air high on the hill. It glittered in a cascade of individual flakes directly in front of them, fell in sheets of gray-white specks out over the Salzach, and on the opposite bank, covered the old city and fortress in a soft gray mist.

They stood in the supernatural calm, cocooned within the cape, hearing nothing but their own breathing and the hiss of the falling snow. Warmth rose from the space between them and wafted in soft waves around Katherina's throat. It smelled pleasantly of the faint residue of perfume and of Anastasia's hair. Resting her head against the fragrant hair, Katherina whispered, *"Like a sign from heaven, too much, almost, to be endured,"* from the duet they had sung only an hour before.

Anastasia relaxed against Katherina's embrace and murmured the next line from the song. *"Where was I ever so happy?"*

"How did she come to me and I to her?"

"I feel it, this world and the next, in this sweet moment."

"Until death," they whispered in unison, as they had sung it, but without orchestra and stage, the declaration became their own. They stood in silence for an agony of time, as if before a threshold where both were fearful. Then Katherina whispered, "Anastasia."

Anastasia turned around inside the sheltering cape and inside Katherina's arms. With eyes closed, she rested her cheek softly against Katherina's and slid her hands around Katherina's waist to her back. They stood in the gentlest of embraces without speaking, and with each breath Katherina could feel the rise and fall of Anastasia's breasts.

Gathering courage, Katherina pulled the other woman closer and turned her own head just slightly. The corner of her mouth touched lightly against Anastasia, who did not pull away. She moved again, brushing her mouth across Anastasia's and pressing, tentatively, on dry, uncertain lips.

The hissing curtain of snow around the balcony seemed to sequester them from the world, shielding them from judgment. Katherina withdrew the tiniest fraction, then covered the yielding mouth again, with slightly greater urgency. Anastasia's lips were passive, waiting, but not resisting. No, not resisting at all. The coldness of their faces made the warmth of their mouths deeply comforting, like the fire they had just crouched over, sharing secrets. Katherina sensed a faint pressure of welcome, of timid invitation, and she lingered delicately at the edge of entry. Anastasia's hands were at the small of her back, each fingertip seeming to draw her in. The warmth of her exhalation streamed across Katherina's cheek, a whisper of acquiescence that came with the falling, then the rising of her chest.

Katherina became conscious of the entire length of Anastasia's body pressed against her own, and the heat of arousal began like a small flame between her legs. She ventured farther in over gentle teeth, exploring. Still Anastasia stayed within her arms, breathing heavily, holding the pressure of Katherina's leg between her thighs, her mouth pliant. For a long moment they stood in each other's heat, the one imploring, the other considering, as if some great thing hung in the balance. Anastasia did not kiss back so much as she seemed to surrender, and Katherina was ablaze.

Then Anastasia broke the kiss and laid her cheek against Katherina's again. "I don't know," she murmured. "Forgive me."

"Of course you know. You knew on stage tonight. In the trio."

"Yes, at that moment." Confusion showed on her face. "But this is—"

The phone rang.

It was as if an axe fell between them, severing the fragile tendrils that held them.

"I'm sorry," Anastasia breathed. "No one would call this late unless it was important." Inside the room she caught the phone on the fourth ring. Slightly bewildered, Katherina pulled her cloak around herself and followed her.

The call was short and Anastasia set the phone down finally. "My agent, calling from New York. She's gotten me an offer from the Met and couldn't wait to tell me."

"New York. That's wonderful." Katherina wanted desperately to step back into the embrace, but the moment was gone. She took a step forward, longing for touch, for anything, but Anastasia took a step back. Katherina searched for something tender to say, to at least return to that mood.

Someone knocked. A male voice sounded dully through the door. Anastasia's look of panic told all.

Defeated, Katherina drew her cloak around her. "I guess I should go now," she said, and opened the door.

Boris Reichmann stood massive in front of her, filling up the door frame, arriving to claim his wife. A man in his late fifties, he had a full head of graying hair and a well-trimmed black beard. His small eyes over ruddy cheeks registered surprise and slight annoyance, and Katherina remembered the late hour. She felt suddenly criminal.

"Sorry, I'm just leaving," she apologized awkwardly, and stepped past him into the corridor. Behind her, she heard the door close. She could not remember ever hating anyone as much as she hated Boris Reichmann at that moment.

XXI
DECRESCENDO

It was well past midnight but Katherina lay awake, staring into the darkness. She replayed every moment of the embrace through her mind, ending always with Anastasia's words, "Forgive me." Katherina kept seeing the fear on her face. Or was it regret?

She had taken a huge risk kissing her, and it had proved a mistake. The embarrassment, then the humiliation, of surrendering Anastasia to her husband had drained away the pleasure of the evening's stage success.

Finally she dozed, her father's voice sounding at the back of her troubled mind. "Nothing is given. Everything is paid for."

She slept fitfully, fragments of nightmares keeping her from rest. A line of phantoms formed before her dreaming eyes. Her mother, then her father, then Detlev; all wandered off one by one into the fog, abandoning her. She shivered, until, at the sound of her name, she pivoted and saw another figure on the opposite horizon. Gregory Raspin.

She awoke with a start. As if fleeing the dismal landscape of her unconscious, she got up. To clear her head, she opened one panel of the window. Snow still fell silently on the empty pre-dawn street below. The cold air roused her, and she closed the window again, fully awake. There was no way she could return to sleep now. She might as well continue reading the journal.

She was nearly at the end, and the later entries were more widely spaced. But now that she had begun to digest the fact of her father's "disposition," as she decided to call it, she wanted to know more about it. What was life like for a homosexual in 1960s Germany? What did her father think about it all? Katerina thumbed through the journal with curiosity that she realized bordered on the prurient.

But the remainder of the journal was devoid of introspection and was simply a series of accounts of meetings with men at the Insel: Germans, Italians, Turks. He went there more or less twice a month and almost every time he was with a different man. Finally, he no longer noted their names or appearances, and his accounts of the meetings with them became dreary. It seemed that he had begun to find them dreary too. No longer shocked, Katherina read quickly, superficially. Then, the final brief entry that ended the journal brought her up short.

August 25, 1965
I am where fate and my own nature have brought me. It's senseless to speak at this late date of regret. I had the gift of Lucy and then Katya. I only hope I haven't failed them. Still, a question always burns at the back of my mind. What might life have been like if we could have stayed together, my precious Florian?

❖

There were four more performances of *Rosenkavalier* in Salzburg and, emotionally, Katherina was in free fall.

Boris had stayed in Salzburg, and though he still resided at the Hilton Hotel, he was suddenly the doting husband. On non-performance days, the couple was usually absent from the hotel, and after performances, Boris picked Anastasia up from her dressing room, rendering her unavailable to anyone else.

Octavian remained, however, and so Katherina embraced the woman she desired four more times, though only in the form of a boy in silver-white coat and breeches, or in hunting green. Octavian was always ardent in her arms, and for two and a half hours of the performance, they acted out love.

Katherina discovered what she had missed in her thirty-three years of life: not sexual excitement or even tenderness, but romantic obsession. Now she suffered under it, in full force. She woke every morning wondering where Anastasia was sleeping, ate breakfast imagining Anastasia across the table, walked along the Salzach with Anastasia's phantom at her side.

Her heart quickened when they were on stage together, when the rose duet finished and the scene of their gradual infatuation began. It was mind twisting, to sing a role that replicated her own experience. The audience was titillated to see her feigning romance with a woman dressed as a boy, when in fact, it was the very falseness that she feigned. For she loved and lusted after Anastasia.

She grasped that now and felt desire with a ferocity she had never imagined. Each day in feverish fantasy she let herself seize Anastasia, undress her, ravish her, take every part of her in her mouth, set her groaning, thrashing with want—and each evening she sang with Viennese sweetness of attar of roses in the lightest of embraces with Octavian.

And since she could not give herself to Anastasia, she gave herself to the role, to the thrilling, shimmering, immoral ecstasy of the music.

Was it her overheated imagination, or did Octavian sing with more ardor than before, glance at her a moment longer, court her more urgently than in the first performance? It was demonic, trying to separate theater from reality.

Then, in the last moments of the last act in the final performance, when both of them were physically and vocally spent, something happened. The orchestra played the final musical fillip of the opera while Sophie and Octavian exited arm in arm through the center stage. In the forty seconds, in which a "Moorish child" ran on stage looking for a handkerchief, they stood in the darkness at the edge of the stage set.

Always before they had simply caught their breath after the exhausting final duet and then stepped out toward the waiting stagehands. But this time Anastasia pressed suddenly against her and whispered into her ear, "Oh Katherina, I am so sorry about everything. If only you knew how much I've wanted it to be more."

A stagehand stepped toward them and reached out a hand. Anastasia was startled, then smiled at him and hurried away to join the other singers for the curtain call. Katherina followed, bewildered.

Surely there would be a moment later, when they could talk. Backstage, at the hotel, anywhere. Only a moment.

As always, Boris waited in the dressing-room corridor. He glanced at Katherina from under his thick eyebrows and nodded once, acknowledging her. She tried to read his expression, but there seemed to be none. Did he resent her as much as she resented him? No, of course not. She was nothing to him. He had no idea.

Boris's glance shifted away from her to linger for a moment on Gregory Raspin, who stood talking to Joachim von Hausen. His attention seemed riveted on the two men. Was he planning a new recording with the conductor? Presumably that's how things went. You saw someone backstage, exchanged a few words, and things developed. But Boris made no attempt to talk to von Hausen, who turned and strode toward Katherina, hands outstretched.

"Ah, Katherina, my lovely Sophie." He kissed her lightly on both cheeks. "We were fantastic tonight, weren't we? And you, my dear, were glorious." He stood back, holding her by her upper arms. "You *are* coming to my ice-skating party tomorrow, aren't you?"

"Well, I'm—"

"*Of course*, you're coming. The whole cast is invited. I shall be deeply, *deeply* wounded if you don't."

"But I don't have any ice skates." She stated the obvious.

"Of course you don't, my dear. No one does. We'll take care of that, so there's no excuse."

"The whole cast will be there?" Katherina asked. "Hans, Sibyl, Radu…Anastasia?"

Gregory Raspin had joined them. "Yes, Madame Marow. Everyone but me. I have business to attend to, so you must celebrate for both of us."

A line of opera fans was beginning to approach and Katherina let herself be drawn toward them, relief spreading through her.

She smiled radiantly. "Yes. I'd love to," she said, suddenly buoyant.

XXII
QUARTETTO GIOCOSO

Katherina made her way gingerly along the slippery path that led down to the water and stopped at the edge. While light snow fell, she surveyed the pond. It was some two hundred meters in diameter, with a field of dead cattails poking up through the ice on the far side. On the near side, men were chipping with shovels at the irregular surface of the pond trying to smooth it. Behind them, where someone swept away the chips, a half dozen Salzburgers skated.

She followed the pleasant smell of wood smoke and frying sausage to a campfire on the slope. A handful of people sat on low benches in a circle around a rectangular fire pit. On one side of the fire, a grill held roasting sausages and onions. On the other side, a small cauldron hung from an iron tripod. In a handsome parka with a fur-lined hood, Magda von Hausen was just stirring it with a ladle.

"Ah, just in time for some *Glühwein*," she said, ladling the steaming liquid into a cup and handing it to Katherina. "We have plenty of schnapps too, if you'd like something stronger to heat your blood."

Katherina warmed her mittened hands on the cup before sipping the hot mulled wine. With no singing engagements for the next weeks, she could let herself enjoy the two excesses: going out in frigid weather and drinking scalding wine. In fact, the wine was delicious, and it went immediately to her head. "Well, you couldn't have picked a better day, could you? Just a little snow falling and no more performances to worry about. The only way you could have lured us out of our nests."

Magda ladled a second cup for herself. "That was the whole plan. We've done this every winter we could, though it's not always cold enough. Of course, it's especially fun when there's snow."

"I had no idea so many people still skated on ponds," Katherina said, gesturing toward the skaters. Anastasia, she noted, was not there, but she recognized several of the others. Sibyl and her husband skated awkwardly together, and just on the other side of them were Anne and Chuck. They skated arm in arm, tilting toward the left, then toward the right, obviously hugely entertained.

"It's like a Flemish painting," Katherina added.

"Opera people venture out here only if someone gives them the skates. So we bought a dozen of them a few years ago, the kind that you can adjust to any shoe. It's 'ice-skating lite.' You make a couple of rounds of the pond, and when your ankles begin to hurt, you come back for more Glühwein."

"And there's no danger of falling through the ice?"

"Heavens, no. The pond is frozen solid, and the water is only a meter deep anyhow."

"We haven't lost anyone yet." Joachim von Hausen was just crunching through the snow with an armload of firewood.

Radu Gavril arrived right behind with a crate of wine bottles. "Not to the ice, anyhow." He set the crate down in the snow.

"We lose a few to the Glühwein every year, but it's painless." Magda chuckled, emptying another bottle into the cauldron.

The men fed new logs into the fire, then accepted their portions of hot wine and sat down on one of the benches. A comfortable silence fell over the group as they sipped from steaming cups.

Katherina heard boots crunching on packed snow and allowed herself a glance toward the path. Finally. In a blue anorak and ski pants, Anastasia strode toward the group. A Russian Octavian, except for the blond hair that fell from under a fur cap. Boris appeared directly behind her, dispelling the fantasy.

Von Hausen stood up and held out his hands. "So glad you could come, both of you. We haven't seen much of you otherwise." He shook hands vigorously with Boris who, in sheepskin coat and hat, seemed more massive than ever.

The two new arrivals took their places around the fire. Boris picked up one of the double-bladed skates and turned it, running his gloved thumb along the edge. "Children's skates?" he asked in a deep bass.

"Yes, of course. We're all amateurs here." Von Hausen handed him the other skate. "You'll both take a turn on the ice, won't you?"

"I don't think so." Boris dropped both skates back onto the ground. "No high-risk sports for me."

"What about you, Anastasia? Give it a try. It'll remind you of your childhood."

Katherina wanted to add to the encouragement, but Anastasia seemed to be avoiding eye contact. It was awkward, even painful to sense that the woman she had been embracing for the last two weeks on stage would not even acknowledge her. She turned the wine cup in her hands, her heart sinking.

"Oh, that was *so* much fun!" Anne and Chuck lurched gleefully in from the pond and dropped onto a bench. "I'm going to get complaints from a whole new set of muscles tomorrow, but it was worth it," Anne said. Red-cheeked and merry, she pried off her skates and continued. "Snow is just magical, isn't it? Is there anyone in the world who doesn't love snow?"

"I don't. I hate it," someone said, and Katherina looked around. "Sorry," Radu amended. "I didn't mean to bring down the mood."

"What could you possibly hate about that?" Chuck thrust his thumb toward the idyllic scene on the pond.

"Not ice skaters, of course." In the all-white landscape, Radu's eyes seemed even redder than usual. "Just snow. Put it down to an old man with bad war memories."

There was an awkward moment. Then von Hausen said, "We all have war memories. You have to let go of them."

"I agree," Chuck added. "I don't have 'em, but my father fought on Omaha Beach. One of the lucky ones that made it back. But that's old news, from forty years ago."

"You were on the Eastern Front?" Katherina asked Radu, her curiosity piqued.

He nodded. "In the winter of '43, I was an eighteen-year-old in the Romanian army—20th Infantry Division—fighting the Russians just west of the Volga. They were the most terrible months of my life. It wasn't just the fighting. I'm talking about the snow."

Sitting across from him, Boris nodded faintly but said nothing. Katherina wondered where *he* had been that winter.

"It was deep and hard to wade through, and when you sweated, the sweat froze inside your uniform. There were nights when it was minus twenty-five degrees. In the forests the bark of trees burst. You could hear it sometimes—a sharp crack. In our engines, the oil became a glue that brought everything to a stop. Wounded soldiers froze to death a few minutes after they fell. Even when we escaped the guns, every day was a fight to survive. We had to hack through our food with saws. And the snow never stopped."

He stared into the fire, clutching his warm wine cup. "One evening, my rubber boot soles snapped. I knew my feet would freeze that night and if they did, I'd die. So I went back to where I had seen a dead Russian and took his footgear. Valenki, they're called. Big thick felt things they wore. They saved my life."

Katherina listened to the old soldier and wondered where her father had been on the day that the young Romanian had pilfered a dead man's boots. Was he crouched behind a wall in Stalingrad shooting at Germans? Random chance, that Radu Gavril found life-saving footgear while Sergei had snatched up a costume gauntlet from the Stalingrad Opera. What possible reason could he have had for saving it?

"My father also fought at Stalingrad," Katherina blurted out suddenly, then instantly regretted it. What was she thinking? Now she would have to explain what side he fought on, and why. A question to which she had no answer. She poked the fire, nervously while all eyes turned toward her.

"Oh, Kätchen! Stasya! You're both *here*!" Detlev skated to a sudden stop at the edge of the pond next to the campsite and clapped his gloved hands. Hans Stintzing stopped just behind him with slightly less grace.

Katherina was reprieved. "Yes, we got here only a little while ago."

"Well, you just put on some skates right now and get on out here. I'm not letting you sit this one out, you two!"

"Don't make us climb up there and drag you out," Hans threatened in his rich bass voice.

Katherina seized the moment. "All right. I will, but only if Anastasia does too." She dropped a pair of skates between them and began to buckle one on herself. Anastasia hesitated for a moment, exchanging glances with her husband, then accepted the skates. In a few moments they were on the ice, Detlev and Hans urging them away from the shore.

"There now. Aren't we having great fun?" Detlev cajoled, obviously pleased with himself.

Hans skated alongside Katherina, stumbling occasionally,

humming one of the waltzes from *Rosenkavalier*. She elbowed him amiably. "I see that you ice-skate pretty much the way you fence."

"Mamselle," he said, using one of Baron Ochs' expressions, "I am not skating, just as I was not fencing. I am *acting* like I am skating. That is all an opera singer ever needs to do."

"Hans, honey. I think the ladies would like a little time alone," Detlev interrupted gently. "Sooo, we'll skate around the pond with both of you because we all look *fabulous*, but then we'll take you back to the far side and leave you on your own, *n'est pas*?"

"That's a wonderful idea." Katherina half glided where the ice was smooth and minced delicately whenever they hit lumpy patches. "Hmm. Not so easy to be an ice ballerina, is it?"

Anastasia also seemed to be concentrating on her feet. "It didn't look this difficult in all those Breughel paintings," she muttered. "Do you think they had better ice in the sixteenth century?"

"Painters are liars too," Detlev said. "Do what Hans and I are doing. Pretend to ice-skate."

"What if I pretend to fall down? Will you pretend to pick me up?" Katherina laughed again. She was giddy and happy again after weeks of brooding. Though they seemed to be casual friends skating, a subtle feeling of conspiracy existed among the four of them. Something almost familial tied them together and separated them from the others on the shore. She ached for it to last, then glanced toward the distant campsite where she could see Boris watching.

Detlev skated adroitly in a small arabesque, which brought him alongside of Anastasia. "What were you talking about so seriously back at the fire? You all looked so solemn, like you were discussing death."

"We were, sort of. War stories," Anastasia answered, keeping her eyes on her feet.

"Oh, that. What a waste of time. Everyone over fifty fought in the war and everyone under fifty has a father who did. Time to get over it."

They had reached the far side of the pond. "All right, my pretties. We've rescued you from the nosy neighbors and now you're on your own." Detlev made a graceful curve around them and the two men skated off.

Katherina guided Anastasia so that they skated back and forth at the far edge of the pond, rather than follow the periphery, which would take them back too soon to the campsite. It was awkward to talk because the strain of skating kept them both slightly breathless, and the cold kept their faces buried in layers of scarf. Shoulder to shoulder, they began to breathe in rhythm, and each of their moist exhalations joined in a single sphere of steam before evaporating in the frigid air.

"What were you going to say about your father?" Anastasia resumed the campsite conversation.

"I didn't mean to mention him at all. It just slipped out. I have no idea what he was doing at Stalingrad since I can't read his Russian notes. As for the rest of his confessions, I can't really discuss them with anyone, except maybe Detlev."

"Detlev? Why him?"

They skated slowly, meandering now in curves, their gloved hands brushing past each other, touching lightly.

"Because, from what I've been reading in his journal, he was mixed up with some gangster lowlife named Schalk. Plus, he was homosexual," she added suddenly. "He had a whole other life even after I was born. A secret life within a secret life, like Russian nesting dolls."

"How awful for him. But homosexuality used to be a serious crime, didn't it? After the war, too. I'm sorry."

"I don't want to talk about my father. I want to talk about us."

"Us?" Anastasia shook her head. "There can't be an 'us.' Not just now."

Katherina skated around in front of Anastasia, stopping her.

"There *was* an us, that night on the balcony and onstage in the last performance. It was *not* my imagination. Please don't try to wish that out of existence."

Anastasia pulled her scarf away from her mouth, revealing lovely full lips. "I admit, something happened. Something exciting and precious. Completely new to me. But there is so much that I can't do, that we can't even talk about yet."

"'Yet?' What are waiting for?"

"Please. This is the wrong time in my life. I'm caught and can't do anything now." She glanced to the side. "Besides, Boris is watching us and wondering what's keeping us out here so long. You have to let me go." Anastasia covered her face again and began skating back across the pond.

"Wait!" Katherina held her by the arm and pulled a wad of paper from inside her cape, four sheets of handwritten paper folded into a small package. "It's the Cyrillic pages of my father's journal. I made a copy of them. Remember? You offered to read them. It doesn't have to be right away. I just want you to have them. Whatever's in them, I want to share it with you."

Anastasia looked down at the wad, then slid it into the pocket of her anorak. "Yes, I remember, and I meant it, too. But I don't know when I can do it. So much is happening now, so much up in the air. I'll have to mail it to you."

"It doesn't have to be word for word. I just want to know the subject. It can't take more than ten minutes for you to read them. Whether it's something dangerous, or intimate, I don't care. Maybe we could just sit down over a cup of coffee tomorrow morning. Ten minutes alone, the two of us, that's all I'm asking."

"I don't know. I can't promise anything. We may not have time."

They were near the campsite again and Boris was on his feet, obviously waiting for them. In a moment he would be within earshot.

Katherina felt happiness slipping away. "Please tell me what's going on, why you're avoiding me."

Anastasia took a breath. Though she dropped her voice almost to a murmur, her answer struck with violent clarity. "I'm pregnant."

XXIII
"SOLA, PERDUTA, ABANDONATA"

With her baggage packed, Katherina went early to the common breakfast room and waited. She felt small, foolish, waiting in a public place like a lovesick fan. She sipped at her third glass of orange juice, pretending to study her music, but thoughts of everything but music swam in her mind.

Pregnant. That pulled the ground from beneath any plans, or hints of plans, even the flimsiest of hopes of plans. Katherina felt cheated, then angry at her selfishness. After all, it was Anastasia who had the crisis. Would Boris curb his philandering to be a father? He had, after all, stayed two more weeks in Salzburg. Surely that was a sign that the marriage was working again.

Katherina brooded. What was she doing anyhow, waiting like an infatuated schoolgirl for her favorite teacher to pass in the hallway? Could the whole situation be any more humiliating and absurd? She had to have a final talk with Anastasia, if for no reason other than to put it all away and regain her senses. She hated losing Anastasia to some banal family life in a Munich suburb, but she needed to get Anastasia to talk about it, to wring from her an admission of love, however unconsummated. Katherina hungered to hear the word as much as she hungered for touch.

"May I join you?" Gregory Raspin was suddenly beside her table, immaculately dressed. He indicated the chair across from her.

He was the last person she wanted to see. "Yes. Of course," she said, forcing a smile.

A waiter set down a cup and saucer and poured steaming coffee from a silver pot.

Raspin stirred in sugar. "The reviews are splendid," he said, sliding two Austrian newspapers across the table toward her. "You'll see. Salzburg has been a major success for you."

"Major success? You really think so?" She turned her juice glass in her fingers.

"I do indeed, and since you will soon be inundated with offers, I would like to settle our unfinished business. I mean, of course, the *Walpurgisnacht*. This is the moment when you must make up your mind. I happen to have the contract right here."

He drew a long envelope from his inside jacket pocket. "I presume you've read it," he said, unfolding two copies onto the table and brushing them flat. "It is very straightforward. I have spoken at length with your agent, and she finds no fault with the terms." He held out a ballpoint pen.

"I'm sure she doesn't." Katherina did not take the pen from his hand.

"You might be interested to know that Radu Gavril will be acting as stage manager. I know you trust him. I trust him too. I'm certain that he'll once again reveal his genius in the staging on the Brocken Peak. Incidentally, the DDR has agreed to film it for a broadcast on the real Walpurgisnacht on April 30. I had hoped for a live performance, but a filming of a live performance is nearly as good. Film royalties are discussed in the contract and are generous."

At that moment, Frau Semmel passed by them with a handful of cut flowers for the tables. "Excuse me." Katherina touched her on the arm. "Has Anastasia Ivanova come downstairs yet?"

"Oh, I'm sorry, dear. She checked out last night. It was very late, but she said she had to catch a flight before dawn. She didn't tell you?" The plump matron stood holding her bouquet in front of her.

Katherina felt sudden nausea. "I see. Thank you." She stared into the empty air for a moment, as if reading something only she could see. Then, almost angrily, she took up the pen that lay on the table and signed both copies of the contract.

Raspin beamed. "I know you'll be pleased. It will be a new experience for you, for all of us." He held up his coffee cup. "Let's toast our exciting new venture." She lifted her empty juice glass and brought it toward him as he swung his cup forward. At the tap of heavy porcelain against crystal, the glass broke. Tiny shards fell onto the contract.

Katherina brushed them away with the side of her hand. One shard, nearly invisible, pierced the skin at the base of her palm, bringing forth a tiny drop of blood. A second sweep of her hand smeared the droplet diagonally across the page, through her signature.

She looked down, horrified, at the bloodstained contract. "Oh, I'm sorry."

"Waiter!" Raspin called. "We have some broken glass here." He touched his linen napkin to Katherina's palm. "I hope that's not serious."

"No, it's fine," she said, embarrassed, as the waiter swept together the fragments with a hand brush and removed them from sight.

"Well, then, that's it, I guess. I'll see you in on the Brocken." He stood up with the blood-marked contract and offered his hand. It was as cold as ever.

XXIV
DA CAPO

It was dawning as Katherina waited on the platform at the tiny train station at Drei Annen. She peered down the track, searching for the steam locomotive that would take her up to the Brocken Peak, but still saw no sign of it. Idly, she watched the stationmaster sweeping snow off the platform onto the tracks. He pushed his broom lightly, mechanically, as if accepting the futility of his work, and, in fact, the light snowy mist that still drifted down soon recovered the portions of the platform he had just swept.

The voice rehearsals that had taken place the previous week in rooms all over Drei Annen had gone well. Practicing in school classrooms and private houses was a bit primitive, but that was often the case with festival operas staged outside of a permanent theater or large city. You went wherever you could find a piano and a room large enough. The singing cast of nine included one voice for each of the seven sins and one for Mephisto. She herself, in the role of Woman, made up the ninth. They were mostly "young" singers, starting their careers, hungry for work and willing to take risks. Now the new mountaintop theater was finished and everyone was ready for stage rehearsals.

Katherina was glad to be moving on to the more active phase of the performance, though the intense week of voice rehearsals had begun to relieve both the mourning for her father and the longing for Anastasia. Still, both losses were unhealed wounds, and when she tried to rest, a soft ache settled over her like a pall. She needed to work, to be outdoors, so it felt good to focus attention on the snow-laden fir trees and the cold air in her nostrils carrying the fragrance of pine.

A bird chirped somewhere behind her, signaling daybreak, and Katherina caught sight of it fluttering from under the station roof into nearby trees.

"Snow finch." The stationmaster stopped sweeping and leaned on his broom. "Been here as long as I have—since '59. Even blizzards don't faze 'em. Pretty little things, too." He nodded toward a second bird that swooped past them, its open wings revealing a striking black-and-white pattern.

"You one of those show people got permission to go up on the Brocken, Miss?" He started sweeping again, desultorily.

She lifted the collar of her coat and blew into her gloved hands. "Show people? Yes, I suppose I am. They've just built a performance space for us, I hear."

"Uh-hunh, over the Brocken Stones. That's got to be bad luck, seem to me."

"Bad luck? Why's that? It's just a pile of boulders."

"Two piles. Devil's Pulpit and the Witches' Altar, Miss. I'm not saying that there were real witches up there, carrying off souls. But there's such a thing as an evil place, you know, haunted like, where things happen. So just be careful's all I'm saying." He started sweeping again, Sisyphus-like against the forces of winter.

Katherina stared at his back for a moment, bemused by the warning. The opera they were about to present was all about evil. The seven deadly sins, in fact. She considered Magda's mock declaration that evil was sex and smiled. She rather doubted she'd encounter any of that on the weather-beaten rocks of the Brocken.

"Good morning, Madame Marow." A short bulky man with an enormous mustache appeared at her side. He looked familiar, at least the mustache did, though she could not recall where she had seen it before.

Her expression must have revealed her puzzlement, because the stranger added, "Friedrich Diener at your service." He executed a slight military bow.

"Ah, the composer." Katherina offered her gloved hand. A pudgy hand emerged from the sleeve of his enormous winter coat and touched lightly against her palm.

"So happy you are joining us," Diener said, and slipped his hand back into his pocket.

Katherina endeavored to make conversation. "I understood you are to be anonymous. Why is that?"

"Mr. Raspin has requested that I remain unknown. He has

compensated me for that discretion and I have no objections. He has also contributed a number of his own ideas."

"Morning, all!" The bass, Matti, waved at them from farther down the platform. Other cast members were joining him, and Katherina spotted Radu Gavril among them.

The sound of a steam-locomotive whistle pierced the air, and a moment later the train became visible in the distance, chugging up the incline to Drei Annen, pouring out sooty black smoke. When it drew into the station and stopped, the soot disappeared and gray steam escaped into the icy air.

It was a wonderful antique locomotive, a massive black iron-and-steel barrel covered with countless fixtures, valves, wheels, pipes, and lights. The lower portions of the steam engine were painted red, along with the fully exposed wheels and the armature that turned them. Three lights burned at the front, now superfluous in the snow-augmented morning light, and a wide steel plate between the lights bore the engine number. An open red car directly behind the locomotive held coal, and behind the coal car were six small green passenger cars. Like a child's train set replicated in real-life format.

A conductor opened the passenger-car door from the inside and reached out to help her up. The moment seemed fairy-tale-like. As she clasped the proffered hand, she glanced sideways down the platform, taking one last look at the charming nineteenth-century train station.

With a jolt, she saw Sabine Maurach stepping into the next passenger car.

❖

Katherina stared out the train window at the Alpine landscape, listening to the ever-accelerating *bedattabedatta* of the train wheels. The morning sunlight that shone with double intensity on the snow cheered her immensely and allowed her to forget about Sabine Maurach and most of her other cares. Some of the trees, she noted, had collected snow on only one side. The constant wind had blown it outward and it had frozen in ragged horizontal shapes. They made her think of witches flying into the wind. Could the strange phenomenon be the source of the Witches' Sabbath legends? She wished that Anastasia were at the window with her, explaining snow myths.

"May we join you?" Katherina smiled welcome as Radu Gavril and Friedrich Diener sat down on the seats across the aisle from her. When the train passed through clearings in the line of trees, the newly risen sun was just high enough to shine through the coach window, warming the side of her face.

"Lovely morning, isn't it?" Radu said. "Is this your first trip up to the peak?"

Katherina nodded. "Yes. But I'm curious why we are allowed to perform on the Brocken Peak. As I understood it, it's a high-security area used by the East German government and the Soviets."

"You're quite right, Fräulein Marow," Friedrich Diener said, small now on his seat, all mustache and coat. "It's surrounded by a concrete wall, too. The transmission tower there not only broadcasts East German television, but probably monitors signals from the West. Nasty business."

"It's hard to believe they would allow something like this. I mean the orchestra and conductor are from the DDR, but the soloists are West German."

Diener nodded pedagogically. "Quite so, but it is a work that from its conception was intended to be performed at this location. Mr. Raspin has spent a lot of money and called in a lot of favors to get the DDR to agree to this production. An amazing achievement."

"We'll have to go through border control, then?"

"Yes, two times, in fact. At the Brocken station and again as we pass through the security wall around the transmission station. You have your temporary visa, don't you?"

"Of course. My agent took care of all that." She held up her shoulder bag, which now had a fastener holding it firmly shut.

Friedrich Diener bent toward her from his seat across the aisle. "I trust Herr Raspin has discussed with you the…uh…novel aspects of this opera."

"Yes, briefly. But perhaps you can fill me in on more of the details."

He clasped his hands in front of him. "The novelty is both in the musical structure and in the staging. You see, we return to the roots of the theatrical experience. The performance will be anti-Goethe, even anti-Brecht. We don't want any intellectual detachment. That is the art of the weakling. We wish to initiate a complete abandoning of the self to the musical experience."

"I'm sorry. I don't follow you. I don't know what that means."

Diener continued with what was apparently a little speech he often gave. "Since the onset of the technological age, people have become emotionally lazy, intellectualized. They sit passively in movie theaters having their excitement poured into them from outside. We're going to excite them from the inside. Using the historical-literary nomenclature, we offer a return to pre-classical Greek drama, which was a religious rite—the sacrifice of Dionysius."

Pre-classical Greek drama? Katherina realized now who the composer resembled. Friedrich Nietzsche. Had the man read so much of the nineteenth-century philosopher that he decided to grow a bushy mustache to look like him? Or did the mustache come first?

"How, exactly, will you do this?" she asked.

He smiled with his eyes, though it was not possible to see whether his lips did as well. "Mr. Gavril will be taking care of that."

Radu Gavril cleared his throat as if being handed a microphone. "Part of the performance design is for you to provoke the audience to join in simple tunes and chants. We'll be blocking that out today."

"How can you rehearse that aspect without an audience?"

"We can't really, but spontaneity is part of our challenge and our strength. Dress rehearsal will have an invited audience selected by the East German government, and by opening night, with a different audience, you will all be veterans. You'll see."

An ominous question occurred to Katherina and she felt foolish not having wondered about it sooner. "Mr. Diener, if the Brocken is a restricted high-security area, how do you plan to invite a public to see the performance?"

"Don't you worry about that, dear," Diener responded gently. "You just concentrate on the music. We'll address the question of the audience when the time comes."

Katherina was a little put off by the condescending answer, but saw no point in pushing for more information. It was, as he said, their problem.

"Well, hello," a familiar voice sounded over Katherina's head. The shadow, two shadows, moved along the aisle into view. Sabine

Maurach stood next to a tall, pale-skinned man. His square face with its somewhat large nose and cleft chin gave him a certain masculinity, offset by a wide mouth with high-arched sensuous lips that all but rippled. He seemed unable to hold them still for very long, first pressing them together, then running his tongue quickly over them. The effect was a sort of drawing of attention to his mouth rather than to his whole person. He had also shaved away his eyebrows.

Sabine laid her hand on his shoulder, positioning him for introduction. "Have you met Gustav?" she asked. "He'll be your Mephisto."

XXV
Pericoloso

The guards of the *Grenzpolizei* at the Brocken Peak sprang to life as the steam train disgorged its passengers into the station. The soldiers were all young men in medium brown, lightly patterned field camouflage with the usual chest pockets and epaulets. They wore soft caps, and their unmilitarily long hair offered a stark contrast to the severe haircuts of the Wehrmacht. Each one had an assault rifle slung on his shoulder, which seemed excessive for monitoring an opera company. Two of them had huge binoculars hanging from their necks, and a third stood off to the side taking photographs with a bulky camera. Though Katherina suspected they were glad to have something official to do, the guards scrutinized each pass and visa meticulously, as if the safety of the entire DDR depended on their weeding out spies from among the opera crew.

The pass controllers asked every one of the newly arrived visitors the same two questions: "What is your reason for entering the Brocken security zone?" and "Are you carrying instruments that could be construed as dangerous to the installation?" Then, after a brief pat-down of each person, carried out with the same gravity as the interrogation, they stamped the papers presented and waved the visitor on.

Gustav, who stood just behind Katherina, seemed to share her annoyance. "Amusing for the first time," he whispered, "but two times every day will become boring fast."

After some twenty minutes, all the company members had passed through control without incident, and they moved in clusters up the long path to the performance site. Though the sun was already high, the temperature was still at freezing and the snow on the path was frozen hard.

Long before they arrived at the opening in the concrete security wall, Katherina could see the two transmission towers: the old concrete block tower and the newer and far higher one. The column of steel painted in three bands of red and white and standing on three legs looked more modern but was just as ugly as its predecessor. Katherina had a vague idea that the two structures were for broadcasting both television and the FM radio system of the DDR but was not sure if both were operational.

As they approached the gateway, two guards stepped forward to check their papers yet again, though this time with less rigor. By their uniforms it was evident that one was an East German "Vopo" and the other a Soviet. Katherina had heard that the Red Army maintained a barracks on the Brocken Peak, but had not thought about it until now. One of the women walking ahead of her addressed the German guard but he looked away from her, refusing to reply. Obviously they had been ordered not to talk to the visitors. An unpleasant welcome.

At the foot of the new transmission tower, cars and service trucks were pulled up in a circle. Trabants painted in camouflage had the circular emblem Grenzpolizei DDR on their sides, and dull green minivans were stenciled in black on the rear with *Fernsehen der DDR*. Shabby air-polluting vehicles Katherina had not seen in the West for years. A third building stood next to the towers, she presumed for administrative functions, and attached directly to its wall, a row of cages held German shepherd dogs. They erupted into a frenzy of barking as the visitors streamed through the gate.

Some hundred paces away Katherina and the other cast members stopped and formed a loose semicircle around the performance space. It was as primitive a thing as Katherina could imagine. A natural rock formation, which she assumed was the Witches' Altar the stationmaster had talked about, formed the center. Behind it, temporary wooden flooring had been laid over the rocky ground for the orchestra and conductor. Directly in front of it, a pit had been dug. The only stage was a thin strip of platform a few centimeters off the ground, which surrounded the rock pile and the pit. A circular pine roof supported by beams covered everything but the fire pit, and the wide hole in the middle of the roof, some two meters in diameter, was obviously for smoke ventilation.

Two rings of wooden pillars supported the roof, though the inner pillars were doubly thick. She quickly saw why. Four of them held small platforms where a person could crouch. A narrow ladder ran along the column from ground to roof. A technician with *Fernsehen der DDR* on the back of his overall had just climbed down one of them with a coil of cable over his shoulder. She could see now that he had just installed a length of cable along the column up to the elevated workspace.

"What are those for?" Katherina asked, pointing to one of the platforms.

"Camera emplacements," Radu answered. "DDR television will be filming from three of them."

"Hollywood on the Brocken, dear," Gustav quipped. "Aren't you excited?"

In fact she *was* a little excited, but also a little unnerved. Any error would be recorded forever. Every note and action, for better or for worse, would be irrevocable.

She was also not particularly happy to note that the audience had no seats but only narrow benches. Mere planks, the kind that did not encourage sitting. The audience would thus be standing, just as the chorus would do. Like Medieval spectators. It was an arrangement that encouraged noise.

"Where will we dress and make up?" a dancer asked.

"There are rooms and toilets down there." Radu pointed to a long rectangular shed lower on the peak. "It's not what you're used to, of course, but don't worry. It will serve for dressing rooms for that one performance night."

One of the younger singers warmed her hands under her armpits. "I don't know how we'll be able to sing for two and a half hours in this air. This 'theater' has no walls and it's freezing up here."

Radu shook his head. "It won't be. There will be a fire right here in this pit, a big one, as well as a ring of torches around the whole theater. That, plus some two hundred spectators will provide all the heat you'll need. More than you'll want. You'll see."

Katherina exchanged glances with the singer, who shrugged, obviously unconvinced.

Sabine Maurach was suddenly at her elbow. "So, how have you been?"

"Fine, just fine." Katherina mumbled, her eyes wandering again to Gustav, who stood nearby. The two seemed connected, although the dancers had only just arrived a few days before. Had Sabine already made yet another conquest? Katherina's face burned as she considered the possibility that Sabine had already told him of her *Carmina Burana* seduction.

Sabine touched Katherina's forearm, as if the thought had just occurred to her. "Look, why don't we get together this evening after rehearsal, you know, for dinner?"

Katherina tried to formulate an evasive answer.

Radu Gavril clapped his hands suddenly, interrupting. "Come on, everyone. Let's get started." He ushered his cast to the center of the performance space. On a patch of hard-packed ground, the accompanist was just removing the tarp from the small rehearsal piano.

Radu seemed more edgy than he had been in Salzburg, his rapid-fire manner tense and hurried. He had just finished stage directing in Stockholm a few days before and was obviously under enormous pressure to realize an avant-garde work in a brief period of time. That would take its toll on any man, however brilliant.

He addressed the four female dancers. "Witches, you'll be onstage at all times after the opening. Remember, you'll be the ones to pull people into the ensembles."

"We'll begin with the Prolog," he said without pause. "God and Mephisto." He swept his hand in a wide arc across the audience space. "As you wager for the soul of Woman, you will make a full circle around the audience. The chorus will enter at the end."

The lyrics of the Prolog sounded familiar, and then Katherina remembered her last course in German literature. Though the drama was about the Witches' Sabbath, it began with a near duplication of Goethe's *Prolog im Himmel*. The difference, which she found gratifying, was that it was not a temptation of Faust standing in for Man, but of herself, standing in for Woman. The difference seemed significant.

Moreover, the Devil was rather less threatening. In spite of Gustav's robust stature, Katherina noted, to her amusement, he would sing his Mephisto as a counter-tenor.

Satisfied with the run-through, Radu turned the page in his score. "All right. The first sin is Envy. Katherina and Stefan, this is your duet and then trio with an audience member. Stefan, give us some good tenor excitement. One of the witches"—he pointed toward Sabine—"will pick out someone and get them to sing the refrain. Don't worry about how bad they are. They're there for emotion, not tonality."

Since the singers had rehearsed the vocal parts thoroughly in Drei Annen, they performed them only at half voice with the piano, pulling in a random colleague to stand in for the audience member. Radu seemed satisfied.

He turned his page again. "Let's move on to Gluttony. Thomas, you'll start the baritone while the witches distribute doughnuts and gelatin. The orchestra will be at full volume, so at the beginning of the third verse, I want you to start the food fight. Just mime it right now. We'll have real gelatin on performance night."

He signaled the piano and the team rehearsed all three scenes. Even without the pleasure of a gelatin fight, Katherina had to admit, it looked like it would be fun.

An hour later, Radu called the next sin. "All right. Pride. That's your first aria, Katherina. Mephisto will spot audience members for you, so you should move toward them. Make eye contact, reach out and touch people."

"The witches will bring up more people to the rock to make a pile for you to mount on. Mephisto will help you climb them, where you'll sing the climax of the aria. Are the volunteers ready?" Four young people, music students from town, as Katherina learned, moved to the center of the Witches' Altar. The scene had to be rehearsed several times while Katherina learned how to sing at the same time she clambered over the unstable bodies.

"We'll work on this again tomorrow." Radu looked at his watch. "Let's move on to Greed."

"Here the idea is to get the audience angry and ready for the two final scenes. Katherina, on your duet with Barbara, you go with the witches into the crowd and reach into people's pockets. Whatever you find, wave in their faces before dropping it on the floor. We'll also have handfuls of coins to throw."

The duet worked well musically, with the feigned annoyance of the music students a lively foil. But would a real audience, caught off guard by the singers' abuse, react with the same docility? Katherina had misgivings. Soon, however, Radu's confidence in staging their movement and his frequent laughter swept them away.

It was midafternoon by the time they had rehearsed Sloth and Pride, and Katherina was muscle-sore. Radu's energy was unflagging. "Wrath. That's you, Matti." A bulky, bearded man nodded. "You and Katherina will circulate during this duet, punching and slapping the audience. Just hard enough to get them riled. The vocal range is from forte to fortissimo. The orchestra will be pumping out the rhythm. Bump pah boom, bump pah boom." He imitated the bassoons.

"All right, witches, students, take your places. We'll run through it from the bass entrance. Matti, are you ready? And let's pick up the pace. We've still got some big sins to commit."

❖

It was four in the afternoon when Radu finally announced, "All right. This is the climax of the opera."

Katherina rubbed her neck, imagining a hot bath back in her hotel.

"Mephisto?" He addressed Gustav, who gripped a gardener's rake in place of the scythe he would carry in the performance. "This is where you begin the Dance of Death. The witches will herd people into a line behind the seven sins. The line will follow you around the hall while the chorus sings the *Dies Irae*. Lead them around once and return to this spot. By then, Woman will be up on the Witches' Altar.

"Katherina, this is where you sing your big aria. The orchestra will diminuendo so your entrance can be heard. The conductor will be behind you, so you'll have to listen for the A-flat chord to start. Mephisto will be right below you and will approach while you sing the first four measures. Ready?"

He called to the pianist, "Two measures before the beginning of the aria."

Katherina knelt on the rough, slightly tilted rock of the Witches' Altar, supporting herself on her hands. At the sound of the chord, she began. *"Es wird Tag! Der letzte Tag! Der Hochzeittag!"*

Mephisto climbed up behind her, a leg on either side of her on the rock. Katherina sang the words of the tormented Woman to the empty air over the pit.

"Die Glocke ruft! Krack, das Stäbchen bricht!" She sang of the flashing of the executioner's blade and of a bell ringing out a death knell. *"Es zuckt in jedem Nacken die Schärfe, die nach meinem zuckt! Die Glocke!"*

Mephisto grasped her by the shoulders and tried to cajole her to flee on horses that waited. Quickly, before the dawn. *"Meine Pferde schaudern, der Morgen dämmert auf!"*

Katherina threw out her arms, appealing to the heavens, to the angels to save her soul. Her last note was a sustained tremolo of terror. *"Mir graut's vor dir."*

Then Mephisto forced her down onto the rock surface. Kneeling on one leg over her prostrate body he sang her damnation in a high-pitched fortissimo.

Radu shook his head. "We need much more terror. In case you don't know your Goethe *Urfaust*, there are no angels here. This is where Gretchen is doomed and damned. Blooie. Kaputt." He chuckled. "Here Mephisto has the last say, so put some guts into it. Don't worry about getting a few scratches."

"As for Mephisto…" He addressed Gustav. "Don't be afraid to be a little rough. Enjoy your victory. This is your message, the cold, terrible truth of the world. And to underscore your victory, right after *'meine Pferde schaudern,'* you should rip off her gown. We'll set it up so that it comes off easily.

What?" Katherina jerked her head toward him. "He's going to tear off my costume? In front of hundreds of people?"

"Yes, exactly. As you sing your last line, 'Mir graut's vor dir,' you will be nude."

❖

Corporal Pavel Platinkov was very fond of both dancers and drink. Neither one was much of a liability during his deployment as a border guard at the Brockenberg base. Though his experience with ballerinas had been limited to a single brief and tumultuous affair with a student at the Minsk Ballet School, he harbored the notion that all dancers were open to his attentions. Since ballet was generally not available during his military deployment to the Brocken garrison, he made do with his other favorite thing: vodka. To be sure, he was careful to consume only during off-duty hours. It was rarely to excess, but when it was, his comrades generally kept him out of trouble. They found him congenial in spite of his gawky behavior and his extremely long nose, which had earned him the nickname Vulture.

He happened to be on duty at the security gate when the troupe of civilians passed through and took up position in their newly built shelter over the Brocken Stone. He had no idea what the arrival meant, and when he heard that the visitors were rehearsing some spectacle that involved dancers, he immediately petitioned to attend. Permission, he was told, was contingent on whether troops would be allowed contact with the civilians at all, a decision that had not yet been made.

It was thus that both of his weaknesses fell upon him at the same time, on the second day of rehearsal. While off duty, instead of keeping to the barracks or confining himself to forest outings, which were approved, he consumed a significant quantity of vodka with his comrades and went off-limits to the Brocken Stone.

Pavel and his friends stood partially concealed by a truck, trying to get a glance of the dancers through their binoculars. Finally they did spot one whose peregrinations brought her close enough to examine in the field glasses. She retreated quickly, however, and further study of her seemed hopeless. In any case, Pavel Platinkov was by now quite drunk and needed to relieve himself. It was at this moment that a well-dressed civilian, who had been watching the rehearsal from within the circle, approached the delinquent Russians. At that exact moment, unfortunately, Pavel was relieving himself, although, because his back was turned, this was not evident. When he felt the firm clap of the stranger's hand on his shoulder, he spun around so suddenly that the full stream of his urine splattered on the stranger's shoe.

The civilian looked down at his reeking foot for the briefest second and then, with the hand that had lain on Pavel's shoulder, slapped him sharply across the face.

Reeling from the blow and his own inebriation, Pavel staggered backward. Furious, he regained position and threw himself on the man and would have done him serious damage, had his comrades not pulled him off.

They dragged him back to his barracks where, later in the day, he was called before his sergeant. The gentleman in question had obviously filed a complaint, and for the two violations of going off-limits and attacking a civilian, Pavel was broken in rank from corporal to private, sentenced to punitive bathroom duty, and confined to barracks.

While he scrubbed toilets, stone-cold sober, Pavel had one sole thought. Revenge.

XXVI
BROCKENGESPENST

Though Katherina's legs ached from kneeling on the cold rock, and she almost staggered, she left the performance site the minute rehearsal was concluded. Dazed and furious at the thought of being tricked, she was in no mood to banter with the others. The young ones seemed to cluster adoringly around the frenetic Radu, and she had no patience for that. She wanted nothing more than to get back to the hotel, have a bath, and telephone her agent.

There had been no mention of nudity in the contract, of course. Staging details were never part of a business agreement. But if that was the case, could she be forced to disrobe against her will? Whose decision was it in the first place, she wondered, if not the stage director's? And what would happen if she refused?

As she limped past the soldiers standing guard before the entrance, they seemed to laugh at her, though it could have simply been her grim mood. Sullen, she made her way carefully along the frozen path leading down to the train station. The night sky was beginning to thicken with mist and the air was damp on her face. She formulated phrases of complaint to make to Charlotte or to whoever was responsible for the oversight. Anastasia, she was sure, would not have tolerated such staging.

Finally she reached the station itself, a looming gray-black shadow guarded by another detachment of Grenzpolizei. She was the first of the opera team to arrive and submit her identification once more to scrutiny. The pass-control guard motioned her out onto the station platform to wait. She was sorry now she had stormed off without the others. She did not relish the thought of standing there alone with idle soldiers and so she wandered to the far track along the ridge where, that same morning, she had been able to look over the entire valley.

She sat down on one of the viewing benches and pulled her scarf up over her nose and mouth. The stone bench was cold where she sat, but the rest of her was warm inside her cloak. Below her feet, clouds drifted across the dark valley and lifted toward the ridge. Between them, patches cleared momentarily and revealed other, lower mountain peaks, black in the distance. She stared dreamily at the ragged clouds that blew past her, gauzy variations of the white tree "witches" far below, and drowsiness overtook her. She relaxed, letting herself doze; the train would arrive in a few minutes and the noise would waken her. Her thoughts, of staging details, of sacrificial altars, and of flying snow-witches jumbled in her fading consciousness and she let her head fall forward.

The crunch of footfall on snow awakened her suddenly. Sleep-dazed she stared into the fog that had gathered over the valley. It was a wall of gray, so dense it threw back shadows. She tried to make sense of the terrifying images that suddenly appeared.

Something alien and monstrously long moved toward her on spindly legs, some otherworldly creature, shadowed on the screen of mist, a sphere of light like a halo around its head. The monster wavered, phantomlike, approaching her as from another world. She cringed.

"I'm sorry if I frightened you," a familiar voice said gently.

"Mr. Raspin. No, I was just dozing, I think, and I only saw your shadow." She rubbed her eyes. "You had a halo."

He sat down next to her on the bench, and the gray giant suddenly shrank. "The fog does strange things, doesn't it?" Raspin pointed up at the ball of light that still shone on the fog over both their heads. "It's called the 'Brockengespenst.' Look, the halo is just the station light being reflected back on the water droplets. Apparently it's fairly common here." He lifted an arm that was reflected long and ghostly on the mist in front of them. "You see? Nothing to be alarmed at."

"No, of course not. So silly of me."

"It does throw people. But after a few more foggy nights like this one, you'll become an expert." His voice became lighter. "How was the rehearsal? Did Mr. Gavril explain our new approach to you?"

"Mr. Diener did. A Dionysian opera, he said. But listen, whose idea was it for me to appear half-nude at the end? On a freezing mountain top, that seems ridiculous, and completely unnecessary."

"It lasts only a moment, so there's nothing to be anxious about.

And you won't be cold. There will be a roaring fire right below you. The staging committee thought it would add to the dramatic value. You see, Fernsehen DDR will be filming the performance for broadcast on the real Walpurgisnacht at the end of April. That's what we're focusing on. That very dramatic moment is crucial. I can assure you, you won't mind it at all when you're caught up in the opera. The whole project is groundbreaking: the broadcast timing, the location, the agreement with the East German government. Your name will be known all over Germany, east and west."

"I'm sure the staging committee knows what it's doing, in light of all that, but why must the ending be so…well…demeaning?"

"Demeaning? Ah, but you are taking it far too personally. The opera is about damnation, after all. About ruin, the wickedness of the world. It's not a happy-ending story. The final aria Woman sings is an admission of all human guilt, and once she sings that, she becomes a sort of sacrificial lamb. It is an ancient and very honorable role."

"You're sure that's what the composer had in mind?"

"Absolutely certain. You see, I *am* one of the composers. The opera is a collaboration between myself and Mr. Diener."

"And the final aria?"

"Is from my pen. It is *my* aria, every word and note."

❖

Katherina was still furious. "Charlotte, didn't you read the contract? Why do I have an agent if something like this slips through? Yes, of course I read it myself. There was *nothing* in it about nudity."

Charlotte's response was calm. "Well, dear, I have it here in front of me, and on page three, under 'special conditions,' it says specifically that you agree to all staging, including unusual props and partial nudity. How could you have missed it?"

"I'm sure it wasn't in the draft he gave me. He must have inserted the clause in the new contract, the one he handed me to sign. That's fraud, isn't it?"

"Only if you can prove he did it. Do you still have the draft?"

"Not here. Besides, contracts are your business. I assumed you had your copy and the matter was settled."

"Well, I do have it, and it has the nudity clause. Listen, it's not such a big deal. You are their star. They're not going to throw you out and get someone else just because you refuse to take off your shirt. Certainly not at this late date."

"Are you sure?"

"Relax. Lots of opera singers have costume issues. Beverly Sills once cut hers in half and demanded a new one. Just tell him you overlooked the clause and that it's a step farther than you're willing to go. Period. How long would it take for them to make you a skimpy shift? Something flesh colored. We're not talking the Queen of the Night's costume here. I'll give them a call tomorrow, but they are within their legal rights, so your main weapon is going to have to be your charm."

"I suppose you're right. I just have to stand up to them."

"That's my girl. Oh, by the way. I forwarded a package to you. Someone left it for you at the Salzburg hotel at the last minute and the staff apparently overlooked giving it to you. The hotel sent it to the Festspielhaus and they passed it on to me."

"What is it?"

"I have no idea. It was in a box with the Pension Stein name on it. I just put another label on it and sent it on. You should be getting it in a day or two."

"Were there any other messages for me? Any calls?"

"No. Are you expecting something?"

Katherina's heart sank. "Nothing special. If anyone important calls, you can give them this number."

"If you say so. But it's hard to get through to you. I called several times and they always said you were unavailable."

"Well, I suppose it's true. They work us pretty hard."

"Anyhow, listen, you're settled in on this engagement, and we have nothing on the calendar until next month. I've got my other artists in place for a while so I'm taking a short vacation the day after tomorrow. You can call my assistant for anything you need, and of course in an emergency, she can reach me in Majorca. Otherwise, I'll talk to you in a week."

"All right, then. Have a nice trip." Katherina hung up with a faint sense of abandonment.

XXVII
MOLTO AGITATO

Y ou bastard!" Anastasia crumpled the tiny silk panties she had just found in the bathroom and threw them at her husband. "We haven't been home more than two weeks and already you're screwing your tarts again. In our bed! All that time in Salzburg trying to patch things up, that meant nothing. You are *such* a liar, Boris."

"What do you want me to say? A man has appetites."

"That can only be satisfied by some twenty-year-old who'll let you fuck her to get a recording contract?" Anastasia snapped back.

"No, but by a woman of any age who seems to actually *want* to be fucked."

"What are you talking about? I'm always there for you. For five years I've been there for you."

"That's a load of crap, and you know it. For five years, or at least the last three of them, you've been on one engagement after another. And even when you were home, you seemed always to just be doing your duty."

"Don't twist this thing around to blame me for your acting like a goat. You've been doing those girls for years, getting all the erotic enthusiasm you wanted, and I never complained. I kept waiting for you to grow up and realize that marriage was more than daily orgasms."

"Don't lecture me on what marriage is, Stasya. I never promised you anything except support for your career, and for five years you got what you needed from me. It was never a real marriage. Hell, it was a goddamn business arrangement."

"It was enough of a marriage to make me pregnant, and now I need more from you than recording contracts. We discussed all that in Salzburg. I need a real family now to raise this baby."

He picked up the scrap of red silk from the floor and folded it into his pocket. "You mean you want a nice docile house-husband who doesn't demand sex too often. That's not me, and you know it. Children were never part of our arrangement."

"You want me to have an abortion? So things can go back to the way they were?"

"That's your decision. But you know you can't have everything—a glamorous career *and* a family. If you have an abortion I'll pay for it. If you want to be a mother, I'll send money, but I won't come home at night to a screaming infant."

Anastasia ran her fingers through her hair searching for new terms, trying to reframe the dispute. "Look, infancy doesn't last forever." She heard the whine in her own voice and hated it, but it was the only argument she had left. "We can hire help. A lot of opera singers have children. In a couple of years we can go back to this loose arrangement you are so fond of."

"Listen to yourself. You still don't see what I'm talking about. Our marriage has been theater the whole time, a contract we both agreed on and benefited from. I'm sorry this accident happened, but pregnancy was *not in the contract*." He stormed out of the apartment and slammed the door behind him.

Anastasia stared, speechless, at the closed door. Betrayed. She fumed, less at Boris than at herself. All those quiet conversations in Salzburg with him, all those promises, though she realized in retrospect that Boris had simply repeated that he would support her no matter what. It was on that promise alone that she had made a painful sacrifice. For the word "support" she had closed a door to what might have been real happiness. But it was obvious now that all he had ever meant was money—the one thing she no longer needed from him.

She glanced over at the open score of *Carmen* that she had been reading and sighed. Boris had a point. She *did* want everything. How could a daughter of someone who named herself Olga Adrianovna Romanova not be ambitious? It was that very ambition, after all, that had enabled her to escape the grinding drudgery of Soviet Russia.

Singing with the Bolshoi fulfilled the dream of every music-loving child in Russia, and she had been happy—for a while. But the thrill did not last long. Within the first year, reality set in and she saw that it was a workplace like any other, subject to Soviet rules, overseen by commissars. New employees had to fill out questionnaires to prove they were good communists. The embarrassment of having a faintly Romanov mother, by then deceased, could be offset by producing evidence of a good communist father who fell in the Battle of Kursk, and of Uncle Georgi, who fought at Stalingrad.

But she hated living in the dormitory, since as a single person she did not qualify for an apartment, even a shared one. And she was decidedly single, having never felt the slightest interest in any of the men who courted her.

There were no contracts, only a monthly salary and a work assignment. Like any factory worker with a quota to fulfill, she could be assigned at any time to replace another singer. She could not tour, not even internally, without permission from management. And foreign engagements, even if she was invited to them, were like mountain peaks that she could reach only after she had battled her way through bureaucratic jungles.

It seemed like she was always poor. No matter how much fame she acquired, she earned honors, not money. Not until her last year in Moscow was she finally granted the coveted title "People's Artist of the USSR," which entitled her to a tiny rent-free apartment and permission to travel abroad. Like a bird released from a cage, she sang in Bulgaria and Finland, relearning the old operas in new languages. And she was always under the eye of KGB to guarantee her return to Moscow. Then came Paris, where she'd had enough.

But Boris was right. Her legal identity as Frau Reichmann meant nothing. Like her Romanov names and the pretty roles she was hired to sing, it was all theater. What was left of her behind all the masks? Was there anything still of Anastasia Ivanova? What was real?

The answer was obvious now. The baby was real, and she wanted it.

She wanted something else too, something authentic and untainted that had offered her genuine love. But she had already thrown that away, hadn't she? Overwhelmed with regret, she broke into tears.

What would she do now? She had to take stock. Humbled, she asked herself what pieces were left to pick up. What other things had she neglected that might still be saved?

Then she remembered an envelope of pages in Cyrillic.

XXVIII
Trio Lascivo

The décor of the Drei Annen Gasthof, which Sabine had chosen for supper, was in an Alpine motif. A shelf above the bar held ice picks, spikes, hammers, and a variety of boot crampons. The oak walls were hung with poster-size black-and-white photos of mountain climbers in the early part of the century. Posing in simple wool trousers tucked into leather boots and with cotton ropes looped around their shoulders, they all looked pitifully underequipped for scaling anything more than the modest peaks of the Harz Mountains.

In the dearth of other available social life, Katherina had finally agreed to join Gustav and Sabine there for a post-rehearsal supper.

Throughout the meal, inconspicuously, she hoped, Katherina had been studying Gustav's face. Something about it was not quite right. Or rather, something was just too right, as if someone had designed him. It was not merely that his eyebrows were partially plucked and then drawn in again in a V shape, which rendered him deliberately diabolical. There was something else. Then it came to her. It was his lips.

They were too full and curly, an artist's rendition of sensuous lips that in fact rarely, if ever, occurred naturally. She had seen lips like that only once before, in photos of a famous movie made from an even more famous play.

"Gründgens," she said suddenly.

"Excuse me? Gründgens what?" Sabine asked, her fork raised halfway to her mouth.

"He knows what I mean." Katherina still stared at Gustav. "Don't you? How did you do it? Not the eyebrows. Those are easy to change, but how did you get the lips so perfect? You took his name too, didn't you?"

"What are you talking about?" Sabine apparently did not like to have anything in the conversation that she was not getting.

Gustav smiled with sexually explicit lips. "You have a good eye, Katherina. I'm impressed. It's just a few injections. Approved, oh, maybe a year ago for use. It's good, isn't it?" He sipped at a tiny glass of schnapps, then licked his lips as if to display them in motion.

"More than good. The resemblance is nearly perfect, as much as I can recall from pictures. Gustav Gründgens died in the sixties, I think. Why did you do it?"

"I wanted this role. It suits my voice exactly, not to mention my career. All I needed was the look. With the face of the greatest Mephisto to have ever walked the German stage, how could I miss? And for the chance to perform on television, I'd have done a lot more. Injected anything, slept with anyone, knifed anyone in the back." He raised one of his already-well-tilted eyebrows. "As it turned out, at least the knifing part was not necessary."

Sabine reentered the conversation. "You think sleeping with me got you the role?"

"No, *that* I'm doing just for fun," Gustav said, leaving the more risqué question unanswered.

Katherina moved the conversation as quickly as possible away from sex. "It's an opera, not a movie, after all. You probably would have gotten the role anyhow on the basis of your voice."

"Maybe so. But I don't think the audition counted all that much. It's really a soprano's opera. The high points are all yours, though when you do your final aria, I'm right there and the camera will be on both of us." He signaled the waiter to bring him another schnapps.

"I have the feeling it's *mostly* going to be on me. Remember, I'll be half nude. Obviously the decision-makers are going for the sensational. I don't like it, and I plan to protest, when I work up the nerve."

"There's nothing wrong with the sensational." Sabine shrugged. "I say the wilder the better. Why does opera have to be fat ladies standing in place and singing tunes that everyone already knows by heart?"

Katherina shook her head. "I'm not making a case for stand-and-sing opera. But the idea of stirring the audience to a frenzy frightens me a little. It's potentially explosive. We don't even know how they'll get an audience up here. It's a military zone, and I don't see them inviting hundreds of white-haired German opera lovers inside for an evening. Don't *you* have any misgivings about the whole thing?"

"Not at all." Gustav pursed his Gründgens lips. "Aside from the fact that they're paying us like kings, I trust Radu, and Friedrich and Gregory. They have a revolutionary vision, and I'm perfectly willing to get down in the mud, or rather snow, and pour my guts out for them. As Sabine said, 'the wilder the better,' and with her, that's pretty wild." He glanced sideways in a way that went past suggestive into the lewd. Noting that Gustav had referred to their patron by his first name, Katherina tried to keep the subject on the opera.

"You don't think they're playing with fire?"

Gustav laughed. "Are you joking? The fire's the best part. That big crackling bonfire that'll be blazing along the whole time just *inches* away from us. It's ingenious, absolutely primordial. All that's missing is a human sacrifice, but I don't suppose they've auditioned anyone for that." He laughed again and Sabine laughed with him as he downed his third glass of schnapps.

"And all that talk at the end about being rough with me," Katherina continued. "Just how rough do you plan to be?"

The lewd expression returned. "It's so delicious that you're the innocent one. That practically gives me a hard-on, getting you to surrender that way. Don't worry. I'll only be as rough as you like me to be. But rough can be good. Have you ever tried it rough?" The ridges where his eyebrows would have been rose in two arcs.

Katherina winced at the question. "You're really getting into this demon thing, aren't you? Maybe that's the problem. Maybe I'm a little more nervous than you because the two of you, for that matter, the whole rest of the cast, are playing sins, witches, and demons. I'm the only one who ends up being dragged off to hell against my will."

"That's a small price to pay for having the most glorious aria in the opera. I'd give a testicle to have a solo like that."

"I admit the aria is fairly exciting. But it's just Gretchen's last words in Goethe's *Faust*. They don't even make much sense."

"Oh, but they're a wonderful admission that innocence is crap. We're all going to hell so let's wallow in it. The idea of surrender is such a turn-on. I'm sure it'll be a turn-on for the audience too! You'll be singing your heart out as humankind gives up its soul." Gustav squinted through red eyes.

"That's the problem, though. I don't like being the spokesperson for the human race in damnation. I mean, I prefer to think the human race *shouldn't* surrender."

"That's what I like about you, my dear." Sabine laid her other hand on Katherina's wrist. "You are such a good, sweet person, just begging to be sullied. That is sooo attractive." She paused for a moment, then seemed to take a cue from her companion. "Listen, Gustav and I have been talking. We both think you are very…appealing. Why don't you join us in our hotel and have another drink. The three of us can get to know each other better. I mean, you and I kind of know each other already, but there is *so* much more we can learn. You know that I can make you happy, and Gustav is dying to amuse you in his own special way. Just think of how much fun the three of us can have together."

Katherina slid her hand out from under Sabine's and stood up. "Thank you for the invitation. It's flattering, in a sticky kind of way. Why don't you ask Radu Gavril to join you? I'm sure he'd be pleased." The look that Gustav and Sabine exchanged suggested that they were already considering the stage director.

"In any case, I think I'll hang on a bit longer to what's left of my innocence, or prudery, or whatever you want to call it. I've got a long day tomorrow, we all do, so I'll say good night now."

She dropped thirty marks on the table to pay for her dinner and turned away. By the time she was at the door, coat in hand, she realized this was the second time she had gotten up from a table to flee Sabine's lasciviousness. It had done her little good the first time, though, since she had fallen prey anyhow. The thought sent a wave of excitement up from her groin to her chest, and then to her cheeks. But no, she told herself, she would not become someone's conquest again.

XXIX
SCHERZANDO

Dress rehearsal began and Katherina stood with the orchestra and the other singers behind the Witches' Altar. They would perform before a small invited audience of music students brought up with special permission from Drei Annen. The students, who filled only the front half of the audience space, seemed delighted to be part of the artistic experiment.

Katherina had reached a compromise with the stage director regarding her costume so that she wore a flesh-colored bikini top under a loose gauze shirt. The step back from nudity was small, since her breasts were still largely exposed and her nipples visible through the fabric, but the layer of material gave her a sense of protection.

The Sins were costumed in Greek chitons, all carrying objects that marked their identities. Mephisto's costume, however, stood out from all the others. For anyone with a knowledge of theater, the black tights under a trim black doublet, square cut at the neck and with puffy red satin sleeves, was an homage to the costume Gründgens wore in the famous Hamburg *Faust*. Gustav had also copied the white pancake makeup garishly offset by extreme V-shaped eyebrows and crimson red lips. His head was covered by a form-fitting black skullcap that reached to the back of his neck and was topped with a narrow curved red feather. He even wore the elevated-heel shoes that Gründgens' Mephisto had used to add to his height.

In the midst of the rehearsal another detail of his costume caught Katherina's notice, with such force that she almost missed her cue. His gloves. Black leather, with cuffs reaching halfway up the forearm, they were virtually identical to the gauntlet her father had brought back from Stalingrad.

The orchestra had already begun the overture and on his musical cue, a stagehand ignited the fire in the pit with a pleasant "woooff." Katherina was relieved to see that it was a rather modest fire, fragrant and warming, not at all threatening to the actors moving around above it. Her fears and anxieties now all seemed foolish.

The Prolog in Heaven went quickly as Gustav sang his bantering with God and wagered for the soul of Woman. The voice of God was disembodied, a recording of a bass voice, projected from above at high volume. Katherina recognized some of the text, phrases taken verbatim from Goethe's great work. She smiled at Mephisto's wisecrack-compliment to God for being "mensch" enough to chat with the devil. The audience was attentive and agreeably tense, obviously waiting for the livelier parts they knew were coming.

The first sin, Envy, threaded his way through the audience awkwardly, until the listeners understood that reaction was expected of them. But soon, Katherina's Woman and her dancer "demon" found willing participants who sang their quickly learned refrain with the verve of children chosen for the school play. On cue, the rest of the audience joined for a final repetition, and the opera moved on swimmingly.

The next chorus began sleepily and then was joined by Katherina and the sin of Sloth, as they swept through the crowd drawing in singers to the main melody. Those who were completely tuneless politely held back, letting the more musical carry the sound. It was becoming fun and the audience began to sway, apparently loving it.

At the third sin of Gluttony, people seemed to not believe their good luck. Katherina and the demon began their duet while the dancers threw out doughnuts and balls of lemon gelatin, trying to elicit a rebellion. The response was playful. The audience seemed anxious to please and did not step far over the line of propriety. It was not so much a food fight as a food disagreement.

Pride worked beyond all Katherina's expectations. Mephisto and two dancers chose their audience "bodies" very carefully and drew them to the Witches' Altar. With the pulsing of the woodwinds in the orchestra behind them, they formed their little pyramid with the dancers and Katherina sang her first aria kneeling precariously, but successfully, on their backs.

By the time they arrived at the sin of Greed, Katherina was buoyant.

She was embarrassed that she had ever doubted the showmanship of the three men in charge of the production. It was a charming opera, innocent and playful, and the giddy audience obviously thought so too.

Even Wrath, with the huge Finnish bass slapping people around, never moved the audience "victims" beyond faint annoyance. How could she have ever thought it would be otherwise? The raucous, rhythmic music merely stirred the audience to a loud mumbling, as they tried to sing along.

Lust, which had worried her most of all, was no worse than some Salome performances she had seen. She had to feign group sex with some of the demons, but it was all obviously play-acting, and though it was difficult to sing lying down, the scene worked marvelously. Even the audience, caught up in the ritual chanting of the chorus, cheered them on joyfully, but did not try to intrude in the lustful pantomime on the rock. How silly she had been to doubt the good manners and restraint of the German opera public.

Before she knew it, the single-act opera was nearly over. The orchestra struck up the *Dies Irae* theme, and Mephisto was already leading half of the audience in a snaking line around the periphery of the hall. Everyone was swaying now and clapping their hands in the air. Mephisto handed off his scythe and climbed up behind her, straddling her in his high-heeled boots.

She sang her heart-rending final aria, fighting off the well-rehearsed embrace of Mephisto, and though she did scrape a knee on the rock surface, his manhandling of her was only "stage-rough" and measured. It would make a great show, after all, she thought.

If this was Dionysian opera, she was for it. If all went well, she would have world coverage and a huge fee—while having the time of her life.

"It's a bloody disaster," Gregory Raspin said, striking the table with the flat of his hand. "I commissioned a Dionysian sacrifice and you gave me a Volksfest. The audience all but ran out and polka'd."

"It's certainly not what we planned," Radu agreed. "It has no edge to it at all. So, where do we go from here?"

"The audience is the problem," Diener growled. "They're like sheep. Bland, dull-witted sheep. There is no blood left in them. What's happened to the German character? If this whole endeavor isn't to go down the toilet and make a laughingstock of us all, we have to find a way to set them on fire."

"I agree. It's the audience," Radu added. "The pathetic fools we had yesterday don't have a single carnal thought."

"I think I have a remedy. A remarkably obvious one." Gregory Raspin took out a leather-bound notebook and fountain pen and laid them on the table. "I spent all last night analyzing the problem." He tapped the notebook, suggesting it was the repository of his ideas.

The other two men looked at him expectantly.

"I had originally thought to bring up an audience from Salzgitter or Nordhausen, with special emphasis on young people. We would give out champagne and schnapps before the performance, to break down their inhibition. I had already agreed with the East German government and the Russians to let some of the border troops attend. I thought it would do no harm. But I was a fool. The solution was right here in front of me. What's more excitable than a drunken soldier away from home?" Raspin took out a ballpoint pen and jotted a few lines in his notebook.

Radu Gavril nodded. "I see what you mean. As long as they're not under close supervision, they behave like all young men do when they're let loose."

"Exactly. The Russians especially would suit our needs. We saw in 1945 what they're capable of. We'll just give them all the liquor they want before the opera starts, and in the Gluttony scene we'll give them even more."

Diener looked ceilingward. "Oh, I like this. They'll be in a perfect mood for Wrath and Lust. But what about the soloists? Will they go along with it?"

"Most of them will. They're in this project for the thrill. They'll go all the way with us, no matter what."

"And Katherina Marow?" Radu asked. "She's the one who'll take the brunt of it, especially at the end."

"But that's what we want, isn't it?" Raspin said softly. "A big climax. We just have to make sure she holds still for it."

"She won't like it. And if she has an inkling of how rough it can get, she could ask her manager to release her from the contract."

Raspin slipped his notebook back into his jacket pocket. "Don't worry. I'll take care of that."

❖

Gregory Raspin strode into the Harzwald Hotel at seven in the morning. Without greeting, he asked, "Has Madame Marow gotten any calls in the last few days?"

The night manager peered nervously into Katherina's mailbox. "Why, yes. She has two messages now, from early this morning. I was about to send them up to her."

"No, I'll take them. If her manager calls, please advise her that Madame Marow is not available and then inform me. I will pass on the information to Madame Marow, of course, and will return the calls myself."

"Uh, yes sir. If you wish."

"It is very important that you are diligent about this. We have our opening night in less than forty-eight hours and everyone is a bit on edge. This great artist is about to perform a world premiere in a very difficult role, and the last thing she needs is to be disturbed. Particularly her agent should not be bothering her with future engagement details. I will hold you personally responsible for delivering all messages to me. As I said, I will return the calls immediately, so there is no need for you to even mention them to Madame Marow. Do you understand?"

The night manager clasped nervous hands in front of him. "Of course, Herr Raspin. I'm at your service."

XXX
MOLTO AGITATO

Stabshauptmann Manfred Exner, Commandant of Grenzregiment 6, Brocken Border Control Unit of the German Democratic Republic, buttoned his dark green uniform jacket. Annoyed, he flicked a speck of dirt from the white *Grenztruppen DDR* lettering around his cuff and prepared to meet his visitor. The call had come from the Ministry of Defense an hour earlier, so he knew the substance of the coming meeting, and he didn't like it.

While he waited for his lieutenant to bring in the visitor, he glanced around his office. He was acutely aware of how shabby the room, the whole installation, in fact, would look to Western eyes. It put him in a weak position, and it galled him to have to talk to the man at all. Exner was a good communist, but he was not a fool. It was clear to anyone with eyes and a brain that the prosperous West had won the ideological battle with their East German brethren. The world had changed greatly in the decades following the war, and in that time, while the West was thriving, the DDR had not lived up to its promise to create a prosperous workers' society. The very fact that East Germans had to be blocked from leaving the DDR under penalty of death was evidence enough of the failure. Even for believers like himself, the dream of a just and egalitarian socialist state was receding ever more into the distance. Some time in the past year he had realized that he and his troops were an anachronism and the state they guarded a failure. But Stabshauptmann Exner was a good soldier, and when he was given an order, he obeyed. He had a border to guard, and that is what he would do until he was commanded to stand down.

The lieutenant ushered in the visitor, a slender, well-dressed man in his sixties with a reserved businesslike smile. The handshake told Exner all he needed to know. It was the smooth cool hand of a rich man with the loose grip of one who could not be trusted.

He sat down again at his desk. "What can I do for you, Mr. Raspin?" he asked, though he knew full well.

"I believe the ministry has contacted you about allowing your men to attend our performance on Saturday. Not the select few we had originally agreed upon, but the entire garrison."

"They have, and I informed them that it is a terrible idea. My men are not palace guards with time on their hands, Mr. Raspin, but battle-ready soldiers. What possible value could an opera have for us?"

"Apparently your government is not as averse as you are. Grenzkommando Nord thinks a completely apolitical performance by both Eastern and Western musicians would have great propaganda value. That is why they are setting up cameras to film it as we speak. A triumph of art over ideologies, in effect. We know, the world knows, that Germans have a tender spot for classical music."

Exner drummed his fingers on his desk in a brief cadence. Whatever truth was in the man's words was undermined by his air of condescension. "We are not talking about a string quartet here, but an entire opera production. An avant-garde opera, as I understand it. I have objected to it from the very beginning. However, I have been ordered to cooperate with your undertaking and I will do so. I warn you that *my* troops may put up with your little spectacle without incident, but I cannot vouch for our Soviet colleagues."

"Forgive me if I find your reaction amusing, Herr Stabshauptmann. But Commander Zaizev of the Russian unit expressed the same misgivings about the German troops when I spoke to him this morning."

Exner did not share the amusement. "Ah, you have already reached an agreement with the Soviets. Well then, so be it. I will supply you with half of your audience, but I have already informed the ministry that this assignment falls outside the articles defining military border responsibilities. You will therefore be held to account personally for any irregularities, either between my men and the Soviets, or between my men and your own team. I presume a similar understanding exists between yourself and Commander Zaizev. My authority—and I assure you I will enforce it—extends only to German border troops and, now, of course, yourself. However, neither German civilian courts nor German military courts have jurisdiction over Soviet troops."

"Understood." Raspin stood up, glanced quickly at his watch, and offered his hand once again. "I thank you for your cooperation, Herr Stabshauptmann. Now, if you will permit me, I have an opera to produce." With the hint of a military bow, he strode to the door, which the attentive lieutenant opened for him.

Exner stood fuming. He remembered now why he hated the West Germans.

❖

Gregory Raspin rode the last steam train of the day down from the Brocken Peak satisfied that he'd solved the last problem. What's more, it hadn't added to the fortune he had already spent on the opera on fees, expenses, bribes, all the rest. Even if it had, he would have paid whatever was necessary. Ultimately, a man had to put his money where his heart was. Besides, the well would soon fill up again, nourished as it was by dividends from shares in petroleum, pharmaceuticals, and armaments. And the investors in his private investment firm, Nibelung, GmbH, would not even notice the temporary vacuum. As long as their quarterly statements showed a profit, they trusted him.

Ah, there was so much money to be gotten from that trust, that is, real money earned from the mere promise of money, the fictional money of quarterly statements. Gullible institutions, mostly music and art foundations, entrusted huge sums to him, and each new investor allowed him to make actual payments to the previous ones, cementing *their* trust. When people trusted you, they stopped making withdrawals and simply re-invested, and so the money poured in.

He congratulated himself. How far he had come since being Peter Stein, a hungry little boy in Rüsselsheim, son of a soldier who had been highly decorated in World War I. But his hero of a father had become a drunk who brutalized his wife and his son and sexually assaulted the serving girl. The concussion he suffered from being thrown against the wall during one of his father's rages had crushed any seed of idealism the son might have had. When he recovered, he swore never again to be weak. But he was still young and he endured abuse for three more years. Finally, when the political atmosphere changed, Peter's first act of revenge was to denounce the drunken old brute to the local *Gauleiter*.

Raspin thanked God that he himself was smart, handsome, and

Aryan-looking. He was a star in the Hitlerjugend and a star at university and had always known which way the wind was blowing. When the war began in 1939, he had already been a party member for a year and was in a good position to make his way into the Gestapo. That's when the game got really interesting. One of his first successes was to uncover two brothers, expert counterfeiters who could create high-quality "Aryan" papers for Jews. It was perhaps the smartest move of his life to *not* denounce them and instead to demand in exchange a new set of identity papers for himself. He had no immediate need for them—his ship was in high sail with the Nazis—but he believed in contingency plans. He even protected the counterfeiters, knowing full well they were letting hundreds of Jews and communists escape. That arrangement paid off spectacularly.

In 1945, when it became obvious that Peter Stein, NSDAP party number 2746 and active member of the Gestapo, was someone the victors would certainly hang, he retrieved the masterpiece of fraudulent papers the brothers had created for him and surrendered to the Allies as a simple, apolitical soldier, Obergefreiter Peter Schalk.

The transition had been seamless, and he immediately joined forces with—and expanded—the business of the counterfeiters. Everyone, it seemed, wanted to be someone else, and would pay a lot for the opportunity. From that business, he developed a whole network of trading partners in medicines and other high-value goods.

Then, in the early 1950s, when the false-identity business waned, he had a stroke of genius. He had already concluded back in Rüsselsheim that men were vile, that they all craved a hot ejaculation that could be spiced by violence, the dogfight, the *corrida*, the grisly public execution. The revelation of the 1950s was that this appetite could provide a market. The "special-entertainment" films that had titillated a few friends, he realized, were a gold mine, and he set about acquiring new ones with higher resolution and better camera work. It required a delicate touch, utilizing the talents of various circles of his business dependents, while calibrating just how much information to give each one. The "actors" ironically were the easiest to manage. Three or four well-paid, slightly drunken soldiers just about to be shipped home, plus a prostitute who would not be in a position to contact the police, a secure location. A certain sensitivity entered the business only with respect to the two-man camera crew, the film developer, and the miscellaneous contacts involved in distribution or disposal. They had to be convinced, absolutely, of the need for discretion.

But the business took off, the appetite of the limited but loyal public insatiable. Ever new waves of viewers, both German and foreign, washed into and out of the city and paid handsomely for their voyeurism. Soon he had access to underground venues in Hanover, Hamburg, Stuttgart, and Munich, and the money poured in. So much so that he could set about laundering it through legitimate businesses.

Then, to make the final transition, he got his clever counterfeiting partners to create a third identity for him, which allowed him to lead a double life. For several years, he tapered off his entertainment businesses, while at the same time investing his new fortune in financial ventures under the name of Gregory Raspin.

He chuckled at the name choice. Only he would ever know that he had modeled himself after the pre-eminent charlatan of the Russian Empire, Grigori Rasputin, who had conned the Tsarina of Russia and fucked every noblewoman in St. Petersburg. Like Rasputin, he grasped that politics, economics, whole societies were largely theater. Narratives, promises, and images of vanquished evil and beautiful, erotically charged success.

No wonder he loved opera, the ultimate theater, in which audiences were moved, often to tears, by the most absurd nonsense.

But alas, opera was his Achilles heel. He did not want to *think* of all the money he had spent collecting musicians, violinists, tenors, conductors. Not to mention his sponsoring of concerts, operas, whole festivals so that his protégés had places to perform. He did not mind the expense. To hear a performance he had organized, by artists he essentially *owned*, made him feel like Caesar.

But he also wanted to feel like Wagner, so he devised his most audacious plan of all. Not to simply finance an opera, but to write one. Or at least collaborate in writing one. He had already read Nietzsche's *Birth of Tragedy* and knew exactly what he wanted, the Dionysian revel.

He did not have the time to compose an entire opera, but he had already collected a composer, movie-music writer Friedrich Diener, who could compose it *for* him. With sufficient compensation, Diener agreed to write 90% of the music and remain anonymous, while Raspin would write the libretto and a few arias.

Then, by extraordinary accident, he happened to be attending a concert, Brahms' *German Requiem*, and he saw Katherina Marow. A gorgeous woman who sang with a crystalline soprano sound he'd never heard before, and the daughter of an old "client." He knew he had to have her for his magnum opus, no matter what it took. He'd tried to make arrangements with her father for an introduction, but the ridiculous man, a pathetic old homosexual, had refused and threatened to expose him. That was a fatal mistake.

After resolving that problem, he had no difficulty luring the charming soprano into the net anyway. He could focus on the climax to his work, the soprano aria of surrender, sung to Mephisto. What better way to bring the reveling audience to vent its fury on her than to present her, morally broken, to their appetites?

If she was molested in front of the cameras, it would make fabulous press and seal the success of the opera, guaranteeing more performances. If even worse occurred—he licked his lips thinking about it—that would steam-drive the success of the work. It would be universally remembered as the opera that "sacrificed" its star. Even if it jeopardized his corporate persona, he was legally protected. The sense of achievement would make it all worthwhile. This was his aria, the culmination of all his aspirations, his masterstroke.

❖

Some outdoor sound woke Katherina from troubled sleep. She glanced at the 3:00 a.m. on the radio clock and sat up. She was used to waking up in strange hotels but this time she felt particularly alone.

Taking a deep breath, she tried to dispel her anxiety. It was just a case of nerves; the opening performance was, after all, the next day. Stupid to worry. It would probably go splendidly and by the same time the next night, it would all be over.

When had she become so easily rattled? She had not been this way before the Berlin *Tosca*, or even before *Rosenkavalier*. What had happened? She felt foolish asking herself the question, because she knew.

Anastasia had happened. From the moment Katherina saw her onstage she felt an inexplicable attraction. No, even before that. From the moment she saw the face of Marguerite on the record jacket of her father's recording of *Faust*. She even remembered the aria she had listened to as she went through his things and found the mysterious note, "Florian, forgive me."

It was an aria every mezzo-soprano knew, Berlioz' adaptation of Marguerite's longing for Faust, *"D'amour l'ardente Flame."* The melodic line ran through her mind and she translated the French in her head.

"Love's smoldering flame consumes my happiness, my peace of mind is gone. His leaving, his absence, is like the grave...His step, his bearing, the sweet smile of his mouth, his eyes, his voice that sets me afire, the caress of his hand and...oh, his kiss."

The irony of it struck her. In French there was no difference between "his" and "hers." *"Sa bouche, ses yeux, son baiser"* could also mean *"her* mouth, *her* eyes. *Her* kiss." She hummed the final lines of the song, thinking of Anastasia. "Burning caresses. I would give up my soul under *his—her* passionate kisses."

She covered her eyes, feeling like a fool. A pathetic, lovesick girl. Marguerite at her spinning wheel. And Marguerite ended up dead.

Why hadn't she heard from Anastasia? No call, no letter, not even the promised translation. But maybe there was something awful in the Cyrillic text, something so appalling that Anastasia had washed her hands of it. No way of knowing.

Katherina peered at the bedside clock again. Four in the morning, and she had no one to call. She couldn't bear to stay alone in the tiny hotel room. She threw on slacks and a sweater and drew a shawl over her shoulders.

The hotel lobby seemed desolate at the pre-dawn hour and she pulled her shawl more tightly around her. The night manager was someone she had never seen before. A bony fellow scarcely out of his teens, wiping down the counter with a cloth. He looked up anxiously. "Is everything all right, Madame Marow?"

"Yes, everything is fine. I've just been wondering if I'd gotten any calls."

He looked surprised at the question. "Yes, Madame Marow, there were a couple. But I gave them to Mr. Raspin, as agreed. I assumed that was your wish, too."

"What? That was not my wish at all. Who instructed you to do that?"

"That was Mr Raspin. I'm very sorry if there was a misunderstanding. I will cancel that instruction if you like."

Katherina forced calmness on her voice. "Yes," she said. "I would like to cancel the instruction." Her heart quickened with anger and a little fear. Was it merely incompetence, or something more insidious? Whichever it was, the night boy obviously had nothing to do with it. "Do you have a copy of the messages, or at least the names?"

Clearly embarrassed, the young man bit his lip and rummaged among papers on the counter. "Uh, no. I'm sorry. As I mentioned, we gave them to Mr. Raspin. He said he would take care of them. Can you…uh…contact *him* about the messages?"

Katherina's anger grew. She did not even know what hotel Gregory Raspin was staying in and thus could not reach him. He had isolated her and for the moment she could do nothing about it. She would not be able to confront him until she saw him on the Brocken, and that might not be until after the performance. It was infuriating.

The young man suddenly brightened. "Oh, but look. Something arrived separately this afternoon, after Mr. Raspin passed by." He held out a carton in brown paper, the size of a shoebox. The mysterious package that Charlotte had forwarded from Salzburg.

Placated, Katherina accepted his contrition. "Thank you, Herr…" She read his nametag. "Herr Dubchek. But in future, please be sure to give all my phone messages to me and me alone."

"Of course, Madame Marow. I'll also inform the day manager when he arrives."

It was still long before dawn when she returned to her room, but with the bedside light on and a surprise package waiting to be opened, the night seemed friendlier. She tore open the outside wrapping from Charlotte's office, uncovering the smaller package that was inside. She still couldn't tell what it contained. It was tied in ribbon with the name of some Salzburg shop imprinted on it. She had no scissors and so she untied the knot, delaying gratification, then removed the lid.

She stared at the object bedded in tissue paper, trying to make sense of it. Was it a joke, a gift from a fan, a mistake? She lifted out the doll and examined it. It was clothed in a broad sweeping coat, a sort of royal cloak or mantle, in ice blue. White fur ran from collar to hem and along the edges of the long dropped sleeves. Embroidered all over the icy blue satin of the cloak were tiny snowflakes. Under the cloak the doll wore white satin trousers and over them high boots made of felt. Valenki.

Katrina felt a sudden rush of pleasure as it dawned on her what she held. And yet, what did it mean? It had been sent weeks before, and since that time there had been no other word. Still. An hour before she had seemed to be in free fall, and now she had something to hold on to. She could almost hear the rich mezzo voice reminiscing about "the symbol for our perfect world, the world of our dreams."

A warm blanket of hope enveloping her, she lay down again on the bed and let herself fall asleep with the doll tucked in her arm, Anastasia's gift of the Snow Maiden.

XXXI
Walpurgisnacht

The overture had begun and Katherina stood with the orchestra behind the Witches' Altar, but already she sensed that something was not right. The invited listeners at the dress rehearsal had waited in respectful silence until they understood what was expected of them. But the new crowd kept up a low, persistent murmur, and they smelled of sweat.

The audience buzz subsided as the overture concluded and Mephisto climbed the Witches' Altar to sing the Prolog in Heaven.

Behind the rock cluster, Katherina could not see the audience, but she could hear that there was no applause. There should have been, and its absence was ominous. Were they bored? A terrible thought. Boredom was a gaping maw that could swallow up the whole performance.

A sudden "whuuupf!" and the sound of crackling signaled that the fire in the pit had been ignited. Overhead sparks shot up through the opening in the roof. Hundreds of voices murmured approval. Good, the audience was on their side again.

At her cue, Katherina emerged from behind the rock for her Envy ensemble, and she saw for the first time who made up the audience. She all but gasped.

By the flickering light of the great bonfire she saw only men. Not just men, but soldiers, in two kinds of uniforms, German and Russia. Obviously, a deal had been struck for the Brocken garrison to fill the house. Warmed now by the flames, the theater air carried the smell of them toward her: cigarettes, sweat, and alcohol, the smell of a beer hall.

She was about to sing the opening night of a world premiere to men in sweaty fatigues. The cameras seemed to be taking note of them too, at least the two that she could see, for they swept across the width of the hall, recording their mass.

Composing herself, she sang her part mechanically, through Envy and Sloth, while the sullen men all around her began to sway slightly with the music. Was it a sign that the men were willing to play along? She couldn't tell yet. Probably no one could tell. They were in uncharted waters.

Gluttony was the turning point, when Katherina realized that not just rowdiness, but danger was in the air. The dancers threw doughnuts over the heads of the soldiers and, instead of eating them, the men caught them and tossed them back, pelting the stage performers. At the same time, it seemed like everyone was drinking from little whiskey bottles. The food fight, which had been so innocent in dress rehearsal, took on aggressiveness as the doughnuts were returned with force. Something sticky hit her on the shoulder and she smelled that it was one of the pastries soaked in whiskey. Her big aria for Pride was next and she had no idea what to expect.

She waited again near the orchestra while the dancers built their pyramid on the rock. Mephisto offered his hand and lifted her up to kneel on them. Singing her Pride aria from the top of the slippery mound, she watched the swaying mass on the other side of the fire. It seemed to watch her back, not amused, but predatory. Was it her imagination, or did some of the faces grimace and make lewd expressions at her?

She turned her attention to the pyramid that heaved beneath her with the rhythm of the music. Three of the five bodies were audience members, and they reacted perceptively to her touch. The huge bonfire had heated the entire rock cluster they were on, and everyone's skin was slick with sweat. When she gripped one of the men by his shoulder, he arched his back, causing her to lose her balance and regain it only after spreading her knees wide. "Jawohl!" someone called out from the audience.

At the end of the Pride aria, the staging called for her to flash open her shirt. It had elicited playful shouts at dress rehearsal, even though the filmy undergarment had covered her. Katherina hesitated, but obviously people were planted in the audience who knew what should happen next, and they started the chanting, "Take it off, take it off."

Hoping that the undergarment would signal that the nudity was only pretended, she opened her shirt to the audience. The crowd roared approval and some men pulled off their own shirts.

One more sin done, she thought. Now it was Greed. Katherina climbed down from the human pyramid for the next ensemble. Although she had rehearsed the scene mingling with the swaying audience members, she decided to stay close to the central rocks. But before she had ventured even a few meters, the emboldened audience came to her. Drunken men surrounded her, clapping and grunting so loudly that she could barely hear the orchestra. She tried to keep her composure, but the lyrics of the song were dangerously provocative. *"Give it to me, give it to me; I want it all,"* she sang, and the soldiers were suddenly roaring with her, full throated, grasping their crotches.

Still bravely singing, Katherina brushed away groping hands and worked her way back to the rock. As she stepped up to the platform only slightly above the audience floor, she caught sight of Sabine, who didn't seem perturbed at all. She danced from soldier to soldier, encouraging any touch. One of the cameras was filming the interaction while the others still pointed toward the stage.

After an orchestra passagio, Wrath began. Now thoroughly frightened, Katherina sang her part from the safety of the rock, letting the huge Matti mingle with the dangerously excited audience. But he too seemed nervous, and where at dress rehearsal he had pushed and shoved people, he now just prodded them gently. Too late, for the element of playfulness was gone. The soldiers continued chanting, supported by the orchestra, but they were clearly becoming hostile. In place of the words the soloists had given them, they chanted curses invented on the spot. Gradually they drove the huge bass back to the safety of the rocks behind the fire pit.

Seemingly oblivious to the heavily charged atmosphere in the hall, the orchestra segued into the sin of Lust. With the change of music, the soldiers stopped cursing and began to clap again in rhythm. But now more of them were shirtless and they shoved one another, vying for a better view of what was happening on the rock.

Lust required another hint of disrobing, but Katherina was too fearful and she played the scene covered, remaining on the stage. Still fearless, the four witch dancers mingled with the audience, led by Sabine naked to the waist. Half a dozen bare-chested soldiers reached for the women and danced, pressing them from behind. None of them seemed to mind. Then Katherina understood why. They all were drunk.

Without pause, the orchestra modulated into the *Dies Irae* theme and Gustav appeared, perfectly on cue, as if emerging from the fire, all the cameras directed at him. Raising his scythe to gather in the Sins, he began his dance of death. With only the slightest direction from the dancers, dozens of drunken and shirtless soldiers joined the line. Lurching and stomping, but more or less in rhythm, the human centipede snaked around the hall and back to the bonfire, followed by the cameras. The entire mass of people now was in motion and in various stages of undress. Above them on the highest rock of the Witches' Altar, Katherina waited for Mephisto to join her for the final aria.

He handed off his scythe and leapt to her side, his eyes red against the dead white of his makeup. His gestures were larger, more dramatic than before, and she guessed he was just as glad as she was that they were at the end. Skating at the edge of danger they had delivered the opera, bringing the unruly audience to a near frenzy. This would be the climax. She inhaled deeply, found her pitch, and, suffused by both fear and dizzying excitement, she began her aria.

"Es wird Tag! Der letzte Tag! Der Hochzeittag!" she sang, full out.

"Die Glocke ruft! Krack, das Stäbchen bricht!" Someone dropped something into the fire and it blazed suddenly higher.

"Es zuckt in jedem Nacken die Schärfe, die nach meinem zuckt! Die Glocke!"

Mephisto grasped her roughly by the shoulders. *"Meine Pferde schaudern…"* At the mention of horses, he straddled her. *"Der Morgen dämmert auf!"*

Mephisto took hold of her around her chest and as she prepared to sing the final phrase, he turned her and pressed her onto her back. What was he doing? She had another line to sing, the final ecstatic climax of Marguerite's surrender, but she had to be able to get up again on her knees to sing it. Mephisto knew that, but he didn't just kneel over her while he sang his own line, as rehearsed. He pinned her down by her arms while the electrified audience swarmed up onto the rock. She lay, bewildered and panicky. What was happening? The cameras were running and the performance had to somehow be brought to a conclusion. But now, she feared for herself.

The chorus sang full-throated, the orchestra continued fortissimo, and chanting men clambered up all around her. Suddenly Mephisto fell sideways and someone else was on top of her, thrusting against her, sucking her breast through the fabric of the shirt. Katherina thrashed. Hands grabbed her ankles and knees and forced her legs apart, tearing at her costume.

The soldier on her chest was heavy and stank of sweat and alcohol, and after a few thrusts of his hips she could feel his erection on her thigh. She struggled beneath him. Someone's hands fumbled at her groin, trying to pull away her underwear and expose her to his penetration. The fabric tore and she could feel his naked member pushing, trying to find entrance.

Panicked, she summoned her last strength. With the only defense she had left, she bit her assailant in the throat. He recoiled, clutching at the wound, and she wrestled out from under him. Scraping hands and knees, she scrabbled down from the rock, her costume torn. She staggered through the crowd, which seemed demented now from the ear-splitting *"Dies irae, dies illa"* of the oblivious chorus and orchestra.

Hands reached out from everywhere to grasp her. Twice she was fully embraced, mouths pressed on her throat or breast, but she scratched and bit her way free and managed to stay on her feet. Some of the men stumbled after her out of the circle, still grasping at her, and she fell, finally, onto the freezing ground.

Something large loomed in front of her, lit by one of the torches. A Soviet soldier, drunker and uglier than the others, gangly and with a huge hooked nose. And this one held a rifle. Shivering with cold and near hysteria, she tried to pull herself up, but was jolted back to her knees as he shot his rifle into the air. The men scrabbling behind her immediately retreated, but by then Gregory Raspin had appeared at her side. For a moment he and the rifleman glared at each other, until Raspin snarled, "Get out of the way," and the gunman retreated. Raspin helped her to her feet.

"The military police are arriving. Everything will be under control in a moment. Please, come back to the rock," he said softly. "You'll be warm and safe there."

Stunned, she let herself be led back, clutching her torn costume around her. He led her down the gauntlet of silent men, toward the fire pit. The crowd was tense and sullen, but the near riot, it seemed, was over.

Raspin drew her gently back onto the rock, though after the first step, she balked. What was the point? There was nothing left to perform. She wanted only to get off the Brocken altogether. But he gripped her hand harder, refusing to let go, and drew her up.

"The aria, you never finished it," he bent down toward her and whispered, his eyes red from the smoke and fire. "Sing it. You were paid to sing it. The cameras are still filming." He took the last step onto the high flat rock of the Witches' Altar and with a final yank brought her forcefully up next to him. She cowered for a moment, fearful and exhausted.

"Sing it once, for me, and then it will be over." Raspin picked up one of the gauntlets that Gustav had discarded and put it on. He glanced upward at the cameras and signaled the conductor who, amazingly, was still in place. The orchestra gave the first chord. E-flat major. Like the *Rosenkavalier* trio, she thought, absurdly. The audience, still drunk, was curiously subdued, as if waiting to see what would happen. "Come on," he coaxed, and sang her first line for her in a soft falsetto. "Day is dawning. My judgment day... "

She sang along with him at half volume, though her throat was now tight and tears ran down her face. Raspin stopped singing then, and she continued weakly. "The blades cut into every neck, into my neck too. I hear the bell..."

Raspin then spoke Mephisto's line, in a toneless whisper. "You can hear my horses waiting, look, the day is dawning." He reached out as if toward the rising sun. Something dropped from the glove into the fire, causing it to suddenly blaze up high. She recoiled from the heat, looking for escape. A single shot rang out and a bright red spot appeared at the center of his forehead. His gloved hand dropped to his side and he toppled into the raging fire.

XXXII
Allegro Furioso

K atherina scrambled down from the rock. She heard the panicked shouting of the other cast members and the orchestra players knocking over their music stands as they fled. Other guns went off somewhere on the periphery. Crouching at the foot of the Witches' Altar over the fire pit, Katherina glimpsed the limp form of Gregory Raspin. His hair had already burned off and flames crept along his clothing toward his impassive face. The inebriated onlookers closed in a tight circle around the pit, but no one tried to help him.

Horror-struck and nauseous, Katherina elbowed her way again away from the fire. The crowd of men, transfixed by the immolation, was no longer interested in her. In a moment, she was outside the ring of torches. More soldiers were pouring in from the direction of the barracks. Military police, she thought, relieved. But she had only one concern now, to get out of the melee and off the mountain. She rushed toward her dressing room in the shed, flinging the door shut behind her, even before she turned on the light. Once the door bolt slammed into its groove she flicked the light switch.

A uniformed figure stepped into the middle of the room. A Soviet soldier. She caught the briefest glimpse of his cap before she spun around again and tugged frantically at the door she had just locked. Better to face the military police than a rapist.

A hand reached over her shoulder to brush her fingers off the lock. "Katherina," a familiar voice said. "Stop. It's me."

The illogic of the situation paralyzed her. "What?" Her hand, pale-knuckled, still pulled at the door handle.

"It's me," the voice repeated as she released the handle and turned around, incredulous. The military cap lifted off and a familiar, faintly Slavic face with mist-gray eyes came into focus. Only the short hair delayed recognition for a moment.

"Anastasia! How—"

"I'm so sorry. I was trying to save you from Raspin but I got here too late."

Anastasia stepped close and touched Katherina on the cheek. "He was planning to have you assaulted, or worse, for his last great opus. But you must know that by now. How did you get away?"

"He's dead. Someone shot him. I don't know who. He was sort of crazy at the end. Radu Gavril too. I think they *wanted* the audience to go wild. When they assaulted me, no one helped." Katherina relived the fear, tears erupting as she talked. Anastasia took the cloak from its hook and draped it around Katherina's bare shoulders. "No, of course not. That was the plan."

Katherina's words poured out in a flood. "I tried to escape, I made it out of the crowd, but Raspin dragged me back to sing his damned aria. He dropped something into the fire that made it blaze up. That's when someone shot him and he fell into the pit. Oh, Anastasia. He burned, and no one even tried to pull him out."

"It was all for his film, dear. He had to make everyone a little savage for that. Obviously it backfired on him."

Katherina sobbed for a moment in Anastasia's embrace. Then she calmed and questions crowded in. "*His* film? I thought it was for the DDR. And how did *you* get here? Why are you dressed this way?"

"It's a long story. I'll tell you on the way down the mountain. Now let's get out of here."

"Yes, of course. Let me just get dressed. There's a steam train at eleven. If they let us all go—"

"I can't go with you. You know, I'm here illegally. If I'm seen, I'll be arrested. That's the reason for the costume."

"Oh, I forgot." For a moment, Katherina was at a loss. "What should we—?"

Someone pounded at the door. "Kommandant Exner here," a voice said. "Open up. I have military police with me."

Anastasia raised one hand, signaling "silence," and stepped back into the bathroom.

Katherina opened the door to the garrison commander. Two soldiers stood behind him with carbines across their chests. Was he here to offer her safe conduct to the train? She hoped so.

"Fräulein Marow. I'm afraid I must ask you to accompany me to my office for questioning."

"Questioning? What for? I've just been battered and assaulted by your men. All I want to do right now is leave the Brocken, safely. I was hoping you might—"

"Leave the Brocken? I'm afraid that's out of the question. A man has just burned to death and you were the only person standing near him."

"What?" Katherina was speechless. Then, "*Of course* I was on the rock with him. He dragged me back there, forced me to continue his grotesque aria. Then someone shot him. You can see it yourself. You have it all on film."

Exner averted his eyes. "Unfortunately not. The cameras were turned off when the riot began. But you will have a chance to tell your side of the story in the interrogation." He appeared to finally notice her state of undress as she huddled under her cape. "I will give you a moment to put on some clothes. Then please come out. My men will accompany you to my office."

"All right. Just give me a few minutes." Katherina closed the door and threw the flimsy lock again. Anastasia stepped out of hiding.

"You're *not* going back with him," she whispered. "Once the news of what happened gets out, he'll have hell to pay. He'll throw you to the wolves to avoid a court martial." Anastasia ran to the window on the other side of the room and yanked it open.

"Good, they didn't send a guard to the back. They must have assumed you'd go quietly. We have maybe three minutes to get to the wall. Never mind dressing. Here, just take your pass." She snatched up the shoulder bag that had hung over the chair back and laid the straps over Katherina's head. Leaving Katherina to follow, she threw one leg over the windowsill and struggled through the opening.

Hesitating only a second, Katherina fastened her cape at the throat and hurried after her.

For some five hundred meters they were on open ground, but the moonless sky gave no light, and Katherina could barely make out the dark form of Anastasia slightly ahead of her. There was no sound of pursuit.

In a few minutes, they confronted the row of high concrete slabs that formed the security wall. Katherina stopped abruptly. Panic seized her as she heard the dogs.

Anastasia dropped to her knees. Thinking she had stumbled, Katherina reached over to help her up.

"No, not me. Take hold of this."

Katherina felt cold metal—the rung of a ladder, invisible in the dark grass. How simple it now seemed. But could they do it fast enough? She could already see the flashlights of the men searching the rear of the shed they had just been in.

The ladder was aluminum, not heavy, but its length made it unwieldy. They struggled for agonizing seconds before getting it upright and laying it against the wall. "Go!" Anastasia commanded in a harsh whisper.

"I have to jump off the other side?" Katherina imagined broken ankles.

"No. Straddle the wall at the top until I get there."

Katherina scrambled up the ladder and swung her leg over the top of the slab. The rough concrete added another abrasion to the inside of her thigh. She curled forward, holding herself with pressure from her knees, sweating inside her cloak.

Anastasia appeared seconds later, then swung herself onto the wall. Taking a quick breath, she grasped the top rung. "Help me haul it up," she grunted, and together they dragged the long metal ladder over the top and slid it down the other side. Checking first that the ladder was well anchored, Anastasia threw herself onto it and descended.

Katherina was suddenly blinded by a flashlight beam. She heard a gunshot and the ping of a bullet striking the concrete just in front of her knee. With a sudden absurd recollection of Tosca's operatic end, she flung herself off the wall, grasping the ladder in both arms, and managed to half slide, half clamber down a few rungs before jumping. More gunshots sounded from the other side of the wall as well as the cursing of the thwarted guards who ran along the concrete barrier to the gate.

"This way," Anastasia said, and set off at full speed toward a line of trees. They had gained precious minutes but the dogs would be tracking by smell, and Katherina had no idea how to escape them.

Her throat was parched and her chest ached from the full-out run.

Even her tiny shoulder bag seemed a burden, as it knocked against her hip with every step. Under the trees there was almost no light, only the alternating vertical patches of dark and less dark and the black form of Anastasia that threaded a way through them.

The sound of dogs baying came again. More of them now. Katherina remembered them in their cages, savage, always hungry. Glancing back, she saw spots of light from half a dozen flashlights sweeping the tree line.

Anastasia halted suddenly, appeared to take her bearings, then pivoted sharply toward the left. Katherina followed, winded, with no strength left to ask why. Their change in direction seemed a mistake as they emerged from the tree cover to an exposed ridge.

Out of breath, Katherina threw her head back, gulping in air. Cruelly, when mist might have hidden them, the mountain-top air was crystal clear. The night sky held countless stars in a swath that swept southwest to northeast.

More important to watch their own feet, so as not to stumble. But below them, the ground dropped away sharply into a steep ravine. The beginning of a footpath was faintly visible where it led downward into the obscure depths. A hiking path, probably, from more innocent days.

"Is that where we're going?" Katherina managed between pants.

"No. Up there." Anastasia pointed in the opposite direction, to another ridge. They would have to climb again. Katherina could see huge granite rocks, gathering starlight.

"There's a van waiting…somewhere…that direction," Anastasia forced out between ragged breaths. "But we need to get…farther away…so they don't hear the motor."

Katherina understood. If the border guards still thought she was alone and on foot, they'd keep searching the mountain, at least for a while. But if they heard a vehicle, they'd block the roads. "But how? The dogs are following our smell." She corrected herself. "No, only my smell. They don't know you're here."

Bracing herself against the cold, she opened her sweat-damp cloak and let it drop from her shoulders. Then, rolling it up into a tight ball, she flung it out over the ravine and it disappeared into the darkness. The sound of barking dogs came again through the frigid air, echoing slightly.

"Very clever." Anastasia had started off again. "As long as we're moving, you should be all right. It's not much farther, I think."

The way became steep and they were soon on their hands and knees again. The rocks were icy cold and the soil between them clammy. Bruised and exhausted, Katherina stopped again for breath. The pursuers were below them now and their flashlights revealed them descending into the ravine toward the still-warm coat. Relieved, but shivering again, she resumed the arduous climb.

"I'm sorry, darling. It's only a few more minutes," Anastasia encouraged, and the word "darling" gave Katherina a surge of energy. "Whose van?" she whispered as they crested another ridge and dropped down on the other side. "And how do you know where it is?"

"I don't, but I have this." Anastasia slipped a tiny penlight from the pocket of her uniform and directed it toward the line of trees below them. She made X-patterns in the air, once, twice, three times, then clicked the light off. A moment later, a tiny light among the trees signaled with an O, also three times, then extinguished.

"That's it. We've found him." Anastasia seized Katherina's hand and pulled her toward the signal.

"Him? Who's down there?"

"Long story," Anastasia panted as they neared the cluster of pines. They were thicker now, their resin pungent. Still Katherina saw no sign of life until they arrived under a cluster of trees and she spotted the rear of a minivan. It was identical to those used by the technicians at the Brocken transmission station. Anastasia clicked on the penlight again. Yes, there it was, stenciled in black on camouflage green, *Fernsehen der DDR*.

A man stepped out from behind the vehicle. "Finally. I was about to leave without you," he grumbled, obviously agitated. Without waiting for introductions, he yanked open the cab door and helped Katherina inside. There was a blanket folded behind the seat and he opened it for her. She took it gratefully, still wondering who he was.

The stranger hurried to the driver's side while Anastasia got in beside her and then they were moving. Without headlights, they could only creep along downhill in low gear.

"Katherina, this is Johann."

"Ah" was all she could think of saying. Knowing the man's name did little to dispel her fear and bewilderment, but it seemed unwise to demand an explanation at just that moment. Every lurch told her they were on a steep and precarious slope, and she had no idea how he managed to keep from crashing in the darkness. She could make out the trees, but not the rocks, and the vehicle heaved and tilted wildly each time they ran over one. If they capsized, which the van threatened to do once or twice, she wondered how far they would tumble and how much noise they would make.

They rocked sideways and lurched forward for some fifteen minutes before they dropped onto a narrow gravel service road. Johann exhaled audibly as the level of incline reduced to near horizontal. They might still be shot, but now they would not tumble to their deaths.

Though still without headlights, the van picked up speed and the driver relaxed visibly. "What took so long?" he said, finally. "I was sure they'd got you."

"A lot of the unexpected," Anastasia replied. "Raspin was shot. To death, it looks like. And then he burned. All hell broke loose. Then, when things began to settle and I reached Katherina, the commander showed up to arrest her. He backed off so she could get dressed, and that's when we made the break. The ladder worked perfectly, by the way. Will they be able to trace it back to you?"

"Naa. I took it out of old storage. They don't even know what's down there. But once we get off the mountain, we've got to make up for lost time. I have to have the truck back in place and refueled before dawn."

"Can I ask now to what I owe this rescue? And how did you both know I was in trouble?" Katherina judged it was the moment for explanations.

"Don't ask me," Johann grumbled. "I'm doing this because I'm bloody nuts."

"He's doing this because he's an old friend of Boris," Anastasia said. "From the Eastfront days, right?"

"Yes. We worked together for the Ministry of Propaganda filming Wehrmacht victories. Regular Leni Riefenstahls, we were. I stayed in filming and Boris decided he could make more money in sound. Seems he was right."

Katherina was warming to her rescuer. "Why didn't you move west after the war? There was a lot more work with the Americans."

"Not a chance." He spat out the window. "I'm from Dresden. My family was there, plus all our relatives from the east. Refugees. They died in the firestorm. You can imagine how. After that I never wanted to shake hands with an American or Brit. Still don't," he added quietly, the rage in his voice obviously undiluted by time.

Katherina moved away from the dangerous subject of Dresden. "But I still don't know why you thought I needed to be rescued in the first place. Even I didn't know how crazy Gregory Raspin was until I was up on the rock with him facing a wall of flames."

"Flames, eh? That sounds like the sort of theatrical touch he would like," Johann said, full of contempt. "Looks like this one blew up in his face, so to speak. It was a fitting end. I hope they got it all on film."

"How can you say that?" Katherina was shocked at the remark. "That's so callous. He might have been unbalanced, but he didn't deserve to be murdered. I feel sorry for him."

"Don't." Anastasia joined the conversation again. "The man was vile. You have no idea what he used to do and what he was attempting to do to you."

"What are you talking about?"

"That's what I was trying to rescue you from. Gregory Raspin used to be Peter Schalk, a sadist and a murderer."

"Schalk? The man my father wrote about in his journal? How do you know?"

"Boris put the two together. When I translated the pages from Cyrillic and told him about Schalk, he insisted that he'd seen the man in Salzburg outside your dressing room."

"How is that possible? They're from two different worlds." Katherina pulled the blanket up closer around her, fending off new, incomprehensible information.

"Believe me, it's true. We checked the Salzburg anniversary program that has his picture. Boris was absolutely certain it was Schalk. You won't doubt it either when you hear the story."

"Of Gregory Raspin? You already told me he was a big investor."

"Yes, that's what he did with the money he acquired in the 1950s. After the war, while he was Peter Schalk, he not only ran a large black-market network, he also made pornographic films. Not the usual fare, but films involving torture and murder. Not faked murder, but real. At least in one or two cases, anyhow."

"The kind of creepy shit that makes me ashamed to be a man," Johann grumbled.

Anastasia went on. "The way Boris told it, the business started almost accidentally, when the Russians invaded Germany. I'm sure you've heard about the raping and the nailing of women to barn doors. Apparently at least once, someone made a film of it, and it was passed around before some Soviet officers found it and destroyed it. But Schalk evidently thought torture was a product he could sell, and he was right. He had women kidnapped, isolated women with no one who would track them down, and he found soldiers who were happy to accommodate him for the rape. With a little extra vodka, he'd have no trouble getting them to do the killing too. The woman belonged to the enemy, after all. The films became more and more sadistic, more and more gruesome, and all of them found audiences. Western troops, especially, paid a lot of money to see them. It excited them and at the same time made them feel superior to the Russian 'animals.'"

Reflexively, Katherina drew up her knees inside her blanket. "But how did Boris know about them?"

"Boris made the soundtracks for them, all through the 1950s. He swears he recorded the tracks on order, without ever seeing any of the films. I mean, he knew it was pornography and assumed it was the ordinary variety. He made tracks of music, non-musical sound, moans, and so forth. Schalk never asked for sounds for the torture scenes. Maybe that part was silent, I don't know. It sickens me to think about it."

"Then how did he find out? Wouldn't he have wanted to see the final product?"

"That isn't how it worked in those days. He said he found out by accident when he heard about a showing at a place called Auerbach's Cellar. He was curious to see how the film turned out, so he simply paid to go in and watch it. He said when the film, which was obviously amateurish, got to the end, he nearly threw up. Right after that, he broke all ties with Schalk."

"Why didn't he call the police?"

"I asked him that too, but he pointed out that he couldn't. After all, he was implicated in the production. All he could do was walk away. Like your father did."

"My father was involved in that?" Katherina could not keep the revulsion from her voice.

"No, not with the films. I don't mean to suggest that. But he was part of Schalk's general network. The team doctor. Eventually he must have also found out about the murders and the children, but he was just as unable to notify the police as Boris was. More so, since he was homosexual and faced certain jail time for that. And Schalk could be vindictive. Your father had to have courage to even walk away."

"So that was going on in the 1950s, in the part of the journal that was torn out."

"Yes, almost certainly by Raspin. He must have had an opportunity to pilfer the book. In any case, by the 1960s, with his network threatening to unravel, Schalk gave up the business. He had a fortune by then, of course, and invested it in the New Germany."

"But why this opera then? Why me?"

Anastasia took her hand. "This was his magnum opus. Not a grainy black-and-white smuggled into basements for drunks, but a full opera in color, with an authentic setting, fire, and a famous high-class victim who would go along with the whole thing until it was too late. And it would be broadcast to millions all over Germany. Pornography as high art."

"But he was known as the producer. He would have been arrested, ruined."

"Not at all. First of all, if it had ended in gang rape, that alone would have made it a success. He couldn't be held responsible for the behavior of drunken soldiers, especially Russian soldiers who already have the reputation. It would have shown up in the papers as 'a terrible accident.' He would have acted shocked and horrified, and the film would have been worth its weight in gold."

"But the DDR would never have released it, in that case. Besides, the commandant said the Fernsehen DDR cameras had been turned off."

Johann spoke up. "He was probably lying, to cover his troops, but even if they had shut them off or destroyed the footage, Raspin had a fourth camera of his own. My office lent him a cable for it. He would have enjoyed a certain notoriety for a while, claiming that he had 'misjudged the savagery of his audience,' and then begun marketing the film through some third party."

"It's grotesque," Katherina said weakly.

Anastasia nodded. "I think that's why your father refused to introduce you to Raspin. He suspected that he planned to use you in some awful way."

"But why? He didn't need the money anymore."

"Money wasn't the reason," Johann added. "I only talked with the man a couple of times but I could see he was really obsessed. This 'ultimate-opera' project was the realization of some sick fantasy he'd carried around for years."

Katherina was silent for a long while, shivering again. Anastasia fussed with the blanket, tucking the edges under Katherina's legs. "There's something else I have to tell you. I don't know if it will bring you any peace, but one of Schalk's businesses after the war, when he was still trading black-market goods, was selling war souvenirs. Objects from both sides: SS uniforms, concentration-camp objects, medals, passbooks, and most of all, small arms, both Nazi and Red Army. He specialized in sidearms, like the pistol that killed your father." Anastasia paused, to let the implication sink in.

"I don't think your father committed suicide at all. It probably was not even his gun. I believe Schalk murdered him after he refused to let him meet you. Schalk simply forced him outside at gunpoint, thinking to avoid being heard by the housekeeper, and shot him in the garden."

Tears filled Katherina's eyes. "Murder makes much more sense. There simply was no good reason for suicide, even if he was homosexual. After all those years, he didn't have to fear blackmail any longer. Yes, I'm sure we can prove it now." She stared for a while through the windshield, not seeing. "Imagine. My father, who called himself a coward, lost his life trying to protect me."

"I'm sure you're right," Anastasia said. "The police just never considered investigating for murder. Unless Raspin's body is completely charred, they could get prints and match them with the gun. It seems unlikely, though, that the Vopos will cooperate with the West-German police."

"So why are we running away? Why can't we just explain everything to the garrison commander?"

"Ha," Johann snorted. "Do you think for a moment anyone in the DDR government will admit they were tricked into signing a business agreement with a sadist, to broadcast a gang rape and possible murder? Anyhow, now that he's dead and someone in the DDR's own border guard apparently killed him, you can be sure the evidence will disappear."

"How filthy it all is. You're right. I just want to get out of here."

"That's the idea." Johann finally turned on the headlights and pressed the pedal to the floor.

XXXIII
Accelerando

Katherina was grainy-eyed with exhaustion when they reached Wernigerode, but the clock on the dashboard of the van read only a little before two in the morning. They had arrived with time to spare at the featureless concrete building that was their destination. The metallic sign across the top row of windows read *Fernsehen DDR/ Wernigerode*. There was no sign of life anywhere around the building when they pulled into the lot behind it.

When she and Anastasia descended from the service van, Johann was taciturn and businesslike, waving off their thanks.

"Just tell Boris we're quit now. I don't want any more of this." With that he drove into a garage to park the van and remove all evidence of the night's undertaking.

"The car's over there." Anastasia pointed toward a dark blue rental car parked half a block away from the television substation. "There's a change of clothes for both of us in the trunk."

The night-quiet of the street was suddenly broken by the sound of a truck engine. Before the two women could get out of sight, a military truck swung around a corner and rumbled toward them. They froze, caught in the truck's headlights.

Katherina muttered, "Scheisse." Her mind raced as she tried to think of a plausible explanation as to why a Soviet soldier and a half-naked woman in a blanket would be standing in the middle of the street at two in the morning. There was none. None whatsoever. Her instinct was simply to run, but Anastasia took hold of her arm.

"They're Russians. Let me do the talking."

Katherina frowned. "No argument here," she muttered back. "Your uniform. Are you an officer, or what?"

"I have no idea. This is one of Anne's costumes. Let's just hope it's dark enough so they don't notice." Anastasia adjusted her cap and tugged her tunic down over her hips.

The truck stopped directly in front of them and they both moved around to the side of it, out of the blinding headlights. Katherina could see now it was a Soviet troop carrier. The motor continued pounding noisily even in neutral, and the gray-painted fender, which rose almost to her shoulder, was slightly dented. At the rear, the truck bed was enclosed by low wooden siding. Poles at the four corners held a canvas roof that was rolled up, and some dozen men in field kit sat huddled beneath it. Most of them seemed to be hanging over one side staring at them.

The driver poked his head out through the truck-cab window and Anastasia saluted him. Katherina fervently hoped it was the right kind of salute. The two began talking in a rapid Russian and Katherina tried to detect signs of anger or suspicion. Would there be any point in running from twelve men with service rifles?

Anastasia's voice had dropped to a lower register, below the pitch she had used for Octavian, but still high for a mature man. Would she be able to pull it off? What could she possibly be saying that would explain them?

Oh, hell. The driver was opening the cab door, stepping down onto the ground. He was dressed almost identically to Anastasia, except that he had a sidearm. A critical difference. He gawked for a moment at Katherina, and she realized, for the first time since fleeing the Brocken dressing room, that she was still in full stage makeup. Half naked and painted like a clown, she must have looked like a madwoman to him.

Anastasia seemed to realize the problem as well and laid her hand on the man's shoulder, turning him away from the bizarre spectacle and guiding him toward the street corner. Was she giving Katherina a chance to flee in the other direction? She waited for a signal, anything that would tell her what to do. But Anastasia simply continued in Russian, gesticulating and pointing up the street.

When the two returned to the truck, they seemed to be arguing, though without anger. The driver kept repeating, "Nyet, nyet!" and Katherina's heart began to pound again, ready for flight.

But whatever was wrong, it did not involve attack or arrest, and though the driver was still agitated, he climbed back into the truck cab and put the engine into gear. In a moment, the truck had turned around, leaving Katherina in full view of the soldiers squatting in the wooden truckbed. One of them called out something, and then all of the soldiers joined him in their calls. She recognized only one word: *suka*. Bitch. She didn't mind the seemingly automatic hostility. As long as the word was not preceded by "Someone should arrest that…"

Then, mercifully, the truck pulled away and rumbled up the street they had just come with Johann ten minutes before.

"What just happened?" Katherina asked.

Anastasia guided her over to the blue Mercedes. "Come on, get in the car where we won't be seen again, and I'll explain." She opened the car trunk and lifted several articles of clothing out of a suitcase. "We can change in the backseat." She handed Katherina a dark skirt and a sweater.

The two of them climbed into the car. Relieved to finally be free of her blanket, Katherina pulled on the sweater first, relaxing into the warmth. The skirt, she noticed, was a bit long. In spite of the urgency of the moment, Katherina chuckled as she rolled it at the waist. "I see. The soprano gets the skirt and the mezzo wears the pants."

"Hey, I just saved our lives out there. It was the toughest trouser role of my career."

"Gods, yes, and you were superb. We both owe Anne a lot for that. Who could have known she'd be accurate enough to fool the real thing."

"Apparently I am a *praporshchik*, a warrant officer. While it's obvious I was in violation of regulations being with a woman on the street alone at two in the morning, I was one rank higher than the soldier in charge of the transport, who was only a *podpraporshchik*. While theoretically he could have reported me, I think I won him over." She slid off the military trousers and pulled on blue jeans. "I had no good excuse ready, so I just suggested they had interrupted me in the middle of something manly, and he was momentarily distracted trying to imagine what you looked like under the blanket."

"Oh, so that was dirty guy-talk you were having with him."

"It started that way, but then I recognized his accent. He was from Leningrad and I got him to talk about that. You know, the two of us, homesick for the Neva and hot Russian women." Anastasia struggled out of the officer's tunic and drew a sweater over her head.

"But you were gabbing there for five minutes. All about Russian women?"

"No, we traded opinions on the subject men talk about everywhere. Sports. I said I'd been away too long and asked if he knew how Zenit, the Leningrad soccer team, was doing and whether Nikolai Larionov was still their top scorer."

"You follow Russian soccer?"

They moved to the front of the car and Anastasia started the motor. "No but Boris does. Zenit is a famous team. Fortunately I just remembered the name Larionov. One of the few times I spent a Sunday in front of the television with him."

"So what were these guys doing here at two in the morning, anyhow? Obviously not on patrol."

"They were lost. They were being transferred from the base at Sperenberg, just south of Berlin, up to the Brocken garrison and they made a wrong turn. Their radio was out too—to give you a sense of the efficiency of the Soviet military—so they couldn't radio for help. They just wandered around looking for someone who could give them directions. I explained the way to him. He was so happy to find someone he could talk to in Russian he didn't seem to care much what I was doing with you. I'm sure he assumed it was something unsavory, but had no interest in confronting me about it. He was already in trouble himself. Still, he may report what he's seen, so we've got to get moving."

"Thank God for male bonding." Katherina shifted focus. "Do you have any cold cream or something similar so I can take off this makeup?"

"Yes, good idea. It was so dark coming down the mountain I never thought about it. There's hand lotion and tissues in my bag."

While they drove, Katherina rubbed a layer of lotion over her face and throat and removed as much as possible of the pancake and mascara. A final washing would have to wait until they were safe and near hot running water. "Okay, then. What now?"

"Now we cross the border. "It'll be risky, crossing at this hour, but it's still our best chance. If we're lucky, the Brocken guards are still stumbling around on the mountain. Tomorrow they'll know for sure you've escaped and they'll have sent out an alert for you at the border. You do have your pass and visa, don't you?"

"Of course. It's the only thing I grabbed from my dressing room. What about you? I thought you were persona non grata in the DDR."

"I am, but I'm carrying a fake passport. It's not a very good one, though. Boris used to deal in those, after the war, but he's lost contact with the people who made them. He had to patch one together from an old counterfeit he still had. So we have to hope no one scrutinizes it too closely. I tried to warn you that I was on my way, but I couldn't get through to you."

"You tried to call me?"

"I did. Several times. I always left my number. But you didn't call back. I thought at first you were angry. Then it occurred to me that Raspin would try to isolate you."

"Good guess, he did isolate me and blocked my messages. But I got your package. My agent forwarded it to me. The doll that you left for me in Salzburg. Very sweet."

"I'm glad you liked it. Though it would have been more to the point if you'd gotten it in Salzburg so you'd have known I didn't dump you. I *had* to leave, but I didn't want you to forget me."

"I never did for a moment. If you only knew."

Anastasia let the remark stay in the air. Katherina wasn't sure whether she wanted to avoid a dangerous subject or was simply exhausted. Katherina was beat too, battle-fatigued both physically and mentally.

They were outside of Wernigerode now and on the highway, alone on the road. "Do you really think Raspin murdered my father?" she asked suddenly.

"Yes, though I doubt we can ever put together the whole story. My guess is that first he tried to denounce your father to the police, for homosexuality, or identity fraud, or both. If so, the issues were probably so trivial and obsolete that the exposure had no effect except to put the government machinery in motion that identified Sergei Marovsky as a survivor of the Battle of Stalingrad. With the possibility of blackmail now removed, your father was free to turn Schalk in to the police at any time."

Katherina stared out the car window, embarrassed. "Do the Cyrillic entries also tell about his being homosexual?"

"Yes, in a very poignant way. You can read the translation as soon as we're safe. Right now, let's decide what to do at the border crossing."

"One obstacle after another," Katherina muttered. "So this is what it feels like to be a fugitive. Which one of us is the bigger liability, I wonder. You, who are wanted for defection, or me, who's wanted for murder?"

"Let's hope the border guards are so enchanted by our pretty faces that they don't stare too long at our documents."

"Let's also hope there are no opera lovers on duty who might recognize us."

Anastasia laughed. "Opera fans on night duty in the backwoods of Sachsen-Anhalt? How likely can that be?"

Jörg Menger slouched against the wall of the guard station at Seesen trying to stay awake. At four in the morning, with nothing to do but paperwork, he kept feeling consciousness slip away. His sergeant was sick and so only two men were on duty, and still nothing for them to do. Seated at the station table, Theo rolled himself another cigarette and leafed through his television magazine. Having contempt for both diversions, and no radio to listen to, Jörg felt stupor encroach again. If he could have gotten away with it, he'd have snatched a nap, but the military had removed all sturdy horizontal surfaces that could be adapted for dozing. Even the worktable was metal, with metal stools rather than wooden chairs, and the unheated station was so cold that he preferred to stand through his shift.

His boredom lifted momentarily when he saw the headlights in the distance. On the other hand, it was his turn to go out into the cold. He zipped up his field jacket to the throat and shouldered his rifle. As military protocol required, Theo watched from inside, the phone to headquarters at one hand and his rifle within reach of the other.

The car pulled up to the barrier and Jörg relaxed immediately. Two women in their thirties. Attractive ones, too. But then he was suspicious. It was almost 2:30 a.m.

"Passports, please," he said, with just the right balance of authority and courtesy, and perused the documents by the light of his flashlight.

He read the name on the first one and stared at the picture. It looked familiar, but the name said nothing to him. The second passport gave him a start. It was a name he recognized, but the impossibility of it being her was so great he was sure it was simply a coincidence. He shone his flashlight on the passport holder on the passenger side, and his jaw dropped. The woman was a little disheveled, but he recognized the face from the newspaper photographs. He couldn't believe his luck.

"You are Katherina Marow?"

"Yes," she said meekly.

"The opera singer?"

"Yes."

It was true! His heart leapt. He had never met an opera singer face-to-face, and now a beautiful and famous one was right there in front of him. He wished he could invite her in for coffee. Her papers seemed in order, but he didn't want to let her go without at least exchanging a few words with her.

"I read about you. You sang Tosca in Berlin, didn't you?"

"Yes, I did," was all she said again. The repetition was getting monotonous and Jörg wished she'd say more. What was the point of meeting an opera singer if she had nothing to say? The encounter would make a good story when he called his mother, but there would not be much to tell. He had to think of a good question to get the singer talking.

"I love opera. My mother sang in a choir and we listen to opera on the radio all the time. Last week they played *Rosenkavalier*. Have you ever sung that one?"

"Yes, last month, in Salzburg." Katherina's voice was very small.

"I've always wanted to go to Salzburg." Jörg persisted, trying to elicit conversation. Why was she so stiff? And who was the other woman?

"It's a nice city," Katherina said.

"Do you sing too?" He shone the flashlight on the driver who seemed paralyzed. Then he recognized her. The famous Russian mezzo-soprano. He nearly fainted; he had two beautiful opera singers in front of him. No one would ever believe him.

"I love *Rosenkavalier*," he said, unable to think of anything better at such an early hour. "Especially the end, you know, the trio. Uh, well,

I guess everyone loves that part." He was beginning to feel foolish, saying stupid things, but he didn't want them to leave. He wanted to invite them in, maybe have his picture taken with them. Something to show his mother and his friends.

"How was the performance?" he asked Anastasia.

"It went very well, thank you." She avoided eye contact with him at first, then abruptly seemed to change her mind, as if suddenly she found him interesting. She glanced up and smiled, and then he knew for sure it was her. She was so beautiful, more than on the covers of the recordings his cousin had smuggled in for him. He was surprised at her short hair, which is why he didn't recognize her at first, but at second glance, he liked it.

"Not everyone likes *Rosenkavalier.* It's an acquired taste," she said, with the warmest, sexiest voice he had ever heard. "It's wonderful that you're such a serious listener. Do you like the other Strauss operas? *Electra*, for example?"

Jörg blinked, speechless that she had actually complimented him. A beautiful and famous opera singer had noticed his existence long enough to say something nice about him, and to ask him a question! He was utterly smitten. Had she invited him to give up everything and flee with them both, to simply sit in their dressing rooms every evening while they went onstage, he would have gone. What had she just asked him? Oh, about Strauss.

"Some Strauss is a bit too modern for my taste," he said. "I prefer Mozart. Do you sing Mozart? Oh, of course you do. What a dumb question."

She continued to smile, engaging him, tugging on his heart. He draped his arm over the roof of the car and leaned his hip against the door and would have loved to settle in for a long chat as between friends.

But it was the middle of the night, they were on their way someplace, and he had a job to do. Ladies, even great ones, respected men for doing their duty. He swept his flashlight over the driver's passport again. Something was wrong. The name didn't go with the woman.

He met her eyes again and she held his glance, her lips opening slightly and hinting at a smile. No woman had ever looked at him with such intensity, such openness. He seemed to fall into her; he had the feeling that, had she been standing in front of him instead of sitting down, she would have allowed him to embrace her.

Somewhere in the distance he heard a telephone ring. The glass front of the guard station was reflected in the rear side window of the car, and without turning around, he saw the figure of his comrade waving at him, signaling wildly. He felt suspended, for just a heartbeat. Then something in him broke, or blossomed, or changed. He handed back the two passports, the real one and the counterfeit one, and raised the barrier.

"Have a nice evening, ladies."

❖

For several minutes the two of them drove in silence, as if talking would set off some alarm and they would be pursued. But when it became clear that no one followed them, relief settled on them like warm air. Katherina was fully awake now, excited by the near disaster they had weathered. The danger was past, she was in West Germany again, with Anastasia, and she had never felt happier.

"So what do we do next? I mean, we're driving west, but I live in Berlin, which is in the other direction. Inconvenient, I realize." Lightheartedness crept into her voice.

Anastasia also seemed a bit giddy at having succeeded in what amounted to heroic rescue. "Yes, I vaguely recall where Berlin is. Right in the heart of the DDR. Don't worry. It's all pretty easy from here. We just drive to Hanover, where we leave this car. If you feel that you need to rest, we can stay in Hanover at the hotel where I was living. But we'll be arriving in the morning, so if you have the strength, we can fly directly from Hanover to Berlin. There's a ten a.m. flight to Tempelhof."

"I'd prefer that. You're doing all the work, after all. If you can hold out, I can. Besides, I want to show you my house, cook you a nice breakfast." Katherina imagined showing Anastasia from room to room, preparing a meal for both of them as if they were a couple, leading her upstairs. Then uncertainty clouded the picture. What would happen in Berlin, she realized, was not at all clear. Murky, even. She inhaled deeply and posed the question she had to ask, but which could ruin everything.

"Boris. So you are reconciled with him now? Has he agreed to the baby?"

"No, just the opposite. We made a different deal. He agreed to help me sneak in and get you out of the DDR."

"And what did *you* agree to?" Katherina held her breath.

"I agreed to give him his divorce."

Katherina felt a guarded joy at the announcement, still new, still fragile. She wanted to be sure she'd heard correctly. "So, you don't have to go right back to him? I mean you can stay in Berlin…for a while?" She was careful not to say "with me."

"Would you like me to? I mean, now that you're rescued, you don't really need me any longer."

"Oh, but I do need you. You can't imagine. I want you to come home with me. Stay with me. Sleep with me." The moment she said the words, warmth spread upward from her sex to her chest, then to her face. The admission was as powerful as their kiss had been, and just as fraught with risk. Had she taken a step too far?

Anastasia let a long agonizing moment pass. "I'd like that too. Although I don't quite know what to do. I mean, the sleeping part. I've never…"

Katherina dared for the first time that night to touch Anastasia's shoulder, then her neck, playing with a lock of hair curled over her ear. "I know what to do. I think." She laughed softly, nervously. "I've thought for months of what it would be like, every moment of it. I've felt a strange and wonderful sort of desire that I never knew before. The kind that makes people write sonnets, I suppose."

"I love you, you know," Anastasia said simply, as if she were talking about the road.

"Oh, God. I hope so."

"But I'm pregnant. You know that. I've left Boris, but I can't mess up your life. I have enough money to support myself and a child."

"Don't talk about messing up my life. You've just given life back to me. And right now I don't want to be with anyone but you. Tonight…" She looked at her watch. "Well, tomorrow morning, I want to be in your arms. I want to feel you, smell, taste your skin, touch you, excite you, lie on, under, next to you. I want to do all the things I've imagined doing since Salzburg."

"I imagined them too. Or tried to."

"Why didn't you let them happen? If I had thought for just a moment you'd let me, I would have come to your room and ravished you."

"I think I knew that and was terrified of it."

"You broke my heart leaving that way, so suddenly."

"I'm sorry. It broke my heart too. But so much was at stake, so many decisions to make. The first was actually the easiest. To not terminate the pregnancy. Then there was Boris. We were never in love, but he was a part of my life. I owed it to him to try to work something out, to give him a chance to be a father. As it turned out, fatherhood was never in his life plans. But you understand, I couldn't make these life decisions on the basis of a kiss on a balcony in the middle of a snowfall. Even if it had also made me want to write sonnets."

"Does he know about our *Rosenkavalier* kiss?"

Anastasia smiled. "*Rosenkavalier* kiss. What a nice word for it. I was still half Octavian that night, wasn't I? The entire evening was operatic. But no, Boris doesn't know about the kiss. He doesn't need to. He'll simply accept that we're together. He has no reason to be jealous, and he likes you, anyhow. If he hadn't alerted me of the danger you were in, and helped me set up this whole operation, you'd still be on the Brocken, who knows in what state."

"I guess I wasted a lot of time disliking him, didn't I?"

"Yes, you did. He's a decent man. He was part of that gangster world in postwar Berlin, but when times got better, he became a better man. You'll see."

"Will I?" Katherina wondered how her future would intersect with that of Boris Reichmann. Then she remembered Anastasia's baby. To her surprise, it filled her with such tenderness that she almost cried.

XXXIV
Adagio et Passionata

It was noon when they arrived at the house on the Schlossstrasse. "That's it," Katherina said, pointing to the red-brick structure just ahead of them. Old trees grew on both sides, and a wall of ivy covered one corner of it like a shawl.

"Your father's house?"

"My house now." *Our house, if you want,* she thought, but didn't dare say. It was too soon to offer marriage.

As they parked the car along the side, two familiar figures emerged from the house to welcome them. Katherina was relieved. The house would be heated and clean and ready to receive company. "Casimira, Tomasz, this is my friend Anastasia Ivanova. Anastasia, these are my… well…family. They took care of my father and lately they've been taking care of me again, too."

"Enchanté, Madame," Tomasz said, grasping Anastasia's hand with cavalier formality. Casimira made a tiny curtsy.

"What's this? You never curtsied for me."

"Ah, but Madame Ivanova is a great lady of the opera stage."

"*I'm* a great lady of the opera stage, too."

Kissing Katherina on her forehead, Casimira remarked, "If you say so, dear."

Next to her, Anastasia murmured comfortingly, "A prophet is without honor in his own house."

"So it would seem."

Thomas lifted Anastasia's suitcase from the trunk and they entered the house. It smelled of fresh bread, Katherina noted with both gratitude and nostalgia. It was as if Casimira had known someone special was arriving.

"The bread is just out of the oven, so you can't touch it until supper. Shall I cook something special tonight, or leave you two on your own?"

"Thank you, Casimira. I think we'll just throw something simple together ourselves. Please don't worry about us."

"Of course, my dears. Call me if you need anything." Then housekeeper and gardener retreated to their own sphere of activity where, Katherina knew, they would stay until summoned. That was what she appreciated most about them, their acute sense of the value of privacy.

"Are you hungry?"

"No, surprisingly, I'm not. But tea might be nice. Then you can show me around."

❖

"This is my father's study." Katherina wandered along the bookshelves. "I've left it as it was the day he died, though I suppose that's rather morbid. I just haven't gotten around to moving anything. Too many concerts." She ran the fingertips of one hand along the edge of a shelf, then found herself at the oaken desk.

Anastasia stood in the doorway, her steaming tea mug in hand. "Is it strange for you to be here, knowing that it all belongs to you now?"

"No, I haven't digested that part yet. But it *is* strange being here with you. Look." She picked up the jacket cover of Berlioz' *Damnation of Faust* with Anastasia's face gazing heavenward. "This seems to be the last thing he listened to." A sudden sense of gratitude washed over her. "Yours was the last kind voice he heard."

"Please put it away. I don't like to think I had anything to do with his sorrow."

Katherina slid the cover back into the bookshelf with the other vinyl records. "None of us did, really. He carried it around inside of himself." She urged Anastasia again toward the doorway. "Let me show you the rooms upstairs."

At the top of the stairs, Katherina pointed toward the left. "That's my father's room. It's spacious and bright, and one of these days I'll use it again. For now, this is my room over here."

Less sunny than the master bedroom, Katherina's room was nonetheless warmly furnished and inviting. Anastasia stood at the center of the room, surveying the walls. A row of shelves on one side held sheet music, histories of opera, libretti, a German-Italian dictionary, a biography of Wagner, a few novels. On the other side stood an upright piano with the score of *Rosenkavalier* open to the "Rose Duet." Next to it, a small wooden desk was comfortably cluttered with letters, papers, and a cup of pencils.

"It suits you, I think, though it doesn't look all that much lived in. Rather like my—well—like Boris' house in Munich."

"Yes, we're vagabonds, aren't we? But we don't have to be." She stopped. Letting the conversation drift farther into future plans would be premature before they had even embraced. Instead, Katherina drew Anastasia toward her. "I have longed for a month to hold you in my arms again."

"I have, too. Please, it's time."

They embraced gently, unhurriedly, kissing softly on necks and cheeks, exploring each other's outlines with arms and hands. There was at first no urgency in their kisses, only great joy in having found their way to one another. Then Katherina's body took over, sending a wave of warmth up from between her legs, the delicious tightness of sexual hunger. Their kisses became harder, more ardent, more invasive, until Katherina broke away, breathing heavily.

"I've waited too long for this to let it be less than perfect. And I will not seduce you in my current squalid state. In the last twenty-four hours, I've sung an opera to savages, been almost raped on a rock and thrown in the snow, then run half-naked for my life down a mountainside. I need a bath."

Anastasia leaned back into the embrace. "You smell of stage makeup and lotion, and other, uh, more natural things. And by now, so do I. Is your bathtub big enough for two?"

With the steaming water pouring into the vast tub, they stood in front of each other. "Please let me do it," Anastasia said, and gently drew Katherina's borrowed sweater over her head.

"Oh, my god. I didn't see it when you dressed in the car. You're covered with bruises. And there's a big abrasion on your back. You must have been in pain all night. Why didn't you tell me?"

Katherina looked down at herself. "It must have happened on the rock, when Gustav and the soldiers were throwing me around. But I don't remember any pain. Just fear. Then you arrived and all I cared about was escaping. I don't think anything's serious, though. Nothing a good washing won't fix."

Anastasia kissed Katherina's wounded back, a safe distance from the torn flesh. "This could become infected, though, and the bruises can get worse if you're not careful. My poor Katherina!"

Katherina turned in her arms. "Oh, I love that," she whispered. "No one has kissed my bruises since my mother."

"What about Casimira?" Anastasia unbuttoned the long skirt at Katherina's hip and let it drop to the bathroom floor. Katherina realized she still wore the underpants that were torn from the onstage assault. She removed them unceremoniously and tossed them into the trash.

"Casimira? No, she arrived when I was twelve. Her kisses were limited to my forehead, and then only for good behavior."

"Good. Then I can be your kisser of bruises. And your throat kisser and your breast kisser…" She demonstrated each responsibility.

Katherina drew back. "Wait, I want to see you too. I've wondered for so long." She pulled off Anastasia's sweater and let her eyes sweep over the landscape of Anastasia's body. Full womanly breasts rested in a lace brassiere. Katherina unhooked it and kissed the warm creatures that emerged. They embraced again, warming themselves against one another, and Katherina felt the pounding at the center of their joined chests. Was it her heart or Anastasia's?

Katherina undid Anastasia's jeans and underwear and slid them down. The triangle of light brown hair that emerged caused a sudden thrill of excitement. When had she last seen a woman nude? Like this? Never. She ran the palm of her hand over the swelling beneath the navel.

"The pregnancy is beginning to show, isn't it? Do you feel anything yet?"

"No. I think that will happen in about a month."

Katherina pressed her own abdomen gently against the roundness.

"I love it that you have that little life inside of you. Really. And I love us being here this way, the three of us."

"I do too, but our bath is getting cold and, frankly, we both stink."

They climbed in and lay carefully side by side in the old tub, exhaling with the pure animal pleasure of soaking in warm water.

"Mmmm. I've never done *this* before." Anastasia sighed.

Katherina smiled into her neck. "Not even with a boyfriend?"

"Forgive me if I laugh, darling. You forget, I grew up in Soviet Russia. It's not the sort of thing you can do in a dormitory bathroom or a collective apartment with five people's laundry hanging over the tub."

"I've never done it before either, but I've wanted to. How fortunate that we both needed a bath at the same time."

"Here, let me clean that that horrible scrape on your back." Without moving from the embrace, Anastasia reached behind Katherina and gently drew the soap back and forth over the abrasion. "Is that better?"

"Yes, better. So much better." Katherina took the soap from Anastasia's hand and dropped it over the side of the tub out of reach. The urge to be clean had given way quickly to a force less civilized. Hot wet mouths on hot wet skin seemed a part of the steaming pool itself, a floating together in the primordial element. Something ancient and ancestral reminded her that the purpose of life was more life, and every nerve urged her on to couple. Katherina slid her leg between Anastasia's thighs to begin the act.

Anastasia opened to straddle the leg and undulated against it. "Yes," she breathed. "But not here. It will go too fast. I want to do it to you too, and make it last."

They staggered out of the bath, toweled just enough to avoid leaving a stream of water behind them, and moved to the bed. It seemed they had said everything already and what remained was the wordless talk of lovemaking, the rhythmic give and take of intimate exploration.

It was as natural as growing warm in the sun. Katherina embraced Anastasia unreservedly, licking, sucking every sweet part of her that she could take into her mouth. No longer passive, Anastasia moved over on top of her, biting gently along her neck and shoulder and beginning a delicious friction along the length of their bodies. Katherina was slick now with new wetness, every inch of her skin aroused, every touch electric. But she would be the seducer, not the seduced, at least this first time, and so she regained the upper position. Anastasia seemed to understand the game and yielded, whispering, "Yes." In charge now, Katherina slid loving insistent fingers along Anastasia's thigh and entered her. Anastasia opened, inviting more, moving her whole body in rhythm to each gentle thrust, and invaded Katherina's mouth. Katherina shifted once again so that their two bellies touched, and while she stroked she sensed the third life that pulsed between them. A delicious mix of images swam in her head, of a boy in white silk, smelling of roses, of the snow maiden lying beneath her, harboring within a tiny precious being that grew with each of their panting breaths. "Oh, stay with me," Katherina murmured. Anastasia breathed, "Always," and her wrenching climax was the consummation of the *Rosenkavalier* kiss.

Then, feeling Anastasia drift off in her arms, Katherina herself fell into soft dreamless sleep.

❖

Several hours later she awoke, her head on Anastasia's chest. "Your heart's beating," she whispered.

"Oh, thank goodness." Anastasia laughed.

"I mean it's pounding." Katherina raised her head. "I can hear your blood flowing through your body. It makes me so grateful that we're alive, and together. And it makes me all the more sorry for my father. I wonder if he was ever really in love."

"He was. And this is as good a time as any for you to read about it." Anastasia slipped out of bed and retrieved her shoulder bag. She drew out a large gray envelope with two folded packets of paper. "This is the copy of the Russian pages that you gave me." She dropped it back into the envelope and handed over the second packet. "And this is the translation. I feel like I've looked into this man's soul. Do you want to read it now, lying next to me?"

"I can't think of a better place." Katherina raised herself up on one elbow and withdrew the folded pages. "Is it terrible? I mean, is it full of war horrors?"

"It's terrible and beautiful. No war horrors, just a personal tragedy. I'm surprised you couldn't read the first lines. They were in French."

"French? Really? Well, I was in shock when I found the journal in the first place. I only flipped through these pages and saw they were written in Cyrillic, so I never even attempted to read them." She unfolded the packet and laid it flat between them.

"*'D'amour l'ardente flame...'*" she began.

XXXV
Lacrimoso

Stalingrad, January 31, 1943

"D'amour l'ardente flame consume mes beaux jours." The words of my favorite aria go through my head as I lie here next to him, my lover. Don't be shocked. You, the Russian who is reading this page now, let me tell you of something precious and pure.

First, here's the irony. I was one of Russia's children, like you with a Russian child's memories. My grandmother had a parrot called Zharptitsa, the firebird of our fairy tales, and in my mind I can still taste sweet samovar tea. It was your revolution that drove us out, to Germany.

But Germany sent me back, so I'm yours again, at least my frozen cadaver will be. And since I'm dead, I don't have to see the disgust on your face when you read that I am lying here next to the man I have made love to. If you find our remains side by side in this basement, please lay us together, even in the common pit.

I never wanted to come here and fight you. We're brothers, after all. But the Third Reich doesn't like my sort any more than you do and so gave me an interesting choice: rot in a concentration camp or practice medicine under fire. That is, die in Buchenwald or Stalingrad. I made my choice, and with my medical kit I followed the Wehrmacht into hell.

And second, here is the lesson: that love can appear,

persistently, miraculously, even here. My lover lies next to me, keeping warm against my side, and this is the third time I mention him because it thrills me to see the words as I write them. I have just sewn the wound shut where his last two fingers used to be, without anesthetic. His body shook the whole time, but he didn't scream. It's a clean shrapnel wound that he could survive—if this were a real field hospital instead of just a basement full of dying men, a charnel house. We have no more medical supplies, only a few bandages, some surgical thread. We can't even wash out wounds, except with freezing-cold water. But you know that. If you're still here in Stalingrad you're probably not much better off.

But the first thing I see when I wake by kerosene light is his face, his fine nose, his eyelashes long as a woman's. He has lips like a Renaissance cherub, and I have known such happiness, kissing them in the dark. I call him Zharptitsa, my miraculous bird. I forgive you for your contempt, my Russian brother, and hope that one day you too find love as pure and precious as the one that burns between Florian and me.

Katherina gasped. "Florian! That's him. The man my father named his son after and the last word he wrote before he died. Florian was his lover. He must have died in Stalingrad, while my father made it back. No wonder he felt guilty."

"The story's a bit more complicated than that," Anastasia said. "Keep reading. It's all there."

February 3, 1943
Yesterday General Paulus surrendered the German Sixth Army to the Russians. It's over for us. Hitler ordered us to fight to the last man and the last cartridge, but we're out of ammunition, food, clothing, and the will to fight. Goering's promise to supply us by air was nothing but shit. All over the city our troops are freezing to death or dying of hunger. We're beyond savagery and live like beasts. There are rumors of cannibalism. Some of our officers are shooting themselves, and an SS demolition team has just blown itself up. Common

soldiers run out into the open and empty their magazines until they are mowed down.

This place, Collection Station N. 6, keeps operating, but the last flight out carrying wounded was a week ago, so now it's just a place to die. The walking wounded are not even brought here but are rounded up for captivity. The only men they bring are the ones too far gone to stand up. Some of them are carried in screaming, broken bones protruding, viscera exposed, but soon the cold gets to them and they quiet down. Then they die. The stretcher-bearers carry them out again, stack them up in the yard.

There are always about twenty-five men, with the new arrivals replacing the dead. Every second day they bring us soup, just hot water with barley in it. Sometimes there's bread, a scrap for each man. Hard to sleep for very long, but the cold keeps the lice from crawling.

One of the guards, a man they call Kolya, seems to be assigned to this side of the cellar. He has seen me embrace Florian and I can feel his contempt when he's near. Still, he's not brutal. He knows I speak Russian and so stops by sometimes to tell me what's happening outside. He has a strange scar across the bridge of his nose, as if someone had struck him with a sword but stopped short of slicing through his head. Today he mentioned that the bombed-out building overhead used to be the opera house. Nice touch, dying in an opera house.

We're all just waiting to be told what to do, everyone thinking the same thing. How much longer can I hold out? A week, a month, a year? I worry most about Florian. Can I protect him in captivity?

An hour ago I went to the "latrine." Just a pool of shit in one of the back rooms. Frozen, but it still stank. My urine gave off steam; a little more precious body heat lost. On the way back I stepped over plaster slabs and thought I saw a hand.

But it was a glove, a black gauntlet, with a wide cuff. Part of a costume but still good, one more layer of protection against the cold. I put it over Florian's injured hand, which was so cold I could feel no pulse in it. He keeps up a brave front, but when I hold the lantern over him I can see that his bright blue eyes are glassy with pain. To keep him talking, I asked him what opera he thought the glove might be from. *Faust*, he whispered. *Faust*, for sure, and it was the devil's gauntlet. He could tell by the fire in his missing fingers.

February 4, 1943

There are things worse than dying. Being eaten by rats while you're still alive is worse. They don't like the frozen corpses and prefer the bodies that are still warm. One of the jobs of the medics is to keep the rats away from the feet of the wounded who are too weak to fight them off. The mice are a plague too, and have caused outbreaks of tularemia among the troops. Since I can't sleep much anyhow, I make rounds continuously, without medicine or morphine, simply talking to the men who want to talk, lying to the ones who are afraid. I promise to take messages to their families, as if it were certain I would make it home myself. Then I go back to our corner and hold Florian in my arms.

February 5, 1943

Florian is feverish. He keeps saying that he hears music, like a chorus singing. I tell him it's only the wind outside. I hold him in my arms and feel how frail he's gotten. "Don't leave me," he begs, and I promise not to.

I fell asleep, keeping him warm, and dreamt the opera house over our heads was still there. I was outside in the snow, but I could hear the orchestra and a woman singing. *"D'amour l'ardente flame..."* Then I saw soldiers riding toward me on horseback. They stopped in front of the opera house and one of them offered me his hand. It was the devil wearing the black gauntlet, and he asked me if I wanted to go home. I said of course I did, and I was suddenly on horseback, riding away with him, going back to St. Petersburg. Strange. I left St. Petersburg when I was seven. It's the last place I would consider home.

Kolya the guard woke us up with his foot. "Hey, you sweethearts," he said sarcastically. Then to me, "Get your kit and report to Major Karlovsky."

"I want to bring my comrade," I said. "He's my assistant."

Kolya said no, but I could come back for him later. Meanwhile, he'd keep an eye on him. I don't trust Kolya, but had no choice. I left Florian, making sure he had his glove on.

February 6, 1943
We may be saved after all. With thousands of wounded men and few surviving medics, a major named Karlovsky has been put in charge of rounding up the German doctors. Because I spoke Russian, Kolya separated me from the rest of the group and took me alone to Karlovsky's headquarters, a primitive enclosure dug into the cliffs overlooking the Volga. He must have thought that Karlovsky was alone, but he wasn't. One step into the dugout and we were facing both the major and General Vasily Chuikov, Commander of the 62nd Army that had just taken Stalingrad. Karlovsky saw my German uniform and was furious. "Get that prisoner out of here," he snarled. Chuikov stood a meter away from us, waiting for the interruption to end. He scratched his jaw with swollen fingers and a bandaged hand. The rumors were true, then. He had eczema. Without thinking, I pulled away from Kolya and said in my best Russian, "Commander, I'm a dermatologist. I can cure that."

"This one speaks Russian," Chuikov remarked, surprised, of course. I talked fast. "My name is Sergei Marovsky, General. I was born in Leningrad. I'm a dermatologist," I repeated. He glared at me, I suppose trying to decide which was worse, a Wehrmacht soldier or a Tsarist. But his hands must have been hurting a lot.

"I can cure that." I lied again, pointing to the red swollen things protruding from the bandaged palm. Open sores, some infected, were on the knuckles. He lifted one hand, I thought to slap me, but it was to wave me away. "Wait outside," he said, and Kolya took me outside the dugout. "Don't talk about yourself. That will remind him you are a Russian fighting with Germans. We execute men for that. Talk about medicine. Promise him cure."

"Yes, I will. And I'll tell him I need my medical assistant."

Kolya shook his head. "Pretty Face? Forget him. He's wounded, no good to Russian hospital. Maybe good luck can save him, but not you. Two of you together is death for sure."

Just then, Chuikov came out alone and signaled me to follow him. His dugout was close by and like Karlovsky's, only larger, set back farther into the cliff and with an improvised door. Inside, I saw he even had electricity, and lights were on over a small table. I unwrapped his bandages under the lightbulb and saw swelling, blisters, open sores. His doctors had been telling him it was nerves. Idiots. But none of them were dermatologists. I told him it was simple eczema, exacerbated by dirt. He ordered hot water from his cook and I washed his hands to stop the itching and clean out some of the infection. I told him to send for vegetable oil from his field kitchen and rub it in to stop the dryness. "Clean cotton gloves," I added. "Get two pairs, not too tight. I'll wash them for you and you can change them every day. That will make all the difference." I made him promise to drink nothing but clean water, and lots of it, to hydrate his skin. He must have been desperate, because he agreed to everything. He even smiled and I saw that his front teeth were capped in gold.

I thought he would send me back to the German field station, but instead he ordered one of his men to take me to a soldiers' bivouac across the Volga. I was to be a "free" prisoner encamped with his troops and had to treat his hands every morning. My new guard took me to a supply truck and a bivouac where soldiers were sitting around a fire. He ordered me to take off my uniform tunic and gave me one of their padded winter jackets. I'm here now, warm for the first time in weeks, but I *must* get back to the opera-house medical station for Florian. I'll try to find Karlovsky in the morning.

February 7, 1943
The Russians need front-line surgeons, since their losses were just as great as ours. Though everyone is wary of me, they put me into the surgery to assist when I'm not tending the commander. The soldiers have the same wounds as the Germans, and the care is almost the same. Except they use pure grain vodka both as anaesthetic and as antiseptic.

Time is running out to save Florian. He has no idea what happened to me. While I washed Commander Chuikov's hands this morning, I asked if I could return to get my medical assistant, but he said to forget about the Germans. The subject was obviously closed. My only chance is with Karlovsky, but I don't have much mobility and I can't find him. How much time do I have left before Florian is moved?

February 8, 1943
I've been watching them all day, the surrendered men, the whole Sixth Army and the armies of the Hungarians, Romanians, Italians, in a five-man-wide line slogging across the frozen Volga and disappearing over the horizon. Like a gargantuan, and endless, gray serpent. Most of them have only their issue denims, lightweight coats. Their leather boots are caked in ice that will soon freeze their feet like so much bad meat and cripple them. A few of them have thrown their deadly boots away and shuffle along in straw sentry shoes. Others have feet wrapped in strips of wool cut from coats.

The ones who could find blankets have them draped over their heads, keeping the wind away from their emaciated faces. A few Russians, still in their white camouflage cloaks, herd the POWs, but mostly they are unguarded.

I watched my comrades of a few days ago shuffle along dumbly like they already know they're dead. I could be shuffling with them. And Florian?

Still no sign of Karlovsky and I'm desperate to find him before it's too late.

February 9, 1943
I finally found Major Karlovsky, standing together with Kolya, and I begged him to let me return to get Florian as my medical assistant. Kolya whispered something in his ear, the bastard, and Karlovsky was suddenly suspicious. "What's the hurry? Is that your butt boy? If he is, you can just go on back to him, for good. But you can't bring him along. There are no butt boys in the Red Army."

"No, of course not," I said. "He's just a comrade, a very good medic."

Karlovsky laughed. "Well then, you'll have *new* comrades here on this side of the river. Make your choice. Go back to your pretty friend and join the long march to a POW camp or be a man in Chuikov's Army. Go on." He took a step backward to let me pass him, even stretched out an arm toward the opera-house collection station where Florian waited. All I had to do was walk. Kolya looked away but I knew he had betrayed me. I hesitated, speechless.

"Smart choice," Karlovsky said, and the two of them marched away.

February 10, 1943
I was sick all night with regret. I had to see Florian. Maybe

together we could work out something to save us both. I tracked down Karlovsky again and begged him to let me return to the German medical station to "fetch my medical instruments," although it was obvious I already had my medical kit with me. He must have been in a good mood this morning because he agreed, and I hurried through the wrecked city back to the opera-house cellar.

When I arrived, I felt like I'd been shot. The cellar was empty. Where Florian had been lying there was only the leather gauntlet, covered with plaster. Did he leave it as a sign for me, or did it drop when he was carried away? Did he freeze during the night without me to warm him? Had the rats… I couldn't finish the thought.

The corpses were still piled up like cordwood outside. Like a madman, I rushed along the rows, poking among them, brushing snow and ice from the dead faces. I would have collapsed in grief if I had found him, but it was almost worse that I didn't. If he's not dead, then he's among the prisoners force-marched eastward through the snow. He can't survive that.

God, he's gone. He's gone. Oh, Florian. If I knew where you were in that endless trudging line, I'd run after you. How far can you march before you fall? They're pulling us apart, dragging you eastward and forcing me toward the west. I have the glove, the sign of my cowardice, but where my heart was there's a stone. How can I live, day after day, imagining you lying by the roadside, covered with snow? I bought my life with yours, and now I'm an empty shell.

Katherina's hand shook as she folded the pages of the translation and tucked them along with the original into the journal. Next to her, Anastasia was silent, watching her.

"So that's where it all came from. The uniform, the glove, the guilt that was hanging over our family."

"Your father obviously felt like he'd made a devil's pact, to the point of being superstitious about it. And then, of course, Schalk showed up, offering him even more deals."

"That explains his cynicism, too. I remember from my earliest years that he said 'you have to save *yourself,* because when you need your friends, they will abandon you.'"

Anastasia took her hand, kissing her palm. "But he didn't abandon anyone. The guards took him out of the cellar at gunpoint. And then, when he had to choose between life and loyalty, all he was guilty of, really, was hesitating. It was just his dream that made him think it was a 'pact.' He kept that black gauntlet for forty years, to torture himself, as if it were his contract. But there never was one, even in the abstract sense."

"He thought there was. It colored his whole life."

"I know. We all make up our life stories, don't we? My mother lived in Tsarist Russia in her head, long after it was gone. But your father lived with the devil. Get rid of the glove, darling. Break *his* fake contract the way you broke that insane contract with Raspin."

"Raspin? Yes, he was demented, wasn't he? It took me far too long to realize it. The aria he made me sing at the end. The Mephisto aria. The words are from *Faust.* They're the ravings of poor Marguerite, who was forced by the devil to kill both her mother and her child. A totally broken spirit who is then executed. That's what he wanted me to be, a sacrifice, to get back at my father."

"I think he was demented long before your father met him. War brings out sociopaths and there were plenty on both sides. But he was smart enough to create a philosophy out of it, and a business too. Plus he knew how to manipulate people so that they played out his master-morality. It was a sort of Faust meets Nietzsche. You got drawn in because his last illusion was that he could write an opera to reveal the beast in men."

"I can vouch for the 'beast in men.' I had some of them lying on top of me on that damned rock. But I particularly resent it that he used the opera stage to 'prove' this hateful world view, and almost got away with it. What does that say about us? We're theater people, after all. Illusion is what we do."

"Yes, but we do it for fun and put away the costumes afterward. We have nothing to prove except that music is beautiful. I don't know.

I've just run down a mountain and made love with a woman for the first time. I'm not ready for hard questions like that."

"I'm not, either." Katherina curved over Anastasia and brushed her lips over tousled hair. Then, abruptly, she sat up again.

"Is something the matter?"

"I have to sing at that concert," Katherina announced. "I'll do it without a fee. They should let me. I'm the daughter of a Stalingrad hero."

"The commemorative concert at Volgograd? Yes, I think you should." Anastasia sat up, enthusiastic. "Maybe Boris can help. He has a few friends in the Soviet State Recording Studio. Ones that will have forgiven him for marrying a defector. They will surely have contacts who have other contacts in Andropov's government. You know how those old war-buddy networks are."

"Isn't that forbidden? Making deals with Western capitalists?"

"Hush. Let me finish."

"I'm listening," Katherina said. "You were saying…Andropov's government."

Anastasia gazed inwardly, as if calculating. "The Andropov government is trying to put a respectable face on communism. You know he's got an anti-alcohol program, and he's trying to live down his past as head of the KGB. I bet the concert was his idea in the first place, and all the scheduled performers are Russians. Just imagine what it would do for their credibility if they also had a German perform. I'm sure they'll snap up your offer in an instant."

"You really think so?"

"Definitely. How can it be a 'reconciliation' if it's Russians performing for Russians? You'd be the only German Stalingrad descendant who could also perform. It would be a public relations coup. It may take a while to reach the relevant people and get them to contact the committee, but it all seems possible."

"Where do you suppose they'll hold the concert? The journal says the opera house was destroyed. Did they rebuild it?"

"There is another concert hall close to the site. The Tsaritsinskaya Opera Company performs there with its own orchestra. It's provincial, compared to Leningrad and Moscow, but the symbolic value of the concert would be stupendous."

"Assuming that we can pull it all together in time, will you come with me?"

"I can't. I'm a defector, remember? But don't worry about me. I'll be here waiting for you. Do you know what you want to sing?"

"Yes, I do," Katherina answered without hesitation. *"Your* aria. That is, Marguerite's aria, from Berlioz' *Faust*. The one you recorded. *'D'amour l'ardente flame.'"*

XXXVI
Aria da Capo

February 2, 1983

The connecting flight from Moscow was late and so the Tupolev 134, with every one of its eighty seats occupied, did not reach Volgograd air space until three in the afternoon. In the mid-winter light, the ground below bore little color beyond the white of snow and the nuanced grays of cities.

As the aircraft reduced altitude in its approach, Katherina stared out the porthole, trying to make sense of the landscape below. She tried to imagine Volgograd as it had been forty years before, as the tenacious Stalingrad. Even in its current so far uninteresting form, it held an almost mythical significance for her.

"If you're looking for the Volga, it's frozen solid and covered with snow this time of year." Her seat mate, a bearded fifties-something man in a slightly rumpled business suit, spoke in thickly Russian-accented German.

"Oh, you speak German," she said. "Yes, of course. I should have remembered that it would be frozen. I'm assuming it's that strip of white snaking along between the gray patches."

"I heard you conversing earlier with the stewardess," he explained. "Is this your first visit to Volgograd? Perhaps to see the historical sites? Our business visitors rarely include such lovely women as yourself."

Katherina glanced briefly at him, reluctant to pull her gaze away from the maze of shapes below. "I'm singing in a concert to commemorate the Battle of Stalingrad. That's why I'm trying to see the city from the air. Can you tell me what I'm looking at?"

He stood up and then bent over her shoulder, supporting himself on the seat in front. "It will be hard to make out the landmarks with so much snow, but in just a minute, you should be able to see the

Mother Russia statue. That will show you the Mamayev Hill where the Stalingrad memorial complex is located."

"Oh yes, that's something I want to visit while I'm here. You see, my father fought at Stalingrad," she said with pride, surprising herself.

"I see. And, judging by your age, it appears he survived. A lucky man. I myself was one of the children hiding in the tunnels and basements." He sat down again.

Katherina twisted toward him in her seat. "So the story is real. I read some place that thousands of civilians were trapped in the city throughout the battle."

"What you read is true. Stalin didn't allow the people to evacuate until much too late. And my family could not evacuate at all because my mother was a worker at the Red October metal factory. After our house was burned by exploding fuel tanks, we slept in the factory, until bombs gutted it. After that, we went into hiding. We had no food or even water most of the time, although I was five years old so I don't remember very much. I *do* remember the soldiers rescuing us and giving us food. We were so hungry, and of course, it's a little boy's dream to be sitting down with real soldier heroes. Ah, there it is!" He stood up again. "There's the 'Mother Russia Calls' statue."

Katherina pressed her forehead against the glass and saw an enormously tall structure, dark against the surrounding snow, drift into view on the right. Although the distance and line of sight did not allow a good view, she knew from pictures that it was a statue of a woman striding forward with upraised arm and swinging an enormous sword.

"She's very tall," the gentleman added. "Some eighty-five meters, with her sword. You can see her from much of the city."

"Very impressive," Katherina replied politely. "And those buildings around her are part of the memorial?"

"Yes. One of them is a burnt-out building they've left to show what the whole city looked like. That cylindrical building there is the Hall of the Warrior Glory. Very beautiful inside, with mosaics of golden glass all around. The names of about seventy thousand of the soldiers are inscribed on the walls. That, of course, does not count the civilians."

"Is there a special cemetery?"

"No, not yet. But one is planned. However, there is a tomb where General Chuikov is buried. Perhaps you don't know the name. You are so young. Vasily Chuikov is one of the generals who were victorious at

Stalingrad. He went on to capture Berlin too. He died just last year and is buried on the Mamayev Kurgan."

Katherina thought of swollen infected hands that saved her father's life and could almost imagine the general's cheerful peasant face with its row of gold teeth. "Yes, I have heard of him," she said softly, and at that moment decided to lay flowers at his tomb.

❖

Katherina stood facing the spotlights of the Tsaritsinskaya Opera Theater. She held the skirt of her white gauze concert dress with one hand and raised the other toward the balcony. The common soldiers sat there, she knew, or rather the white-haired men and women who had survived the "cauldron" of Stalingrad. She wanted them to know she was bringing something back to them.

She sang her father's song, which he had carried with him across the Eastern front. It tied him to his young lover and haunted him for forty years. Upon his death, it had passed through the voice of Anastasia Ivanova to her, Sergei Marovsky's child, and now she gave it back to the air of Stalingrad.

With the full orchestra swelling beneath her, she sang the climax of the aria that belonged to all four of them. In a language that did not distinguish between "him" and "her," she celebrated the mouth, eyes, caress, and kiss of the beloved, of all beloveds.

O caresses de flamme! Que je voudrais un jour
Voir s'exhaler mon âme Dans ses baisers d'amour!

When it was over, she curtsied deeply. The other performers joined her onstage then, and the audience of politicians, diplomats, survivors, and their families gave them an ovation. The survivors, especially, clapped long and passionately, acknowledging not only the concert but, of course, themselves. For everyone among them, the Battle of Stalingrad had been the nadir of their existence; for everyone, the memory was a deep and twisted scar. And yet they had emerged from the chasm and could celebrate in music what hardly could be said in words. Katherina felt it in the air around her: gratitude, reconciliation, and fathomless melancholy.

When the cheering stopped, all the artists gathered at the reception in the entry hall of the theater.

She shook hands with a dozen Russian politicians, whose names she knew she would never remember. Then the crowd parted and Yuri Andropov himself stepped forward.

The premier, who had gained a reputation for ice-cold and sometimes ruthless calculation in his long career as head of the KGB, looked surprisingly weak. His bland face, rendered even blander by his growing baldness, was pale and slightly jaundiced. Katherina recalled that men like Yuri Andropov were part of the reason that Anastasia had defected to the West. But for all that, he seemed sickly, and the head of the vast and all-powerful Soviet Union looked like a banker in need of a vacation. After working his way down the line of musicians, he shook Katherina's hand and, in awkward German, thanked her for her performance. A secretary handed him a series of small bouquets, which he presented with presidential formality to each of the performers. After a few additional words, presumably about international cooperation, he left the hall with his entourage.

After the premier's departure, the corridor returned to its previous liveliness, and people once again crowded around the singers. The high emotion of the concert still lingered, in spite of the extreme age of many of the audience members. Some wore their old military uniforms, ill fitting on aging bodies, and all of them, even the ones who attended in civilian jackets, wore their ribbons and Stalingrad medals. That was what they still carried after forty years: memories, medals, and long covered-over wounds. A few were scarred in a more obvious way, with missing arms or a limp that betrayed a prosthetic leg.

Katherina looked around for the German survivors, knowing there would not be many. Practically the whole of the Sixth Army marched into POW camps where some 90 percent of them perished. Only a lucky few were seriously wounded early in the battle and carried by their comrades to the airfields, from where the Luftwaffe flew them out. In the final weeks, when the casualties were massive, such evacuations ceased. To be a German survivor of Stalingrad was to be extraordinarily tenacious or extraordinarily lucky.

They were also difficult to identify since, unlike some of the Russians, they had no old uniforms hanging in their closets. Few German soldiers cherished their identification with the Wehrmacht of Nazi Germany, and any who had been captured had worn their uniforms to shreds. It was not until a cluster of some dozen old men in business suits shuffled toward her that Katherina recognized the German veterans.

Surely these were the early escapees, the wounded ones saved by the Luftwaffe before the Soviets captured the last airstrip. The number of leg-amputees and variety of prosthesis hands seemed to verify that assumption. She could not imagine that a POW would want to return to the country that had kept him in purgatory for years, even if the government paid for his visit.

One after another, the mostly handicapped German veterans greeted her. *"Sehr schön,"* they said. Lovely that the daughter of a Stalingrad man could sing for them. None of them remembered Sergei Marovsky but, given the size of the city and the number of medical personnel, it was not surprising. The concert program, she recalled, had listed Sergei Marovsky among the Germans and made no mention of his service with the Red Army. Did the German government not know? Or care? Katherina supposed that highly political events such as the Reconciliation Concert would wish to gloss over such facts as the heroism of a turncoat. In any case, she was relieved that these old men in their sorrowful nostalgia would have nothing with which to reproach her.

After nearly an hour of handshaking and a few tears, the crowd thinned out and the general manager of the Tsaritsinskaya Opera Company arrived to offer his congratulations. She accepted his handshake and then excused herself for a moment, asking him to wait. A few minutes later she returned to the entrance hall with a package wrapped in brown paper and addressed the manager in German.

"Herr Direktor. My father found this in the basement of the Stalingrad Opera House, during the battle which destroyed it. He took it due to a misunderstanding, and it has stayed far too long with my family. I believe you are its rightful heir," she said, presenting the package to him.

Clearly surprised, the general manager opened one end of the package, revealing the desiccated and dusty leather of a black gauntlet. He smiled, slightly nonplussed, and drew it out.

"I thought it might have some historical value," Katherina explained. "I suspect there is little else left of that opera house."

The general manager studied the glove, holding it gingerly, then nodded. "Yes, you're right. I believe it does have great value for the Museum of Stalingrad. Thank you for returning it." He held up the glove for a press photo, standing next to her, and flashbulbs flickered.

At that moment, the conductor appeared in the corridor, adding a third face and another photo opportunity. For the next several minutes, the press constructed a photo-documented story out of the presentation.

When the press interest waned, both general manager and conductor turned away and meandered across the hall toward a waiter carrying a tray of champagne glasses.

Katherina was still surrounded by elderly German veterans who seemed to have run out of small talk. One of them, however, stepped shyly out of the circle. Well dressed, in his early sixties, he was accompanied by a slightly younger man who had stepped out also, but kept a slight distance behind him. Both were attractive, though the closer one, with thinning white hair, had a curiously delicate quality to his face, and under long eyelashes, his eyes were an extraordinary bright blue. He spoke in a soft voice, his manner slightly effeminate.

"The program says you are the daughter of Sergei Marovsky." He held it up as evidence.

"Yes," Katherina confirmed. "He changed his name to Marow after the war."

The old man smiled wanly. "All these years I thought he had fallen at Stalingrad. But he made it back after all. You look a lot like him."

Katherina's heart leapt. Finally, someone who remembered her father. Someone who could describe him, tell of the wounds he had bandaged, men he'd saved. She was hungry to hear it all. "Did you know him as a medic, or were you a fellow soldier?"

"Both, actually. Your father treated me for shrapnel but we were also very good friends. His excellent surgery saved my life. I was sure he had been arrested for something, and I myself was in a bad state, both physically and mentally. But a Russian guard, a man named Kolya, befriended me and helped me survive the first hard weeks after surrender."

"I am so happy to meet you." Katherina studied the veteran's face, an idea forming. But no, it was not possible.

He had been standing somewhat stiffly and bent toward her, with one hand behind his back, like an officer poised midway in a military bow.

She offered him her hand, and he presented his own. It was missing the last two fingers.

"Müller is my name. Florian Müller. I don't suppose he ever mentioned me."

Holding the mangled hand in her own, Katherina felt tears well up. "Yes, Mr. Müller. He did. With great affection. I believe we have a lot to talk about."

POSTSCRIPT

This novel deals with several highly specialized realms: Stalingrad, postwar Germany, East Germany (DDR), Communist Russia, the Faust myth, and the world of opera. While the author has endeavored to avoid stereotypes or errors, the limited scope of a novel inevitably requires a certain superficiality. I beg the indulgence of any readers who have a greater expertise than I do in any of these areas.

Stalingrad: I have tried to do justice to the scope of horror of this battle (July 1942 to February 2, 1943), which is considered the bloodiest in modern history, with combined casualties estimated at nearly two million. It marks the turning point of WWII, which led to the eventual defeat of Nazi Germany.

Most sources indicate a woeful lack of medical supplies on both sides. The German collection hospitals (of which Station Nr. 6 really *was* the cellar of a bombed-out opera house) seem to have suffered the worst, particularly after surrender, when they were simply cellars full of the untreated wounded and dying. Vasily Chuikov, commander of one of the victorious armies, did indeed have severe eczema, although it is highly unlikely that he would have allowed a Wehrmacht doctor— least of all an anti-communist Russian emigré German—to tend him, however effective the treatment was. The Red Army, filled with commisars, ever watchful for the weakening of Stalinist support, would likely have shot so severely tainted an individual as Sergei Marovsky. This, however, is fiction, and our hero has made a pact with the devil and thus achieved this little miracle.

Postwar Germany: The 1940s and 1950s were tumultuous decades for Germany, and it is unfortunately beyond the scope of a novel to do justice to its nation-shaking events: occupation, reconstruction, political divisions, economic crises, blockade, airlift, partition, etc. in their complexity. Regrettably, these have been only hinted at or omitted, though they could be understood to cause a radical difference in the character, that is, the fears and expectations, of the two generations whose lives are described in the novel.

East Germany: The Deutsche Demokratische Republik (DDR) was a self-declared communist state that existed from October 1949 until October 1990. Soviet occupation troops remained in DDR territory throughout its existence. Berlin, completely surrounded by the DDR, was divided into East and West sectors, with the western portion open to Germany by way of three air corridors and various heavily monitored land routes. Thus, in order to escape the border police (*Grenzpolizei*), our heroines had to drive first westward to West Germany and then fly eastward back to Berlin.

The world of opera: The author wishes to point out that it is not possible to become an opera star by selling your soul to the devil. I tried, but the devil never returned my calls. A singer achieves an opera career with a) conspicuous talent that does not wear thin after a few years of stress, b) stamina and patience to get through the long period it takes to establish a reputation, c) financial and emotional support during the lean years, d) a good agent, and e) a great deal of luck.

The author apologizes to any actual opera performer who might read this story for making it seem that fabulous engagements follow one after another, week after week, that performers never catch cold, and that it takes only a few short rehearsals before the show goes on. The author acknowledges that rehearsals are grueling affairs that involve hundreds more people than just the opera stars, and that a breathtaking amount of behind-the-scenes work and money goes into a performance. Given the effort it takes to walk up and down stairs in costume and act out a role while sweating and singing very high notes, it would seem unlikely that one could fall in love onstage. But what do I know? The devil never gave me a chance to try. However, all the singers I have asked have said that the pleasure of being "in voice" and "in sync" with fellow performers on a good night is incomparable.

The following operas and choral works were addressed in the novel and are recommended for your enjoyment. If you consider yourself opera-challenged, you might want to start with "Excerpts from…" any of these works.

Tosca: Italian tragic opera. Giacomo Puccini

Ein Deutsches Requiem: German variation on a requiem mass. Johannes Brahms

Die Zauberflöte (Magic Flute): Comic opera. W. A. Mozart

Nozze de Figaro (Marriage of Figaro): Comic opera. W. A. Mozart

Carmina Burana: Scenic cantata and sometimes ballet. Karl Orff

Rosenkavalier: Comic opera. Richard Strauss

Carmen: French tragic opera. George Bizet

Walpurgisnacht: Fictional, never performed anywhere. Justine Saracen

About the Author

After years of "professing" at universities and writing for international literary journals, Justine Saracen discovered the joy of creating from the imagination and the heart. Trips first to Egypt and then to Morocco and Palestine inspired the Ibis Prophecy books, which move from Ancient Egyptian theology to the bloodthirsty Christianity of the Crusades. The playful first novel, *The 100th Generation*, was a finalist in the Queerlit Competition and the Ann Bannon Reader's Choice award. The sequel, *Vulture's Kiss*, focuses on the first crusade and vividly dramatizes the dangers of militant religion.

The expatriate Brussels-based writer then moved her literary spotlight up a few centuries, to the Renaissance, and a few kilometers to the north, to Rome. *Sistine Heresy*, her most daring work to date, conjures up a GLBT, and thoroughly blasphemic, backstory to Michelangelo's Sistine Chapel frescoes. The newly released work quickly sold out at the 2009 Palm Springs Lesbian Book Festival.

Mephisto Aria, in contrast, deals with devilish things, in a thriller that has one eye on the Faust story and the other on the world of opera. In Berlin, staggering toward recovery after WWII, a Russian soldier passes on his brilliance, but also his mortal guilt, to his opera singer daughter.

Lest anyone think that Saracen is done confronting religion, her current work in progress is about a transvestite in Venice who meets the terrors of the Inquisition and finds out something important—one might almost say appalling—about God.

Scanning a fictional eye along the centuries, Saracen has a self-declared mission, to repopulate history with "the likes of us," by which she appears to mean people who, not by their acts, but by their very lives, still scare the ignorant.

Visit her at her Web site, justinesaracen.googlepages.com, or follow her on Facebook (Justine Saracen) and on Twitter @JustSaracen.

Books Available From Bold Strokes Books

Magic of the Heart by C.J. Harte. CEO Susan Hettinger and wild, impulsive rock star M.J. Carson couldn't be more different if they tried—but opposites attract in ways neither woman can resist. (978-1-60282-131-6)

Ambereye by Gill McKnight. Jolie Garoul is falling in love with her assistant. The big problem is, Jolie is a werewolf. (978-1-60282-132-3)

Collision Course by C.P. Rowlands. Tragedy leaves Brie O'Malley and Jordan Carter fearful and alone. Can they find the courage to take a second chance on love? (978-1-60282-133-0)

Mephisto Aria by Justine Saracen. Opera singer Katherina Marov's destiny may be to repeat the mistakes of her father when she becomes involved in a dangerous love affair. (978-1-60282-134-7)

Battle Scars by Meghan O'Brien. Returning Iraq war veteran Ray McKenna struggles with the battle scars that can only be healed by love. (978-1-60282-129-3)

Chaps by Jove Belle. Eden Metcalf wants nothing more than to flee from her troubled past and travel the open road—until she runs into rancher Brandi Cornwell. (978-1-60282-127-9)

Lightbearer by John Caruso. Lucifer dares to question the premise of creation itself and reveals that sin may be all that stands between us and living hell. (978-1-60282-130-9)

The Seeker by Ronica Black. FBI profiler Kennedy Scott battles ghosts from her past, deadly obsession, and the evil that haunts her. (978-1-60282-128-6)

Power Play by Julie Cannon. Businesswomen Tate Monroe and Victoria Sosa are at odds in the boardroom, but not in the bedroom. (978-1-60282-125-5)

The Remarkable Journey of Miss Tranby Quirke by Elizabeth Ridley. When love enters Tranby's life in the form of a beautiful nineteen-year-old student, Lysette McDonald, she embarks on the most remarkable journey of all. (978-1-60282-126-2)

Returning Tides by Radclyffe. Insurance investigator Ashley Walker faces more than a dangerous opponent when she returns to the town, and the woman, she left behind. (978-1-60282-123-1)

Veritas by Anne Laughlin. When the hallowed halls of academia become the stage for murder, newly appointed Dean Beth Ellis's search for the truth leads her to unexpected discoveries about her own heart. (978-1-60282-124-8)

The Pleasure Planner by Larkin Rose. Pleasure purveyor Bree Hendricks treats love like a commodity until Logan Delaney makes Bree the client in her own game. (978-1-60282-121-7)

everafter by Nell Stark and Trinity Tam. Valentine Darrow is bitten by a vampire on her way to propose to her lover Alexa Newland, and their lives and love are placed in mortal jeopardy. (978-1-60282-119-4)

Summer Winds by Andrews & Austin. When Maggie Turner hires a ranch hand to help work her thousand acres, she never expects to be attracted to the very young, very female Cash Tate. (978-1-60282-120-0)

Beggar of Love by Lee Lynch. Jefferson is the lover every woman wants to be—or to have. A revealing saga of lesbian sexuality. (978-1-60282-122-4)

The Seduction of Moxie by Colette Moody. When 1930s Broadway actress Violet London meets speakeasy singer Moxie Valette, she is instantly attracted and her Hollywood trip takes an unexpected turn. (978-1-60282-114-9)

Goldenseal by Gill McKnight. When Amy Fortune returns to her childhood home, she discovers something sinister in the air—but is former lover Leone Garoul stalking her or protecting her? (978-1-60282-115-6)

Romantic Interludes 2: Secrets edited by Radclyffe and Stacia Seaman. An anthology of sensual lesbian love stories: passion, surprises, and secret desires. (978-1-60282-116-3)

Femme Noir by Clara Nipper. Nora Delaney meets her match in Max Abbott, a sex-crazed dame who may or may not have the information Nora needs to solve a murder—but can she contain her lust for Max long enough to find out? (978-1-60282-117-0)

The Reluctant Daughter by Lesléa Newman. Heartwarming, heartbreaking, and ultimately triumphant—the story every daughter recognizes of the lifelong struggle for our mothers to really see us. (978-1-60282-118-7)

Erosistible by Gill McKnight. When Win Martin arrives at a luxurious Greek hotel for a much-anticipated week of sun and sex with her new girlfriend, she is stunned to find her ex-girlfriend, Benny, is the proprietor. Aeros Ebook. (978-1-60282-134-7)

Looking Glass Lives by Felice Picano. Cousins Roger and Alistair become lifelong friends and discover their sexuality amidst the backdrop of twentieth-century gay culture. (978-1-60282-089-0)

Breaking the Ice by Kim Baldwin. Nothing is easy about life above the Arctic Circle—except, perhaps, falling in love. At least that's what pilot Bryson Faulkner hopes when she meets Karla Edwards. (978-1-60282-087-6)

It Should Be a Crime by Carsen Taite. Two women fulfill their mutual desire with a night of passion, neither expecting more until law professor Morgan Bradley and student Parker Casey meet again…in the classroom. (978-1-60282-086-9)

Rough Trade edited by Todd Gregory. Top male erotica writers pen their own hot, sexy versions of the term "rough trade," producing some of the hottest, nastiest, and most dangerous fiction ever published. (978-1-60282-092-0)

The High Priest and the Idol by Jane Fletcher. Jemeryl and Tevi's relationship is put to the test when the Guardian sends Jemeryl on a mission that puts her not only in harm's way, but back into the sights of a previous lover. (978-1-60282-085-2)

Point of Ignition by Erin Dutton. Amid a blaze that threatens to consume them both, firefighter Kate Chambers and property owner Alexi Clark redefine love and trust. (978-1-60282-084-5)

Secrets in the Stone by Radclyffe. Reclusive sculptor Rooke Tyler suddenly finds herself the object of two very different women's affections, and choosing between them will change her life forever. (978-1-60282-083-8)

Dark Garden by Jennifer Fulton. Vienna Blake and Mason Cavender are sworn enemies—who can't resist each other. Something has to give. (978-1-60282-036-4)

Late in the Season by Felice Picano. Set on Fire Island, this is the story of an unlikely pair of friends—a gay composer in his late thirties and an eighteen-year-old schoolgirl. (978-1-60282-082-1)

Punishment with Kisses by Diane Anderson-Minshall. Will Megan find the answers she seeks about her sister Ashley's murder or will her growing relationship with one of Ash's exes blind her to the real truth? (978-1-60282-081-4)

September Canvas by Gun Brooke. When Deanna Moore meets TV personality Faythe she is reluctantly attracted to her, but will Faythe side with the people spreading rumors about Deanna? (978-1-60282-080-7)

No Leavin' Love by Larkin Rose. Beautiful, successful Mercedes Miller thinks she can resume her affair with ranch foreman Sydney Campbell, but the rules have changed. (978-1-60282-079-1)

Between the Lines by Bobbi Marolt. When romance writer Gail Prescott meets actress Tannen Albright, she develops feelings that she usually only experiences through her characters. (978-1-60282-078-4)

Blue Skies by Ali Vali. Commander Berkley Levine leads an elite group of pilots on missions ordered by her ex-lover Captain Aidan Sullivan and everything is on the line—including love. (978-1-60282-077-7)

The Lure by Felice Picano. When Noel Cummings is recruited by the police to go undercover to find a killer, his life will never be the same. (978-1-60282-076-0)

Death of a Dying Man by J.M. Redmann. Mickey Knight, Private Eye and partner of Dr. Cordelia James, doesn't need a drop-dead gorgeous assistant—not until nature steps in. (978-1-60282-075-3)

Justice for All by Radclyffe. Dell Mitchell goes undercover to expose a human traffic ring and ends up in the middle of an even deadlier conspiracy. (978-1-60282-074-6)

Sanctuary by I. Beacham. Cate Canton faces one major obstacle to her goal of crushing her business rival, Dita Newton—her uncontrollable attraction to Dita. (978-1-60282-055-5)

The Sublime and Spirited Voyage of Original Sin by Colette Moody. Pirate Gayle Malvern finds the presence of an abducted seamstress, Celia Pierce, a welcome distraction until the captive comes to mean more to her than is wise. (978-1-60282-054-8)

Suspect Passions by VK Powell. Can two women, a city attorney and a beat cop, put aside their differences long enough to see that they're perfect for each other? (978-1-60282-053-1)

Just Business by Julie Cannon. Two women who come together—each for her own selfish needs—discover that love can never be as simple as a business transaction. (978-1-60282-052-4)

Sistine Heresy by Justine Saracen. Adrianna Borgia, survivor of the Borgia court, presents Michelangelo with the greatest temptations of his life while struggling with soul-threatening desires for the painter Raphaela. (978-1-60282-051-7)

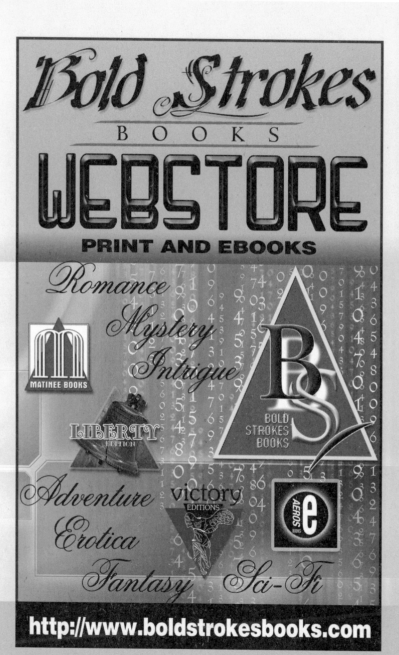